I0451591

Remember Me

OAKVILLE SERIES: BOOK TWO

Remember Me

OAKVILLE SERIES: BOOK TWO

KATHY-JO REINHART

Kathy-Jo Reinhart
Remember Me (Oakville Series #2)

© 2014, Kathy-Jo Reinhart
Self-publishing
(kathyjoreinhart.com)

Cover Design by: Ebook Covers Galore @ Ebookcoversgalore.com
Edited by Monica Black of Word Nerd Editing
Interior Designed and Formatted by E.M. Tippetts Book Designs

ALL RIGHTS RESERVED. This book contains material protected under International and Federal Copyright Laws and Treaties. Any unauthorized reprint or use of this material is prohibited. No part of this book may be reproduced or transmitted in any form or by any means, electronic or mechanical, including photocopying, recording, or by any information storage and retrieval system without express written permission from the author / publisher.

Terms and Conditions:
The purchaser of this book is subject to the condition that he/she shall in no way resell it, nor any part of it, nor make copies of it to distribute freely.

This book is a work of fiction. Any similarity between the characters and situations within its pages and places or persons, living or dead, is unintentional and co-incidental.

I dedicate this book to my beautiful triplet angels and to any parent who has lost a child, no matter the circumstance. There hasn't been a single day over the last thirteen years when my babies haven't crossed my mind. It's always a thought that makes me smile while at the same time causes an indescribable pain in my heart. Thank you for showing me that I am a hell of a lot stronger than I thought I was and to never give up. I wouldn't have my son today if I hadn't picked myself up and tried again.

CHAPTER
One

Amber

THE MOST beautiful voice is singing. He sounds so sad. So heartbroken. Is he singing to me? Who is he? Where am I? Panic starts to rip through me. I try to open my eyes, but it feels like weights are holding them down. The song comes to an end and I hear another voice.

"That was beautiful, Kyle. Sorry, I didn't mean to interrupt," a female voice says.

"It's okay. I was hoping that maybe music would help. Nothing else seems to work." That voice...there's something familiar about it.

I finally get my eyes to open. It takes a minute to focus on the two people standing in the room. A gorgeous man and a very beautiful redheaded woman. Neither of which look at all familiar to me. I can tell that I am in a hospital, but I have no idea how I got here or why.

"I wouldn't be too sure of that," the woman says with excitement before running out of the room to get a nurse.

The man darts to my side and holds my hand. When our skin touches, I feel a jolt shoot through my body. It is the strangest feeling. It alarms me. I grab for the tube in my mouth. I want to ask him who the hell he is. The way he tries to calm me tells me I should know him, that we are close, so why don't I know him?

"Amber, sweetie, calm down. That tube is there to help you breathe. The nurse will be in any minute." He's still holding my hand. He called me Amber. My name is Amber? Too bad, it doesn't ring any bells. This is so strange and scary at the same time. There's something about this guy that... draws me to him. I hate that I don't know him. The doctor comes in, followed by a couple of nurses.

"Kyle, Holly, would you mind going to the waiting room so I can remove Amber's tube and examine her?" So, his name is Kyle, and she is Holly. At least I know their names now.

"Princess, I'll right outside if you need me. I love you," Kyle says as he kisses me on the head.

There is that jolt again as soon as his lips touch my skin. He turns and eyes me warily before walking out the door. The doctor begins removing the tube from my throat. As he slowly pulls the tube out, my eyes fill with tears. My throat burns as if someone has lit it on fire from the inside. Once he has it all the way out, I start to cough. I try to ask for some water, but my throat is so dry, only a squeak comes out. Luckily, the nurse knows what I want and hands me a cup of water. Taking a gulp, the cold liquid soothes the burning and rehydrates my vocal chords. I am able to get out a thank you.

"I'm Dr. Michael Scarn, I have been looking after you for the last three weeks. How are you feeling, Mrs. Connor?"

"I have a slight headache. I also...well, the people who just left, I don't know who they are. I feel like I should, though." I give him a pleading look, hoping he'll tell me that the confusion will go away.

"What is the last thing you remember?" the doctor asks. With a look of worry on his face, he sits down in the chair next to me and writes on the chart in his hands.

"I don't remember anything. I don't even know who I am."

"Your name is Amber Connor. You were in a bad car accident. The man that just left is your husband, Kyle. Your father is also waiting outside."

"Will this go away? Will I remember my life again?" My chest tightens as panic sets in once more. This is all so overwhelming. The dull ache in my head increases and the more I try to remember, the worse it gets.

"It's hard to say. I have seen this type of amnesia go away within

2

hours of waking up. I have also seen cases where the patient never regains their memory. Every person is different. Would you like me to stay and explain it to your family?"

"Yes, please." I barely get the words out. I have a family. My stomach twists painfully and I feel like throwing up. I have a family that I don't remember. My nerves are frayed. Even though I don't remember these people, I feel terrible. By the way Kyle was looking at me earlier, I know what the doctor is about to tell him is going to hurt him. I really don't want to hurt him. I feel a connection to him even without remembering anything about him or us. It's a strange feeling.

The nurse walks back in. Behind her is Kyle and a man that I assume is my father. When Kyle walks in, he smiles at me. I have to look away. I know that none of this is my fault, but I still feel so guilty. Worry and pain are etched into his features and I can't help but feel like I somehow made this happen.

"I have checked Amber over and physically, everything looks great," Dr. Scarn states. He takes a deep breath before continuing. "There is one problem however, and at this point, we have no way of knowing whether it's temporary or permanent. Amber has complete amnesia. She doesn't remember anything or anyone. She doesn't even know who she is."

I avert my gaze to my hands resting in my lap. I can't bear to see the look in his eyes. It's too quiet and I glance up, just in time to see Kyle run out the door. I drop my head into my hands and cry. I wish I could explain how I feel, but it all feels so foreign. I'm upset over a man I don't know, yet feel so connected to. His pain is causing me pain.

"Amber, I'll be back in a few hours to check on you. If you need anything, the nurses will get me," Dr. Scarn tells me on his way out the door. I nod my head and try to smile.

"I'm Lee Beasley, your dad. You can call me Beasley, everyone does. Do you mind if I sit with you for a while?"

"Not at all. Will Kyle be okay?" I ask, wiping the tears from my face. Beasley sits in the chair next to my bed.

"He'll be fine. He's been so worried about you, he hasn't left this hospital in three weeks. I think he's just overstressed and needs to clear his head."

"How long have I been married to him?"

"Well, the accident happened on your wedding day. The two of you have known each other since you were both very young." He smiles, as if remembering something happy. Beasley seems like such a nice man. I must be very lucky to have a father like him. I wonder if we are close.

"Can you tell me what happened?"

"Are you sure you're up for it?"

I nod and he begins to tell me about my wedding day. It sounds like it was so beautiful and perfect. From everything he describes, Kyle and I are very much in love. My heart warms, knowing that I cared so deeply for the man in here just moments ago. Then, he tells me about Beau. I can't help but feel a slight relief at not remembering. Why would someone do such awful things? It doesn't make sense to me. The slight pang in my heart returns as I realize how hard this must be for Kyle. I wish I could take his pain away. I feel something wet on my hand and look down. It's a tear. I didn't even realize I was crying.

"Amber, are you okay? I can stop. I shouldn't have told you this so soon."

"No, I need to hear it. I'm hoping it will help me to remember something. I just... I feel so connected to Kyle even though I don't remember him. I hate that he's hurting."

"That doesn't surprise me. It's going to take a lot more than amnesia to break the bond you and Kyle share."

"Can you tell me more about my life with Kyle? Please?"

"I'll tell you everything I know."

For the next hour, Beasley tells me all about my life. I learn of my grandparents, who sound amazing. He tells me about my mother and Charles and the terrible way they died. Then, he fills me in on the six-year separation between Kyle and me. Finally, he tells me about everything leading up to the accident. By the time he finishes, I'm exhausted. My eyelids flutter as I drift in and out of consciousness, trying my best to stay awake.

"I will come by and see you again in the morning. As long as it's okay with you?" Beasley asks, obviously noticing how tired I am.

"I would really like that. Thank you for staying and telling me all that you did."

"Anytime. Everything is gonna be okay. I promise. We will get through this together. You're not alone, Amber," he says as he kisses my forehead. I give him a smile before he walks out the door. I sure hope he's right.

Kyle

WHEN I get to the bar, I grab a bottle of whiskey and head to my office. I sit on the leather sofa in the corner. Opening the bottle, I lift it to my lips, and take a long swig. I welcome the burn of the whisky as it travels down my throat. I don't care as long as it stops this ache in my heart for just a little while. Why does it seem like the universe is trying to keep Amber and me apart? Every time I think we are finally going to be together and happy, something comes along and fucks it up.

Over and over, I prayed that she would wake up. When she does, I think my prayers have been answered, but I knew by the way she looked at me that something was wrong. I always thought we could get through anything together, but how can we get through this if she doesn't even know who I am? How the hell do I fix that? I take another swallow of the whiskey. It's not helping, only clouding my thoughts. Like I wasn't confused enough. Fuck it. I'm not going anywhere tonight anyway. I might as well drink until I'm numb.

I open my eyes when I hear the door open. Amber is standing there looking at me hungrily. My heart beats faster at the sight of her. She closes the door and slowly saunters over to me. I take in the beauty that is my wife. I just watch her, afraid that if I move or speak, she'll disappear. My pulse quickens and I can feel myself harden. Damn, if I don't calm myself I'll be finished before she even touches me. When she reaches the couch, she smiles that breathtaking smile, and then lowers herself onto my lap. Her short denim skirt slides high up her thighs exposing her soft creamy skin. Drawn to them like a magnet, my shaky hands slowly caress her. Leaning down she begins trailing soft kisses along my neck as she runs her hands through my hair. I close my eyes and enjoy the feel of her body on mine and her warm breath on my skin. I want to tell her how much I've missed her, but before I can, something or someone is ripping her from my arms. I tighten my grip on her but it does no good. As soon as her body leaves mine, I feel empty. "Amber! Don't go! Please don't leave me again," I cry out.

Snapping my eyes open, I realize my head is still foggy from all of the alcohol. Was I dreaming? I hear a screech, then a thud.

"What the fuck?" I shout as I look over and see Holly holding

Leena against the wall by her throat. "Please tell me that wasn't her kissing my neck," I plead.

"Oh, it was. Please tell me you had no idea what was going on so I don't have to kick your ass next," Holly growls.

"He knew what he was doing. He wants me just as much as want him," Leena taunts, struggling to remove herself from Holly's grasp.

"I was passed out. I was dreaming about Amber. I thought I was holding Amber." I'm starting to lose it. Reality is sinking in once again. Not only was Amber not in my arms, but Leena was trying to take advantage of the situation. "I had no fucking idea she was in here doing that shit. Holly, you know I would never do that to Amber." I give her a pleading look, begging her to understand that I would never hurt Amber. Holly is hurting too; I can see the pain in her eyes. She loves Amber and it kills her to see Amber hurt in any way.

Before I can register what is about to happen, Holly's fist connects with Leena's face. *Crack.* Leena wails as blood sprays from her nose. *Ouch.* Holly let's Leena out of her grip and she drops to the floor, crying and holding her nose. Holly grabs a towel out of the closet and throws it at Leena.

"Don't get any blood on the floor. I'm not cleaning it up and you no longer work here. I warned you not to fuck up again." There is so much venom in Holly's voice, I'm afraid she is going to go after her again.

"You can't do that, you're not my boss," Leena whines. Both girls look to me for confirmation.

"Yes, she is. Even if she weren't, I agree with her anyway. You have been asked to stop more than once. This went way over the line." Before she can start to protest, my office door opens and in walks Jax with a bewildered look on his face.

"What the hell is going on?" He looks at Leena and she looks down at her lap. "What did you do now, Leena?" His voice isn't one of concern. He sounds plain pissed. It seems he's used to his cousin's antics. When Leena doesn't answer his question, he looks at me. Great. Just what I need. He already thinks I'm no good for Amber; here is the perfect thing to twist around to make me look like the bad guy.

"I was passed out on my couch and Leena decided to take advantage of the situation," I tell him truthfully. I didn't do anything wrong, so there's no reason to lie. Jax glares at Leena. If this were a cartoon, his face would be bright red and smoke would be coming out of his ears.

"Why? You promised me you would stop going after Kyle. When

will you learn to leave people who don't belong to you alone?" He shakes his head. "I think it's time you go back home to Atlanta. You have caused more than enough trouble here." She starts to protest, but Jax shoots her a look and she stops. "Let's get that nose looked at, I'm pretty sure it's broken," Jax says as he helps her off the floor.

"Sorry, Jax. I didn't mean to hit her that hard. She just..."

"Don't worry about it, Holly. I know my cousin, I'm sure she deserved worse than this. I should be apologizing for bringing her here in the first place. You don't need this shit right now, Kyle. Not with everything else you have to deal with. I'll make sure she gets back to Atlanta," he says as he helps Leena out the door. When the door closes behind them, Holly marches up to me.

"I know you're hurting and I get it, but drinking is only going to make it worse. Next time, I may not be around to keep you from making a mistake that can't be taken back. Go upstairs to the apartment, sleep it off, and in the morning, go see your wife." She walks out the door before I can respond.

Holly is right. Drinking is only going to bring me trouble. I am just so fucking lost right now. I'm so fucking happy and relieved that Amber is awake and doing okay, but the fact that she doesn't know who I am is killing me. It's like being an alcoholic in a room full of booze, but it's just out of reach. You want it so badly, but you just can't seem to get it.

First thing tomorrow, I'll go see Amber. Nothing is going to keep us apart. If I have to, I'll make her fall in love with me all over again. She may not remember all of the things we've shared, but I do. I have to fight for her. I can't give up. Not yet.

CHAPTER *Two*

Amber

J STARTLE AWAKE. My legs are tangled in the hospital sheets and my skin is drenched in sweat. My heart is racing, feeling as though it will beat right out of my chest. Flashes of broken glass and twisted metal play behind my eyes. It feels so real. The sounds of glass shattering and metal crunching. The smell of gasoline, burning rubber, and blood. So much blood. This isn't a nightmare, I'm remembering the accident. I want my memory back, but why couldn't it have been the happy times Beasley mentioned? I sit up and take in mouthfuls of air. Deep breathe, in and out. Trying to calm down, I remind myself that I'm okay. It's over. The accident has already happened and I'm alive.

"Good morning!" Becky beams as she begins to check my vitals. Becky has become one of my favorite nurses. She always has a smile on her face.

"Morning."

"You look tired. Did you sleep well?"

"Not really. I had nightmares about my accident all night. I think they were actually memories; bits and pieces of it anyway."

"That's a good sign. Hey, I know what will cheer you up. That handsome husband of yours is waiting in the hall to see you, if you're up for it." The thought of Kyle being here instantly puts a smile on my face.

"I do want to see him, but can you help me clean up first? I don't want him seeing me like this."

"Of course. It doesn't surprise me that the mention of his name brings a smile like that to your face. He is one fine looking man," she says, giving me a wink as she helps me into the bathroom to clean up. Maybe the bond my dad was talking about yesterday is so strong that nothing will break it. I have no idea. I just know that hearing he is here makes me happy.

Becky helps fix me up as best as she can with the limited resources we have. It will have to do for now. Slowly, I make my way back into bed.

"Ready for me to send in Mr. Hottie?" Becky asks with a giggle. I can't help but laugh with her. Mr. Hottie. She's not wrong.

"Yeah, you can send him in," I say in between my laughter.

When Kyle walks through the door, my heart skips a beat. I can feel my pulse speed up and a smile starts to form on my lips. He looks uneasy. When he notices me smiling, his face lights up.

"Hi. I brought you some breakfast. It's your favorite, an egg white omelet with bacon and cheddar. I made it myself," he says proudly.

"That sounds really good. It's my favorite?"

"Yeah. It has been ever since I can remember," he says as he takes the food out of the bag. When he opens the container, the aroma makes its way to my nose and my stomach instantly responds by growling loudly. I can feel the heat rising in my cheeks from embarrassment. Kyle smiles at me as he hands me my omelet and fork. As I bring the first bite to my mouth, he watches me intently, anxious to see if I like it.

"Mmm," I moan, the flavors bursting along my taste buds. "So good. I think it may still be my favorite." His eyes light up at as his lips curve up into a heart-stopping grin. *Good God.* What a smile this man has. But, it's nothing compared to his eyes. He has the most beautiful cobalt blue eyes. How did I ever do anything other than gaze into those eyes? I hear Kyle chuckle and realize I have a fork full of omelet halfway to my mouth, caught stupefied by his eyes. *Shit. Busted.* He goes from a chuckle to a full-blown laugh.

"What is so funny?"

"I'm sorry. I didn't mean to laugh, it's just...some things never change," he says, trying to stop his laughter.

"What do you mean?" It's nice to see him happy, so much better than how he looked when he left yesterday.

"I catch you zoning out and staring at various parts of my body quite frequently. Though, in your defense, you catch me doing the same to you just as often." He gives me a wink.

"I'm sorry," I reply, a little embarrassed that he caught me gawking.

"You have nothing to apologize for, princess. You can stare at me as much as you like. I don't mind at all."

"Princess? Why do you call me that?"

"When we were kids, you loved the Disney Princesses. You wanted to be a princess, so I told you that you could be my princess. I started calling you princess and it just stuck. You always liked it before. I can try not to call you that any more if it bothers you."

"No. I still like it. I was just curious." I give him a smile, hoping to ease any tension that is building. "I know it must be a pain in the ass to have to explain every aspect of our lives to me. I don't want to upset you by asking a million questions I should already have the answers to."

"Princess, you're not upsetting me. I am afraid I'm going to say or do something wrong and upset you."

"How about we make a deal?"

"What kind of deal do you have in mind?"

"I won't worry about asking you questions. When I have one, I'll ask."

"I can handle that. What do I have to do?"

"You just have to be yourself. Don't worry about upsetting me. If something bothers me, I'll tell you. Sound fair?"

"Perfectly." We both reach out at the same time to shake on our deal. As soon as our hands touch, goose bumps raise on my arms and a zinging feeling like an electric shock rocks through my entire body. I know he feels it too because we both jump a little at the same time. Our hands remain touching longer than they need to as we seem to become mesmerized, peering into each other's eyes. I'm not sure which one of us lets go first, but I feel a loss as soon as his hand leaves mine.

I was expecting it to feel strange between us, but, to my surprise, it doesn't. I'm very comfortable around him. Kyle stays with me for a few hours and every minute is filled with conversation and laughter.

"Good afternoon. I see you two are doing well today," Dr. Scarn says as he enters my room. "I hate to break up your good time, but I have to take Amber for a few tests. All routine, but nothing you can be with her for, Kyle. If you have any errands to run or anything else you need to take care of for the next few hours, now would be a good time. I'll come back in about ten minutes so you have a chance to say goodbye." He smiles at us and walks out of the room.

"I should check in on Holly and Paul at the bar. How about I come back around dinner time with your favorite dinner?" He gives me a shy smile.

"Hmm. That depends," I tease.

"Depends on what?"

"What is my favorite dinner?"

"I can't tell you that, princess. You're gonna just have to wait and see." He gives me a lopsided grin that makes my stomach flip-flop. "I'll see you around five." He walks over to my side and bends down like he's going to kiss me. In that moment, I realize I want him to. I don't miss the look of desire that flashes across his face. My body starts to tremble slightly and I lean forward, waiting for him to make his move. He quickly kisses my cheek, which has me a little disappointed. When his lips touch my skin, my heart begins to race and I'm a little light headed. Wow. I can't help but wonder now what those lips would feel like on mine.

As I watch him walk out the door, I can't stop the smile that blooms across my face. Just before he closes the door behind him, he turns and lifts his eyes to mine. The moment he sees the smile I'm wearing, one instantly appears on his face. I love that smile of his.

Kyle

As I walk out to my truck, I'm on cloud nine. This morning was so much better than I had even hoped. I was scared shitless when I walked in there, unsure of what to expect or how she was going to react to me. As hard as this is for me, it has to be ten times worse for her. She may not have all of the memories of our times together, but I know she feels our connection. I can see it in her eyes. And, I almost fucked everything up by kissing her. Those beautiful brown eyes were begging me to kiss those plump, soft lips. I shake my head, trying to stop my thoughts from wandering any further. I have to control myself. God help me, because I want… no, I need her so fucking bad it aches. If I'm not careful, I'll end up scaring her away.

Before I go check in at the bar, I stop by our house to pick up a few things that will make Amber more comfortable while she's in the hospital; which I'm hoping isn't too much longer. I also grab two photo albums — one from our wedding and one that has all of her family photos and us growing up. Holly put the photo album of wedding pictures together for us. She gathered pictures that our guests had taken as well as the ones from the photographer. She thought it would be a nice thing to have when Amber woke up. Now, I'm only hoping that the photos help her remember. If not remember, at the very least see how perfect we are together. There are so many memories in this house of the two of us; maybe being home will help her regain some of her memories. What is it going to be like when she does come home? Is she going to want to stay here? Is she going to want me here with her? *So much for being on cloud nine.* All of the uncertainty I felt this morning rears its ugly face, hitting me like a fucking brick upside the head.

When I arrive at the bar, I'm glad to see that Holly is gone. I love Holly, but I'm not in the mood for her to grill me about my visit earlier with Amber. I plop down on a barstool and wait for Paul to finish with a customer. He always tells it to me straight. I need to know how to handle this. I don't want to push too hard and scare her away, but at the same time, I don't want to do nothing either.

"You look like shit. Did your visit with Amber not go so well?" Paul asks as he slides a beer in front of me.

"Actually, it went really well. I was fine until I went by the house and started thinking about what was going to happen when she gets out of the hospital."

"What do you mean?"

"Well, is she going to want to come home? If she does come home, is she going to want me there? How the hell am I going to live in the same house and not be with her?" I express my concerns and he just stares at me like I'm crazy. After a few seconds, he begins to shake his head and laugh.

"What the fuck are you laughing at? There is absolutely nothing funny about this situation."

"Calm down. I'm not laughing at the situation, I'm laughing at you."

I flip him off. "I'm so happy my pain and suffering keeps you amused."

"You just need to relax. Take everything one day at a time. Stop getting so worked up over what ifs."

"I know. I'm just so fucking scared I'm gonna lose her. I couldn't take it. I wouldn't survive it again."

"Stop worrying. The only thing you're doing is driving yourself insane. She's not going anywhere. You need to have a little faith," Paul scolds me. Luckily, a big group of college kids walk in and take seats at the other end of the bar. Looks like Paul's going to be busy for a while. After finishing my beer, I wave goodbye to Paul.

I drive to the little seafood place twenty miles outside of town, anxious to get back to the hospital. Back to Amber. As I'm driving along the country road, the memories of the last time I took this particular drive flood my mind — the last time I tried to surprise Amber with this meal. It was the day Beau had taken her, the day I thought I'd lost her forever. I shake my head, clearing away the memories as my heart starts to accelerate. It's over. Amber is alive, that's the only thing that matters. And, I'm not going to give up. Even if she never remembers anything before the accident, she fell in love with me once, it can happen again.

I walk into Amber's room and take in the image before me. Her head is gripped in her hands with her eyes are squeezed shut, pain etched in her features. Before I get all the way into the room, her head snaps up and she smiles brightly at me. She's trying to smooth her features, hiding her obvious discomfort. If I were anyone else, it would have gone unnoticed. But, I'm not anyone else and I hate seeing her in pain while I'm not able to do anything about it.

"Are you okay? What hurts?" She looks at me, her lips forming an 'O' of surprise. She'll learn soon enough that she can't hide much from me. Much like, under normal circumstances, I can't hide much from her.

"I have a nasty headache. They come and go. The doctor says it's to be expected. Eventually, they should go away completely." She gives me another sweet smile. "Is that my surprise favorite dinner in your hand?"

"It is," I reply, starting to lay out our food. "How did all of your tests go?"

"They went well. Dr. Scarn says I can go home in a couple days." We both look at each other, watching the others reaction. I'm thrilled she'll be able to get out of here, but scared of what that might mean for me.

"That's great news. I actually planned to ask you if you have given any thought to what you want to do when you get out? I want you to be comfortable and I'll do whatever you decide. That being said, I'd like you to come home." There. I said it. I want her to come home, to our home. I really don't know if I can handle being away from her any longer.

"Are you sure that won't be too difficult for you? I can't make any promises."

"I don't want you to. I just want to help you. And if I'm being honest, I don't think I can stand being away from you any longer. I will take anything you're willing to give, even if it's living in the same house as friends for now."

"And what happens if I don't get my memories back?" she asks, her eyes no longer meeting mine, but looking at her lap instead.

"I hope that you do. Though, if you don't, it doesn't matter." I pause for a moment, collecting my thoughts. "We have a connection that can't be broken. Even amnesia can't take it away. You've felt it, haven't you?" Amber nods her head. "So, if by some chance you don't get your memories back, I'll just have to start over. Make you fall in love with me again." I move a little closer to her. I slowly lift her face with my finger and look her in the eyes. "I will promise you this, princess, I am not giving up on us without one hell of a fight." That gets her attention. Goose bumps form on her skin as her breathing quickens. Maybe I have nothing to worry about, after all. "Now, let's eat this food before it gets too cold." I shoot her a wink and a smile and her face instantly reddens. It's the sexiest thing I have ever seen. It makes me want to hold her in my arms and never let go.

With a scallop on her fork, she reaches over and dips it in my tartar sauce. I quickly snatch the fork from her hand just before it touches her mouth and she looks at me like I have completely lost my fucking mind. I don't blame her. I'm going to have to let her find out things like that on her own.

"What was that all about?" She has an amused look on her face. At least she's not pissed. I try to recover by being flirty. I smile and pop her scallop into my mouth. Amber scowls at me playfully and I give a little moan as I chew. Watching her tongue dart out to wet her lips, I pick up a scallop with my fork and dip it into the cocktail sauce.

"You hate tartar sauce. You only eat scallops with cocktail sauce," I say as I raise it to her mouth, just barely touching her lips.

She opens her mouth and I ease it in, savoring the way her lips wrap around the fork. Instantly, her eyes light up, just like they always do when she eats these. She may not remember loving them, but she still does.

"Oh. You're right, these are so good." She dips the tip of her finger in my tartar sauce and tastes it. I can't help but laugh. The face she makes is like she's sucking on lemons. "And I still don't like tartar sauce, obviously," she giggles before drinking her water.

We eat in a comfortable silence for a while. I love just being near her. Every now and then, I look up and catch her looking at me. She blushes the instant I look at her. If only she had a clue as to how beautiful and sexy she is without even trying.

"What are those books that you brought?" Amber asks, pointing to the photo albums I brought with me. I had almost forgotten about those.

"Photo albums from home. I thought you might want to look through them. One is from our wedding; the other has pictures of us growing up. Maybe they can help you remember." She pats the spot next to her on the bed as she moves over.

"Bring them over. You can tell me who everyone is." *Is this woman slowly trying to torture me to death? Can I really sit that close and not touch her?* Pulling all of the self-restraint I have to the surface, I sit next to her. Our shoulders gently brush together and I hear her suck in a breath. *At least it's not just my restraint being tested.*

She looks at every picture so intensely, as if she's trying to burn it to memory. I explain each picture in as much detail as possible. After a while, I notice the slight drop in her eyelids and know she must be tired. She snuggles up close to my side, resting her head on my shoulder, and I stop breathing. She yawns as she turns a page in the photo album and I snap out of it, my restricted lungs taking in air again. I barely pay attention to the photos as she flips through, too busy enjoying taking in her scent of coconut. Holly must have brought her favorite shampoo to her today.

Shaking my head to clear my thoughts, I realize she has stopped flipping pages and asking questions. I look down and see that she is sound asleep. I gently take the photo albums from her hands and set them on the table next to the bed. Slowly, I slide out of the bed and lay her down. For a moment, I can pretend everything is normal. She looks like my Amber. So beautiful and peaceful. I can't help myself. I place a kiss on her forehead then the slightest of kisses across her lips.

"I love you, princess. More than you will ever know. You are the very thing that keeps my heart beating. I'm not giving up on us. I need you too much."

As I walk to my truck, I feel a little more hopeful that maybe things can work out. But I can't help but wonder just how bumpy the ride will be.

CHAPTER
Three

Amber

I AWAKE WITH a start. My skin is slick with sweat, my heart racing, and arms and legs tangled up in my sheets. I had another nightmare about the accident. Each night, they seem to become more vivid, more intense. Each time, I seem to remember more than the last. I was screaming something as the truck crashed but I couldn't make out what I was saying. Frustration bubbles up inside of me. Why am I remembering something that terrifies me to my very core? Why can't I remember happy things? Like being with Kyle? Just thinking about him brings a smile to my face.

"I bet thoughts of Mr. Hottie put that smile on your face," Nurse Becky says, giggling.

"Maybe. Am I going to have to watch you around him?" I tease. She's so much fun to be around and the only thing about this hospital I am going to miss.

"No, I can behave. Just know, if you ever get bored with him, you can send him my way. Now let's get you ready to fly this coop. I'm sure Mr. Hottie will be here soon to whisk you away."

"I'm going to miss you."

"No you won't. Your friend Holly invited me to a girl's night at the bar once you are up to it. We exchanged numbers. We also put my number in your phone and she put yours in mine. You really thought you could get rid of me that easily?" I just shake my head and smile. It's nice to be friends with someone who has all of the same memories of our relationship as I do.

"That sounds like fun." And it really does. Holly is a lot of fun to be around also. She's spent quite a bit of time here sitting with me. As I make my way into the bathroom to get dressed, I can't help but feel a little nervous about going home. I'm not nervous really to be around Kyle... well except for the fact that my body seems to take over every other part of me when he's around. I can't seem to control my over active libido. It goes crazy just thinking about him. What the hell is going to happen when we are in the same house together, day and night?

"One day at a time," I whisper to myself in the mirror. I take another deep breath and gather my things. When I walk out of the bathroom, Dr. Scarn and Kyle are standing by the bed talking. They both look up and smile when they see me.

"Are you ready to get out of this place?" Dr. Scarn asks.

"No offense, but yes, I'm ready to go home." I notice the smile on Kyle's face when I say home.

"None taken. I'm happy to see you healthy enough to be walking out of here. I have gotten all of the results back from the tests I did the other day. Everything looks great. Physically, you are one-hundred percent. You will probably continue to have headaches now and then. I have written a prescription for that. I think the fact that you have been remembering parts of the accident is a good sign as well." I look over to Kyle. He looks shocked, but I also see hurt flash in his eyes. I haven't mentioned any of that to him yet. Not because I'm hiding anything, I'm just having a hard time remembering it myself and I know it will hurt him to have to live through it again. I don't want to cause him any more pain or guilt than he's already feeling.

"So, unless something comes up that worries you, I won't need to see you again for two months. Call my office next week. My secretary will make the appointment for you. Any questions?" Dr. Scarn looks between Kyle and me. I'm so worried about Kyle being upset, my mind seems to draw a blank. Thankfully, Kyle is thinking clearly.

"Does she have any restrictions?" he asks.

"No, not officially. I would advise to ease back into things at first.

Don't overdo anything. Most of all, don't push yourself to remember things. If they are going to come back, they will. Don't get too frustrated if they don't right away. It might happen in little flashes here and there, or they may all come flooding in all at once." He gives me a reassuring look. "Is there anything else?" We both shake our heads no. "If you do think of anything later, write it down and call my office." Dr. Scarn gives me a brief kiss on the cheek and shakes Kyle's hand. "You are free to go whenever you are ready, my dear." He smiles and leaves the room.

"Why didn't you tell me?" Kyle asks, sounding hurt. All I do is cause this man pain. If he were smart, he would run as fast as he could away from me.

"I wasn't trying to hide anything. There just isn't anything pleasant about these memories. I only have them at night."

"Like dreams?"

"No. Not dreams. They are nightmares. So real. I can hear the metal of the trucks crunching, the glass shattering. I can smell tires burning, gasoline, and blood. I wake up in the middle of the night or morning in a panic." I start to pace the room, trying to calm my rapidly beating heart. I look out the window, not able to look at him. "I see the pain and guilt in your eyes. I don't want to make you relive any of that and cause more pain and guilt than I already have." Before I can turn around, strong arms wrap around me. My whole body feels like it has been set on fire from the inside, yet at the same time is calm the moment I'm in his arms. He brings his lips to my ear, so close I can feel the heat from his breath.

"Princess, you haven't caused me anything but happiness and a heart full of love. We have been dealt a shitty hand, but, baby, you aren't the one dealing the cards. You didn't cause any of this. The guilt you see in my eyes? That's guilt from not protecting you when I should have. Twice, that bastard got to you. Twice, he hurt you. Twice, I let you down. I tried to protect you, God knows I tried so hard, but I failed." I try to turn in his arms so I can look at him and tell him this isn't his fault either, but he holds me tighter and shakes his head no before continuing.

"I'm pretty sure you've already figured this out, but in case you haven't, let me fill you in. We are both in pain. When you look into my eyes, all you see is a reflection. The pain I feel is from watching you go through so much pain and knowing I almost lost you. Anything that you feel, I feel too. That is just the way it is with us. If you hurt, so do

I. If I'm scared, so are you. You have already realized a little of this, haven't you?" The yes that falls from my lips is a whisper. Between his body against mine and the words he's speaking, I'm speechless.

"I don't care how big or small something is, I am here for you. Always. No matter what it does to me. I can take your pain, your fears, your worries, and help you carry them. Lean on me. Cry on my shoulder. Anything you need, I will give it to you. I love you. I love you so much that if you needed my last breath to survive, I would give it without a second thought." He softly kisses behind my ear and I feel a tear land on my shoulder. This man is amazing.

"Okay," I reply, tongue-tied. What in the hell do I say to that? How can I make this better for him? He's right, I do feel his pain. I do feel his fear — the fear that I will never remember our past and he will lose me forever. I have to remember. I have to fight for us just as he is. We both stay still, neither of us wanting me to leave his arms. I feel so safe and happy when he's wrapped around me like a warm blanket. After a few more minutes, I hear him take a deep breath as he slowly drops his arms.

"Let's get you home, princess," he says, still so close to my ear that I feel his warm breath.

"Sounds good to me." Turning so I can see his face, I smile when I see the love for me in his eyes. Even though I don't remember our life together, I do know I love this man. I couldn't deny it if I tried.

Kyle

THE DRIVE home from the hospital is quiet, but comfortable. I hadn't intended for things to get so heavy at the hospital, but she needed to know where I stand and how I feel. If either of us is going to shoulder the blame for any of this, it should be me. I failed. My purpose is to love and protect her. Loving her is as easy as breathing; it just comes naturally for me. For some fucked up reason, I always seem to fail miserably when it comes to protecting her. Nothing I can do about that now, though. I just have to do my best to be here for her and make up for failing her in the past.

As we park in front of the house, I look over at Amber. She scans everything in her view. The look on her face is unreadable. Before I can ask her about it, she gets out of the truck. I watch her for a minute before getting out and walking up beside her.

"Are you okay, princess?" She looks over at me with tears in her eyes.

"Yeah. I-I'm not remembering anything but it all feels so familiar. It feels like home. Does that even make any sense?" She looks up at me, her eyes full of so many emotions. I can't help myself. I may be moving too fast, but I know her. I know right now in this moment, this is what she needs. I don't say anything. She doesn't need me to. I just wrap her tightly in my arms and hold her close.

"Let's go inside and have some lunch, I'll get your bags later." I lead her into the house and we sit at the bar in the kitchen. "What would you like me to fix you for lunch?" She looks at me with a beautiful smile on her face.

"How about one of my favorite omelets?"

"I had a feeling you would want that. Why don't you look around and get familiar with the house? I'll let you know when it's ready." As she slides off her stool and walks toward the stairs, I grab what I need to start cooking. I pass by my iPod and turn it on, needing something to break the silence of the house.

I crack the eggs into the mixing bowl, then add a little milk, salt, and pepper, and begin to beat it all together. I notice I'm feeling much more at ease just by having Amber here at home. I need to make sure I don't move too fast and spook her. That's going to be my biggest challenge. Anytime I'm near her, I have a need to touch her, hold her. She seems to be happy to be here, and I want it to stay that way. I'm so engrossed in thoughts of Amber, I'm not paying attention to what I'm doing. *Shit.* I was beating the eggs so fast that I splattered egg all over the front of my shirt. I take my shirt off, throw it over the back of the chair, and continue cooking.

Just as I'm finishing up at the stove, a good song starts to play. I begin singing along and swaying to the beat when the sound of Amber giggling breaks through the music. I look over my shoulder and wink at her before turning back to the stove.

"Enjoying the show, princess?" I ask, not missing the want that flashes through her eyes. She may not remember that morning that feels like a lifetime ago now, but it's definitely something I will never forget and I'm curious as to what her answer will be this time. Not that

I'll go as far as I did the last time we were in this kitchen like this, as appealing as the thought might be.

"Eh...kind of." She shrugs her shoulders. The second our eyes lock, we both realize she remembers this moment. She looks over at the counter, the one I sat her up on that first morning after we found each other again. When she looks back at me, I can see the heat crawl up her neck into her cheeks. *Oh, she most definitely remembers.* I can't stop the smile that spreads across my face. Even though it's just one memory, it's a memory of us. Of me.

"What do you remember?" I ask and she blushes immediately. She turns away from me, as if she's trying to gather the courage to say what she sees in her head out loud. She takes in a deep breath before turning around to face me again.

"I remember standing in the doorway, watching you cook breakfast. I was thinking that you were the sexiest man I had ever seen. You were wearing jeans and no shirt. Music was playing, and you were singing and swaying to the beat, just like now. And you asked if I was enjoying the show. I teased you by playing it off and saying kind of. And then..." Too see her so turned on, yet so bashful at the same time is sexy as hell. I'm testing my own restraint but I have to see her reaction. I quickly pick her up and set her on top of the counter just like before. I move to stand between her legs and bring my lips to her ear.

"And then, I did this," I say. I feel her shaking her head yes as her breathing speeds up. *God, I want her so badly.* She's giving me all of the signals that say she wouldn't stop me if I took this further. But as badly as I want and need that closeness, that connection to her, I can't. I'm too afraid it would be pushing too far too fast. The risk of pushing her away from me is just too great. I pull back so she can see how much I want her, even though I am not going any further.

"Princess, I..." Before I can finish, she grips the sides of her head with her hands and squeezes her eyes shut tight. "What is it? Are you okay?" *Shit. What did I do?*

"My head...a headache," she says softly. I carefully pick her up and carry her upstairs. Gently, I lay her down on the bed and kiss her forehead.

"Rest here. I'll get your lunch and your pain medication." She smiles sweetly before closing her eyes. Once in the kitchen, I heat her omelet back up, pour her a glass of orange juice, and get her pills. I really need to keep my fucking hormones in check. What if I caused her headache? I just keep screwing things up at every turn.

When I get back in the bedroom, Amber is sitting up against some pillows. She looks better than she did when I left her.

"You do know this isn't your fault, right? You didn't cause my headache."

"But..."

"But nothing. I get them. You heard Dr. Scarn this morning. It will happen, they will go away eventually. There is nothing you can do to prevent or cause them. Okay?"

"Okay," I concede. She is the same feisty Amber, my feisty Amber. I can't help but feel lighter knowing my girl is coming back. I hand her the plate, set the juice on the nightstand, and then give her one of her pills.

"Do you want me to turn on the television for you while you eat?"

"Sure." I find the remote and turn on the TV.

"I, uh...I'll be down stairs if you need anything." Just as I get to the door, she stops me.

"Wait! Don't you want to keep me company?" She sounds like she is afraid to hear my answer. Of course I want to keep her company. I don't ever want to leave her side.

"As long as you don't mind." She gives me a look that says 'don't be a moron', then pats the bed beside her. We flip channels for a while and finally settle on a *Duck Dynasty* marathon. Those guys always crack us up.

I awake with a start. I blink, trying to clear the haze and focus on the screaming and thrashing that pulled me from a deep sleep. It takes me a minute to realize what's happening. Amber is next to me. She's screaming. She's having a nightmare. I glance at the clock as I go to switch on the lamp. It's two o'clock in the morning. We must have fallen asleep. Amber starts screaming again and I freeze, hearing her words clearly.

"Kyle! Help me! Please! Don't let me die! I don't want to leave you! Kyle, I'm so sorry. I love you." It feels like someone punched me in the chest as the air escapes my lungs. The pain and fear in her voice breaks me. I was there the whole time it was happening and all I could do was watch. I couldn't help her. I couldn't protect her. I would have given my own life for her to not have gone through any of that. She lets out another scream, but this one sounds garbled, like she's in pain. I quickly slide across the bed, scoop her into my arms, hold her on my lap, and rock her back and forth, trying to soothe the bad memories away.

"Princess. Wake up. It's just a nightmare. You're safe. I'm here. Baby, I've got you now." I keep saying this over and over, as I gently rock her. After a minute or so, her eyes flutter open. When she realizes where she is and what has happened, she clings to me and begins sobbing uncontrollably. Hearing the pain in her cries makes my chest ache and my own tears fall. I feel her pain, but more importantly, I want to take it all away from her. I hate that this is the memory she has to continue reliving night after night.

When she finally calms a little, I ease her off my lap and lay her back down on the bed. I start to slip my arm out from under her and she startles.

"Please, Kyle. Just hold me. Don't let me go. Please." She sounds like a scared little girl and my heart breaks further at hearing her so afraid.

"Never, princess. I will never let you go, I promise." And it is a promise I will die to keep. I wrap her tightly in my arms and pull her close to me. Her breathing finally begins to even out and I do just as I promise. I hold her all night while I lay awake, wondering how I'm going to fix my broken princess.

CHAPTER
Four

Amber

THE SUN shines through the bedroom window, heating my face. I stretch and roll over, slowly opening my eyes. I see Kyle asleep in the chair. He looks so uncomfortable with his legs hanging over the arm of the chair and his head hanging at an unusual angle. He has been so attentive and sweet. Every night for the past two weeks since I was released from the hospital, he's slept in that chair. He wants to be close in order to comfort me during the night. Every night, I wake up terrified and screaming. The images, sounds, and smells have been haunting me, night after night. Each night, I remember just a little more than the night before. With each new memory, it feels more and more like I am reliving it all over again. Last night it took almost forty-five minutes for Kyle to convince me that I was home and safe.

On the bright side, I am slowly starting to remember other happier parts of my life. Some childhood memories of Kyle and my grandparents have resurfaced, along with more recent memories of Kyle and me. I was having strong feelings for him before I started remembering anything, but now? Now, I know I'm in love with him. I haven't come right out and told him yet. The time just hasn't been right. Though, it is getting harder and harder to be close to him without touching him. It isn't easy for him either. That's why he's in the chair. He holds and soothes me until I fall back asleep after a nightmare, then moves himself to the chair. He says he can't be that close and keep himself under control. *Fine with me.* That's what I would like to tell him anyways.

"What are you thinking about over there?" Kyle asks in his sleepy voice that is oh so sexy. I swear the sound of his voice has me wet and wanting him. What is the equivalent of blue balls for women? Blue boobs, maybe? Well, whatever it is, I have it. He also has that lopsided smirk on his face. He knows I'm daydreaming about him. The cocky bastard.

"Oh. Nothing really. Just thinking I would like to go to the center today. Maybe it could spark a memory or two." I smile my most innocent smile, playing it off as nothing. Maybe he doesn't know I was thinking dirty things about him again. Just then, he stands up and the blanket falls to the floor. Big, beautiful muscles and black silk boxers are all I see. When he reaches over his head and stretches, those muscles flex and tighten. My mouth is hanging open and of course, he notices. He starts to laugh as he saunters over and sits on the bed next to me. His leg brushes mine and my body is instantly on fire.

"If you feel that you are ready, then I think that's a good idea," he says with a slight squeak in his voice, as his leg brushes mine again. *Ha!* At least he feels it too. Maybe even a little more. He quickly gets up from the bed. "I'm going to take a shower in the guest bath, then I'll make us some breakfast. Come down when you're ready."

The drive to the center is over too quickly. As Kyle pulls into the parking lot, that familiar feeling sweeps over me. No memories, just the feeling that I know this place; that I've been here before. I can feel my palms starting to sweat and it's suddenly hard to catch my breath. How are the people who work here going to react to me? What about the kids? They're going to know me, but I won't know them. Maybe this wasn't such a good idea after all. I'm so lost in my own head that when Kyle grabs my hand, it startles me.

"Princess, you don't have to do this today. We can turn around and go home. I'll be right beside you, whatever you decide."

"I'm okay. I'm just nervous." He squeezes my hand, slowly moving his thumb back and forth along the top. It's such a simple gesture, but it eases my nerves and awakens a fire in my core at the same time. Why does that little bit of contact from him have such an effect on me?

"I know you are. I wish there was something, anything, I could do to make this all go away for you. I would do anything if it meant you didn't have to go through the hell you've been through. I am always here for you. You can hold my hand for comfort." He squeezes my hand a little tighter and gives me a heart-melting smile. "When you're scared, you can find safety in my arms. I will always protect you. When you're mad or frustrated, you can scream and yell at me. Trust me, I can take it. I just want you to be happy and I will do whatever it takes to help make that happen."

Well, if I weren't already in love with him, then I sure as shit am now. He leaves me speechless when he says things like that. And he does, often. But, it's not just his words; it's the look in his eyes as well. They say so much more to me than his words ever could. Lust, love, guilt — the emotions playing across his beautiful blue irises are enough to make me weep. His loves shines brightly, but he thinks he failed me. I wish I could make him see how much I want him. How much I need him to let me shoulder the weight. Gathering my strength, I can only hope that he understands.

"I am so thankful that I have you. I don't think I would've been able to make it through any of this without you. You have been more than patient with me. This whole ordeal hasn't been easy for you either, but you have only been worried about taking care of me."

"As long as you are happy, so am I." He leans over and kisses my forehead. "If you get too uncomfortable, just say the word and we're out of there."

As we walk through the doors of the center, I take in everything. It's all so familiar. I know what each room is for, where each door leads, but I have no idea how I know that. I look over toward the music room when I hear a guitar playing. Angel is in the room with a group of kids. All of a sudden, images start flashing through my head. It's like watching a video in fast forward. My head starts to throb as it usually does when I start to remember things. Kyle must notice because he leads me up the stairs and into an office. My office. I'm remembering. Mainly the day Darcie came and took me to Beau. Why do I have to keep remembering the bad things that happened to me? I sit on the couch. Sometimes these headaches are unbearable. Kyle hands me a glass of water and one of my pain pills.

"Are you okay, princess?" Kyle asks, concern lacing his voice. "You're remembering something again, aren't you?"

"Yeah. Quite a few things, actually. The day I found this place and getting it all ready to open. Hiring Jax and the rest of the staff. All the kids, I remember the kids." I can't help but smile at that. I was so worried I wouldn't remember them. Kyle smiles back at me. As more memories flood my mind, the smile quickly melts from my face.

"What is it, babe?"

"I also remember Darcie and the cabin." I look up at him just in time to see the anger cross his handsome face. I grab his hand. "It's okay. I need to remember everything. Good and bad. Grandma once told me, if we didn't have the bad times, how would we know what the good times were like?" He opens his mouth to say something but before he can, Jax and Angel walk through the door.

"Hey, I thought I saw you two come in." Jax beams as he comes over to kiss my cheek. "How have you been?"

"Really good," I say as I look up at Kyle and give him a smile. "Kyle has been taking really good care of me." It almost looks like that statement annoys Jax. I must be wrong. He has been so great to Kyle and me. The center wouldn't be open if it weren't for Jax being here to take care of everything for me. Kyle has even seemed to warm up to him quite a bit.

"Well, it's good to see you back here again. Thinking of coming back to work any time soon?"

"No. I think it's still too soon for that. Maybe in another couple weeks." I really want to come back, especially now that I'm remembering this place again, but pushing things too fast would be a mistake. Waiting a while longer is the smart thing to do.

"Don't worry. You know I have everything taken care of until you do. I better get downstairs and check on things. It was good to see you both." Jax places a kiss on my forehead before walking out the door. I swear I hear Angel growl when Jax touches me.

"Amber, you look tired. Are you overdoing it by being here?" Angel asks as he looks at me with concern. He can be so sweet. He always treats me like I'm his little sister.

"I am getting a little tired. These damn headaches take a lot out of me."

"You heard the lady, asshole. Take her home and take care of her. If you don't, I will." He looks up at me then, giving me his killer smile and a wink. Kyle mutters something under his breath as he flips Angel off. I love how these guys all joke and tease each other like brothers.

"Okay, princess, let's get you out of here. Want to pick up some food from the bar to take home? I have to check in with Paul anyway. We can watch some movies and relax while we eat. Sound good?"

"Sounds perfect to me," I reply with a smile as the three of us leave my office. It feels good to have regained more of my memories. It seems as though my life is finally coming together and I'm going to be okay. Kyle and I are going to be okay.

The sight of Holly standing behind the bar as we walked into KC's makes me smile. We haven't been able to spend too much time together lately and I've really missed her. She looks so happy to see me as I make my way to the bar and sit on the stool in front of her.

"Hello there, stranger. It's good to see you out and about," Holly chimes.

"It feels good to be out and about. How have things been around here?"

"The same as always. Boring with a capital B. I was thinking...since you seem to be feeling better, maybe we could have a girl's night out soon?" She looks at me expectantly.

That does sound like fun and I definitely could use some fun. I'm sure Kyle could use a guy's night out as well. He has spent every second with me since I came home from the hospital. Not that I mind it, but he probably needs a break from me.

"Okay. How about this weekend?"

"Really? I'm not going to have to twist your arm or beg? Shit. Becky and I have been trying to think of all kinds of ways to convince you for days now." She shakes her head and smirks. "All I had to do was ask? Bitch." We both start to laugh. It feels so good to have the feeling that my life is getting back to normal. Back to what it was before the accident. The thought of all the good things to come makes me smile.

As I look up, I see Paul standing in front of me. He slides a drink by my hand and winks. It looks like some kind of martini. The look on his face is telling me this is something I should remember. Not wanting to put a damper on everyone's good mood, I decide to play along. With a smile on my face, I nervously take the glass in my shaky hand. As soon as I taste the sour apple flavor, it all hits me. All of the times Paul and Holly have made these for me. My favorite drink — appletinis. I remember the playful winks Paul always gave me every time he served me one of these. The time Holly and I got so drunk from them, I didn't think I would ever drink another one again. Yeah right! Who was I kidding? We were back at it the next night.

"You okay, Amber? I know there's nothing wrong with the drink, I made it," Paul states with his usual little touch of cockiness thrown in for good measure.

"I'm fine. Great actually. I was just remembering a few new things." I hear Holly groan and I laugh. She knows what I was remembering and she was a lot sicker than I was that night.

"Of course you did. I'm unforgettable. There is no way you could ever totally forget anything that has to do with me," Paul jokes as Kyle slaps him in the back of his head.

"You are lucky Holly loves Amber so much. She would normally kick your ass for flirting with another girl so openly," Kyle teases. Holly and I sit back and watch the two of them go back and forth until the food we've been waiting on is ready. Holly and I make a plan to have lunch in a couple days to discuss our girl's night. Kyle thinks it will be good for me to get out with my friends and have some fun, but I can tell that he's a little nervous about the idea of me being out of his sight. He's afraid something will happen to me and he won't be around to protect me. The fear that something bad will happen to me again is going to eat him alive. I wish there was something I could do to take it all away.

When we get home, Kyle takes the food to the kitchen to plate while I find a movie to watch. I'm not really sure what kind of movies I like. After giving it a little thought, I choose a horror movie. I figure it will give me a good excuse to snuggle up in Kyle's arms. Every part of me wants him and I am finished denying myself. I need him to see that I'm here, I'm alive, and the fear he feels of something happening to me has to stop. The only way to make that happen is to start living again. Living like the married couple that we are, that I want to be in every sense. We both need to get back to living normal lives, free from drama, and I've regained enough of my memories to do just that. I can go back to working at the center again and Kyle can get back to the bar. Back to playing the music he loves with the guys.

"So, what will we be watching tonight? Some sappy love story?" Kyle teases as he lays my plate on the coffee table in front of me.

"I was thinking something scary sounded better," I say. When I look over at him, he has his eyebrow raised and a smirk on his face. What's that all about?

"Okay. That's fine with me. If you're sure," he says with a hint of a laugh. I wish I knew what he was thinking.

"Do you not think I can handle a scary movie?"

"Well, you've always hated them because they scare the crap out of you."

"Then I guess you will have to hold me if I get too scared." Just a hint of a smile graces his handsome face. I can see how appealing the idea is to him by the way he has to adjust himself in his jeans.

"I think I can handle that," he says as he starts to eat his cheese steak. Clark makes the best cheese steaks I've ever had. My mouth starts to water at the thought, so I begin to dig into mine.

Luckily, my mind is on my food and not on the ear piercing screams coming from the movie. I guess these movies still scare me. When both of our plates are empty, I jump up from the couch and carry them to the kitchen. I was trying not to look at the screen but of course, I do. Why do people like these blood and gore movies? Yuck. I take my time in the kitchen. Putting the plates in the dishwasher then throwing all of the trash away. When I can't find anything else to do, I grab a couple beers and slowly make my way back to the living room. I hand Kyle a beer and sit beside him on the couch.

All of these movies are the same. Some woman is some place she shouldn't be and you know she's about to be slaughtered. I can feel myself shaking. Kyle must think I'm cold. He grabs the throw blanket from the back of the couch and spreads it out over me. But before I can thank him, a really gruesome part comes on the screen. I am practically on his lap with my face buried in his chest and the blanket covering it for good measure.

"Aww, princess, a little scared?" Kyle chuckles

"No. Not at all. Just getting comfy," I say as innocently as I possibly can. Kyle is still chuckling. I do not like these movies. Not. At. All.

Laying against Kyle's chest, wrapped tightly in his arms, is so relaxing. Today was a great day but a little draining. I'm enjoying the feeling of being here with him so close and I don't want it to end, but unfortunately, my body has other plans. I fight it for as long as I can, but after a while, I have no choice but to give into the exhaustion.

Kyle

As I climb the stairs, carrying a sleeping Amber in my arms, I think about the perfect night we had. For one night, it felt like we were a normal married couple without all of the baggage and drama that haunts us. Even though we only sat and watched movies, it was the most fun I've had in a very long time. I feel so relaxed and happy.

The best part of the night was the look of want in Amber's beautiful brown eyes. How in the hell I managed to keep my dick in my pants, I will never know. Every time she buried her face in my chest, the air was knocked right out of my lungs. By the time the movie was over, I was so fucking turned on I wanted to take her right there on the living room floor. But I didn't. For one, she was sound asleep. And two, I don't want to push her.

So, here I am, hard as a rock, tucking my wife into bed so I can sleep in the chair across the room. I try to keep telling myself it will be worth it. When we finally come together again, it will be unbelievable. Thank God, she's already in her pajamas. I would explode if I had to change her clothes for her. I lay her gently down on the bed and pull the sheet over her. I lean down and lightly brush my lips against hers. I miss the softness of her lips. It takes every ounce of strength I have to pull away and not take it farther. Normally, I would be happy just to hold her close to me, but it's been too long, I wouldn't be able to stop there. I make my way to the chair and strip down to my boxers. After about ten minutes of moving around, I finally get comfortable enough to fall asleep.

"Kyle! Kyle! Please, help me! I don't want to leave you! I love you! I'm so sorry, please forgive me!" I jump from the chair the second I hear her screaming. The terror in her voice shatters me from the inside out. My body is shaking as I crawl into the bed next to her. I wrap her tightly in my arms and pull her closely to me, calming her thrashing.

"Shh. I'm here. I've got you. You're okay, baby. I promise," I whisper, holding her tighter. I continue to tell her how much I love her and that she is safe, attempting to break through her cries. I wish I could erase all of the images that torment her night after night. After a few moments, she finally starts to calm, my voice breaking through to her.

"I'm sorry," Amber whispers against my chest.

"Princess, you have nothing to be sorry for." I raise her head so I can see her eyes. "You haven't done anything wrong."

"But you have put your entire life on hold for me. And for what? A wife that doesn't act like much of a wife? We don't even sleep in the same bed. You sleep in that uncomfortable chair every night so you can calm me when I wake up screaming. You spend every second of every day with me. What about your bar? Your friends? Your band? You can't possibly be happy. Maybe...I... maybe I should just leave." She buries her head back into my chest, her wet tears hitting my skin as her shoulders begin to shake from her sobs. She can't be serious. The thought of her leaving sends an unbearable ache straight to my heart. I know she's frustrated and scared — hell, we both are — but there is no way she is leaving me now, we are too close to having our life back.

"Look at me," I demand a little too harshly, needing her to hear me. Her head slowly lifts and her eyes find mine. "Please, don't say you're going away ever again. I've almost lost you too many times. This last time though..." I take a deep breath and shake my head, pulling myself together. "Sometimes you forget that I was there too. I had to helplessly watch the whole accident play out in front of me and there wasn't a fucking thing I could do to help you. I wanted to. So badly." Tears flow down my face and I don't even try to stop them. She needs to see that I am as affected by this as she is. That I'm right here alongside her. "For better or worse...that's what we vowed. I'm not bailing just because we are going through a tough time. Would you?"

"Of course not. You have to stop blaming yourself for everything that's happened. I don't blame you for not being able to do anything. There was nothing you could have done. I know if there was something that could have been done, you would have done it. The person that caused all of this pain for us is gone for good. We have to stop letting him hurt us," Amber says through her tears. I lean down and kiss her lips lightly. She has the softest, sweetest lips. I know that should be the last thing on my mind, they just feel so good against mine.

"Please don't cry. I am so happy. Happy that you're alive, happy you are here with me." I kiss her again. "Every day you remember more and more. My life is not on hold. I am still doing what I want. I am still living my life with you. You don't realize that without you I wouldn't have a life worth living." She takes a deep breath, grabs my face in her hands, and crashes her lips to mine. For the briefest second I hesitate, shocked. But when her tongue sweeps across my lips, I let go. The moment our tongues meet, my body is on fire. There is no hesitation on her part. I feel the want, the need, in the way she's kissing me. I don't remember ever being this turned on in my life. Allowing myself something I have wanted for weeks, I begin to run my hands over every part of her beautiful body. Her skin is so soft, like silk.

"Please make love to me," she whispers. "I want you. I need you so badly. I love you and can't wait any longer."

"Are you sure? I don't want to push you." I must be an idiot, am I really trying to talk her out of this? I have only a sliver of self-control left.

"I've remembered what it's like when you make love to me, but I want to feel it. I don't want to keep worrying about the old memories; I want to focus on making new ones." She looks up at me, her eyes pleading with me to give in. I couldn't say no to her now even if I wanted to, and I definitely don't want to. I take her face in my hands.

"I have missed you so much, princess," I whisper against her neck. "You are so fucking beautiful. I love you and only you forever. Let me show you how much." I gently bring my lips to meet hers, my whole body shaking with a combination of nerves and want. I've missed this closeness to Amber. For a while, it's something I didn't think I would ever feel again.

Moving my lips to her neck, I trail my tongue along her pulse, kissing and sucking gently as I move my way up to that spot behind her ear. Her favorite spot. As soon as my tongue glides across that spot, her breathing instantly picks up, coming in short, sharp pants. Her hands slowly glide down my back as I squeeze her hip, wanting more. I continue to suck and kiss, moving my mouth down once more, my hand moving up to her stomach. Her fingers are still playing along my back; slowly teasing with feather light touches intermingled with light scratches. She finally reaches my ass and grips it tight, pulling my lower body into hers.

I grind my painfully hard cock against the heat I feel emanating through her shorts and panties, eliciting a breathy and deep moan from her lips. I slow my movements, drawing a path with my tongue from her neck to between her breasts in a feeble attempt to keep my control in check. She doesn't need me losing control right now. No, she needs to feel everything I'm doing to her. Really feel how perfect we truly are together as one.

As I kiss along her ribs, I move my hand further up her stomach, pushing her shirt up as my teeth nip at her breasts and my other hand moves around to her ass, gripping the perfection and squeezing. I moan at the feel of her ass in my hand, the tease of her tits in my face still fully covered, the breathy moans she lets out as I touch her. My senses are reeling, my body tense from how turned on I am. My cock is so hard it could cut glass and I love every minute of this sweet torture. I find her nipple with my tongue and swirl around it, bringing it to more of a peak before gently biting through the material.

"Oh, god," Amber moans, deep and raspy, her voice belaying just how turned on she is as her hands grasp onto my hair and pull slightly. Fuck, she's gorgeous. She keeps my head where it is, pressing down slightly, taking control of where my mouth goes, and fuck if I don't feel my cock swell even more. I lick and suck the sensitive peak through her shirt, moaning as I look down at the wet spot revealing just how beautiful her rosy nipples are. I go to move to taste her other nipple when she pushes my head away, releases my hair, and reaches up, pulling her t-shirt off over her head, finally allowing me to see her perfect tits. I groan, and it sounds feral to my own ears.

She smiles down at me when she sees me admiring her, her eyes hooded with desire, her breathing rapid. Fucking perfection. I reach up and cup them in my hands, watching as she licks her lips. In one move, I'm up over her, pressing my body firmly into hers and crashing my lips to hers as I tweak her nipples in my hand. She undulates her hips, trying to find the friction she needs, moaning with each brush of contact against my cock. Fucking gorgeous.

I move lower, taking first one, then the other nipple into my mouth. Nipping, sucking, kissing, licking, and biting. I continue to alternate until she's writhing beneath me and my control is on the verge of extinction.

"Fuck, Kyle, more. I need…" Just like that, I snap. A growl travels up my throat as I pull her shorts off and rip her panties away from her body. The next instant, my mouth is on her, my tongue dipping into her folds to find her clit swollen and throbbing. I moan against her, sucking it into my mouth as I swirl my finger into the wetness around her entrance. Fuck, she's soaked.

"Yes… god, Kyle. Yes," she moans, and that's all the encouragement I need. I thrust two fingers inside of her as I wrap my lips around her clit and moan. She bucks off the bed and my cock twitches painfully. Jesus Christ, I'm so close.

"Does that feel good, baby? God, you're so fucking wet," I say, my fingers still moving in and out of her as my thumb reaches up, applying pressure to her clit, circling.

"Tell me what you need, princess. Tell me." I reach up with my other hand and tweak her nipple between my thumb and forefinger, my eyes transfixed on her beautiful pussy as she rides my hand.

"Kyle, I...I need..." she moans, a guttural moan that comes straight from her lips to my cock. I look up, taking her in. Her eyes are closed, her teeth biting into her bottom lip, a light sheen of sweat covering her body as her tits heave with each inhale and exhale of breath, bouncing so fucking perfectly with each thrust of my fingers. A light blush erupts across her skin. So close, she's so fucking close. I move my thumb away from her clit and lower my head once more. My fingers continue their rhythm as I curve them forward, rubbing against that spot inside of her. I suck her clit into my mouth, swirling my tongue and nipping softly.

"Holy...fuck...mother of..." Amber yells, her body shuddering underneath me as I roll her nipple once more. I remove my fingers and plunge my tongue inside of her, lapping at her juices as she rides my face through her orgasm. As soon as her body calms, I stand up, forcefully removing my pants from my body. I grip my cock, stroking it only slightly as I take her in. She's perfection in every way. And, mine. Mine, still. Mine, again. Mine.

I ease my body over hers, kissing her eyelids, the tip of her nose, her mouth.

"Are you okay, princess?" I ask, gently nipping at her lip as I swirl my cock in her wetness.

"Yes, god, I'm more than okay. I need you, Kyle. Need to feel you, need you to make us one." Her eyes flutter open as the sexiest blush rises to her cheeks. I stare into her eyes through my own hooded lids. She rubs herself along my shaft and I shudder, my body tensing as her eyes reveal everything I need to continue. Love, so much fucking love my heart skips a beat, stuttering in my chest. I have her back. She may not have all of her memories but she's mine, just as much as I'm hers.

She moves her entrance over me, the tip of my cock slipping inside of her.

"Kyle," she moans as she begins to move herself on me, pushing me in deeper with each thrust of her hips. I moan low and push the rest of the way in until I'm fully seated inside of her.

"Amber," her name is a whisper dancing across my lips. A promise in so many ways. Never again will I allow anything to happen to her; never again will she be harmed. Because here, just like this, I'm home. Amber is my home, my heart, my soul, and I'll be damned if anyone takes that away from me.

Her nails scratch down my back and dig into my ass, propelling me forward.

"I need more, Kyle. I need you to move..." She smirks.

"As you wish, baby." I give her my own smirk as I move almost completely out of her and slowly, oh so slowly, push back in. Her jaw slackens and her eyes close. "Amber, baby, look at me," I say as I pull out of her once more, gritting my teeth against my impending orgasm, trying to force it back. The moment her eyes open, I become lost. My eyes never leave hers as I move in and out; moans and heavy breaths are the only sound in the room, like our own beautiful sheet music. A song made just for us.

"Oh, Kyle. Yes, Kyle. I...I love you. I love you." Shudders instantly wrack her body, her pussy spasming against my cock, squeezing it so beautifully I can't help but let go and fall with her. Our eyes never disconnect, our jaws both slackened, mouths open. Absorbing the pleasure running through our veins, humming against our skin, adding to the melody that is ours and ours alone.

"I love you, Amber. So much, baby. So much." I gently pull out of her and lay down next to her. She cuddles up close with her head resting on my chest. As I wrap my arms around her, I can't help but think that I am the luckiest man on earth. I've never been happier. I knew when we connected again it was going to be amazing, but this was so much more than I had imagined. Amazing doesn't even begin to describe it.

"Wow. I know there are a lot of things I don't remember still, but I think it's pretty safe to say that was the best ever," Amber says with a giggle as she places light kisses on my chest.

"It was the best...so far anyway." I look down at her and give her my cocky grin. "Does this mean I don't have to sleep in the chair any longer?" She raises up so that she can look me in the eyes. Is this something she actually has to think about? No. She's teasing me. This is new. Amber never was much of a tease. That was always my job. I like this new part of her, though. It's pretty hot.

"Hmm. I guess it would be okay if you slept here with me from now on, but only on one condition."

"And what would that be?"

"That you promise to hold me just like this all night." I see the blush creep up her face before she lowers her head back against my chest.

"There is nothing I would rather do," I tell her as I squeeze her a little tighter. Again, she lifts her head with a lopsided grin. She's trying not to laugh as she speaks.

"Are you sure about that?" I give her a questioning look. "Are you sure there is *nothing* you would rather do?" I can't help the laugh that escapes me. She is so cute when she's trying to be funny.

"When you put it that way, of course I would rather be doing you. However, I think we should get some sleep." She smiles up at me and snuggles back in as close as she can to me.

"That does sound good. Goodnight, Kyle."

"Goodnight, princess."

I've been lying here watching Amber sleep for the last hour. Several times during the night, I woke up and pulled her closer to me, happy to know it wasn't all a dream. This is how I had always pictured our lives. Making love to her every chance I can, falling asleep with her wrapped in my arms, and waking up the same way. Yes, I could do this every night and day for the rest of my life.

"Good morning, handsome," Amber says with a sleepy voice and a beautiful smile. "How did you sleep?"

"Better than I have in a very long time, thanks to you. How about you?"

"I feel really rested. So rested that I think we should just stay in this bed all day." Oh, how that offer tempts me.

"You have no idea how badly I would love that, but I invited Beasley over so the two of you could spend some time together. I hope you don't mind. I wanted to surprise you."

"Of course I don't mind! Thank you. It will be great to spend some time with him."

"Good, now let's get dressed." I place a quick kiss to her lips and guide her to the shower, planning to take her at least once before the day begins.

CHAPTER
Five

Amber

"So...where are we going?" I ask Beasley as we continue our drive down an unfamiliar road.

"This may sound a little silly, but when you were little I always wanted to take you to the county fair. I never had the chance back then. The county fair is going on right now and I thought, better late than never." He looks at me with a nervous smile. This is the sweetest gesture. I can't believe I am going to spend the day at the fair with my dad. Suddenly, I feel all giddy inside. Now I'm the one being silly. I am a grown woman for goodness sakes.

"It sounds perfect. I love the fair and I haven't been since I was in high school." I bet this was partly Kyle's idea. The other night, he told me about all the times we went to the fair when we were younger. I had remembered how much fun it was and I told him I would like to go again sometime. I wonder why he didn't want to take me. I'm looking forward to spending a day with my dad, but I was looking forward to the fair with Kyle.

"I begged him to let me take you. He mentioned your conversation about the fair and about it bringing back some good memories for you. It really is a place I've always wanted to take you. So much of your time is spent trying to regain old memories, I thought it might be fun and a hell of a lot more relaxing if we just made some new ones." He smiles sweetly, reminding once again how lucky I am to have him as my dad. Kyle put my relationship with Beasley and Beasley's feelings ahead of his own. I should have known better.

"Thanks. Sounds like we have a fun day ahead of us," I say as I smile brightly back at him.

The rest of the drive is relaxing. We chat about anything and everything we can think of. I'm always so comfortable and relaxed around Beasley. It's almost as if I've always known that he's my dad. The second I open the car door, the smell teases my nostrils. I take a deep breathe. God, I love that smell — fried food and cotton candy. It has my mouth watering.

"Today is your day, Amber, so you lead the way. Where do you want to start first?" I look around and think for a minute before grabbing Beasley's hand and pulling him through the crowd. Being here makes me feel like a kid all over again. I look back over my shoulder and see that Beasley is smiling and laughing. At least he doesn't think I'm crazy.

It doesn't take long to reach my destination. I remember sitting on my grandpa's lap in the bumper cars as a very small child. I loved them more than any other ride. When I got old enough to drive my own bumper car, he would always pretend he couldn't get away from me, knowing how much I enjoyed crashing into him. Of course, I didn't know he was pretending when I was little.

"Gene would always tell me how much fun the two of you had riding the bumper cars."

"I was just thinking about that. This has always been my favorite ride. Want to give it a go?"

"You bet I do. Why don't you hold us a spot in the line and I'll go buy us a wristband for the rides. "

"Sounds good to me." I got in the back of the line as Beasley walked over to purchase our wristbands. It's a weekday so the lines are nice and short. Beasley comes back just in time for our turn.

As soon as I'm through the gate, I see the car I want. In the far back corner is a black car with dark purple flames along its sides. Rushing over, I jump in and buckle the straps around my shoulders and lap. When I look over at Beasley, he has a grin on his face that stretches from ear to ear. I can only imagine it's the same look that's on my face. The buzzer goes off, letting us know we can start, and I slam my foot on the pedal.

Before I can get very far, a car slams into me from the side. All of a sudden, every happy feeling I've ever associated with this ride vanishes, replaced with a fear I'm all too familiar with. I freeze, encompassed by the sounds that haunt me in my nightmares. Tires squealing, metal crunching, glass shattering, and me crying out for Kyle to help me. I squeeze my eyes shut as tightly as possible, hoping to get the sounds out of my head. Instead, flashes of myself crashing through the windshield of Beau's truck invade my mind. My entire body begins shaking and drops of sweat drip from my brow. As I open my eyes, the world begins to spin and I can't seem to focus on the man in front of me. How long have I been sitting here like this?

"Amber! Sweetie, what's wrong? What happened?" Strong hands grip my arms and gently shake me. I'm still frozen. I want to respond, but I just can't. I feel him pick me up in his arms. My body feels limp, almost boneless. He places me on a bench and kneels down in front of me. Finally, everything stops spinning and I'm able to focus on Beasley's face. The absolute worry and fear on his face breaks me. Ugly uncontrollable sobs rip through me. Beasley wraps me in his arms and gently rocks me. I feel so foolish for acting this way. Nothing happened that would cause this reaction. Is my brain still just fucked up? The tears are flowing so hard and I can't seem to stop them.

After a few minutes of a full-blown snot-cry, I'm finally able to calm down some. Lifting my head, I see a make-up and tear stained mess on Beasley's white t-shirt. What a mess. He follows my eyes down to his shoulder and sees the mess I've made of his shirt. A warm, sweet smile graces his handsome face. That smile alone makes me start to feel so much better. But it doesn't last long. As if the freak out wasn't embarrassing enough, I start to feel my nose running. Beasley notices too. *Perfect.* Before I realize it, he is using the bottom of his shirt to wipe my nose. I'm not sure whether I should be disgusted or touched. Maybe a little of both. He just shrugs his shoulders as I laugh.

"Being hit in the bumper cars brought back the accident, didn't it?" Beasley questions cautiously.

"Ye...yes," I stammer, unable to catch my breath.

"It's okay. Relax. This is a perfectly normal reaction. You have been through something very traumatic. Have you been talking to someone about how you're feeling?"

"You mean like a shrink?" Slowly, he shakes his head yes. "No.

There's no reason to, I'm fine."

"I don't think you are...not emotionally anyway. There's a lot of shit that's happened to you. When it's all over, you put on a smile and life goes back to business as usual. At some point you have to acknowledge that this affects you."

"There is no point dwelling on something that can't be changed. Forget and move on is the best way to be rid of it."

"This little episode is proof that it isn't forgotten and you haven't moved on. You need to deal with all of the feelings you have. They won't just go away because you want them to. They will eat you from the inside out. What about Kyle, can't you talk to him about any of this?"

"NO! He feels guilty enough. He thinks everything bad that happens to me is his fault. I refuse to make it worse for him."

"I'm afraid until you start talking through all of the emotions you have bottled up, things like today are going to keep happening."

"But why something that I have always loved so much? Something I have always associated with happy memories. Why does it feel like even though he's gone he is still hurting me? It's not fair!" I cry as I feel Beasley's arm wrap around me like a security blanket.

"I know. It isn't fair at all. I wish I could take it all away for you. I would do anything to make it better for you." I look up at him and smile through my tears.

"You are making it better for me. You're here. Comforting me. Wiping away my tears...my snot," I say and I can't help the laugh that comes along with it. I lean over and kiss him on the cheek. "Let's go get some junk food. That makes anything better." He takes my hand and helps me stand.

As we are standing in line at one of the vendors, I hear a familiar giggle. Turning, I see Jax and Leena walking in our direction. There's something strange about their demeanor toward one another. They look more like...like they're dating rather than cousins. The way they are walking so closely together, the way they look into each other's eyes as they laugh. That can't be, though. Can it? I'm the only person who hasn't been suspicious of him. Until now. Everyone else may be on to something. I wonder why she's even here. She's supposed to be back in Atlanta. Neither of them see us as they pass, too caught up in each other. And for that, I'm thankful. I'm going to find out what's going on there. Just not today. No more drama for today. I want to enjoy the rest of my day with my dad.

After we stuff ourselves with all the fried foods imaginable, we decide to check out the games. The first game we come to is one where you throw the darts and try to pop the balloons. Beasley hands the guy two bucks then gives the darts to me.

"Oh, no. I'm no good at this. I might injure someone," I say as I try to hand the darts back. He shakes his head.

"Come on. You can do it. Just give it a try."

"Okay, but don't say you weren't warned," I tease as I line myself up to make my throws. I throw the first dart and pop a balloon. Holy shit! I'm so excited, I do a little victory dance then hug Beasley. I'm sure I look like a child, but I don't give a damn. I throw the second one and pop another balloon. Excitedly, I turn to look at Beasley and see that he has his phone held up taking a video of me. He has the look of a proud father on his face. I quickly turn back around before I get emotional. Returning my focus, I take a deep breath and watch as the dart flies out of my hand and straight into the last balloon. I squeal and jump a little, over excited by this accomplishment. The guy running the booth hands me the cutest purple teddy bear wearing a black bowtie. I thank the man for my bear then run to show Beasley.

"See I knew you could do it," he says proudly.

"That was so much fun. I still can't believe I did it. I've never been able to win a stuffed animal by myself. Kyle and my grandfather always won them for me."

"You did it and I have the video to prove it."

We stop and try our luck at a few more of the game booths. By the time we are done, Beasley has also won me a teddy bear. We decide to sit and get a Caricature drawing done of the two of us. I can't wait to show Kyle. We also take a ride on the Ferris wheel. Before leaving, I buy some cotton candy. I can't go to the fair and not have cotton candy.

As we drive home, I can't help but get lost in my thoughts. What he said during my meltdown has stayed with me throughout the day and talking to someone may not be a bad idea. It might just be time to start dealing with it all and stop pretending.

"Okay, you're right. I need to start dealing with the cabin, the accident, and my memory loss." I glance over at Beasley. He keeps both eyes on the road ahead and nods a confirmation. "I'll ask Becky if she can recommend a good doctor. Thank you."

"What are you thanking me for? I didn't do anything."

"Thank you for being my dad. For being a really good one when I needed it the most."

"Thank you for letting me. You are the strongest and bravest women I know." He quickly glances in my direction and smiles.

Kyle

AMBER AND I are on our way to the bar for a night out. She's having her girl's night with Holly, Becky, and Taryn and I'm working and playing a set with the guys. It feels so good to get out again like we did before the accident. We need to get back to our normal routines and start living our lives the way we had always planned.

"What are you thinking about over there?" Amber asks as she reaches over and rubs my shoulder.

"Just about how nice it is to be going out and doing things like we used to."

"I agree. I think it will be good for both of us. I think it's time I go back to the center too. The sooner we can get into our normal routine, the better." She smiles at me when I glance over at her. As nervous as I am about not being able to be with her, I know this is what's best for both of us.

"As long as you feel ready, I'm behind you all the way."

"I guess we will find out how ready I am on Monday."

"I feel better knowing Jax will be there to keep an eye out for you. Wow, never thought those words would ever leave my mouth," I mutter. Amber laughs but it sounds strained. It's almost as if the mention of Jax makes her uneasy. This is strange. I wonder if they had an argument or if — if he made a move on her again, I will kick his ass. I park in my usual space and grab Amber's hand before she can get out. "What's up? Did Jax do or say something to you?" She scoots over closer to me.

"No, he hasn't done anything that I know of. It's just...well, I'm starting to wonder if you and Angel haven't been right to be suspicious of him." She looks into my eyes and the pain simmering around the edges causes a ping in my chest. She has always been a very trusting and forgiving person; I hate to see that part of her disappear. Hate that Beau took that away from her. Before Beau, she saw the world as roses and cupcakes. All her stories had happily ever after, she never would have imagined that there are monsters lurking waiting in the shadows to steal all the good away.

"What happened to change your mind?"

"I saw him at the Fair. He was with Leena." Just the mention of that bitch's name makes my blood boil and my skin crawl. She isn't even supposed to be in the state, she should be back in Atlanta. "I was wondering why she's still around too, but that's not what is bothering me. The way the two of them were acting was odd. It was more like they were dating rather than cousins. I might just be crazy but I have a really bad feeling about all of this. There is something going on with them. I don't know what or why, but whatever it is, I don't think we're going to like it." She's right. I don't like it already. Why would they pretend to be related? What would they have to gain?

"We are just gonna have to find out what they are up to. I will call Beasley in the morning and he can get us in touch with his P.I. friend." I lean down and lightly kiss her lips, slightly taken aback when she reaches up and grips the back of my head, making the kiss deeper. She moves over, straddling my hips as she slides her tongue along my lips until I open for her. I moan, feeling my cock harden instantly. She grinds herself against me and the heat emanating from her only turns me on more. As much as I want to continue, I know we need to stop. Gathering all of my willpower, I break the kiss. Breathing heavily and avoiding the almost painful need, I curse myself while doing what is right.

"Princess, this is going to have to wait until later when we get home."

"Sorry. I got a little carried away," she says with a giggle.

"Don't apologize." I push up, needing her to feel how she has affected me. "I want to fuck you. I need to feel your heat enveloping me, but this is your night. We will definitely continue this at home."

"Promise?"

"Try and stop me."

Hand in hand, we finally make our way into the bar. It's pretty busy even for a Saturday night. Paul is behind the bar. I know he sees us coming in because he is starts pulling the ingredients to make an appletini. When we get up to Paul, he has the drink ready for a smiling Amber. She thanks him and lifts the glass to her lips. Her eyes close and a small moan escapes her mouth followed by a flirty smile. She can even make taking a drink look sexy as hell. It is going to be a very long night.

"It's about time you got my girl here," Holly says as she comes up behind us and wraps Amber in a hug. "Say goodbye to your man quickly then meet us over at the booth. Girls night starts now." She kisses my cheek and off to the table she goes. That woman is a bundle of energy. I don't know how Paul keeps up with her.

"Well, I guess I better get over there," Amber says. Before she can pick up her drink, I scoop her up and set her on my lap. "Don't worry, you'll be able to keep an eye on me all night." She thinks I don't want to let her go because I'm worried about her. Normally, that would be the case, but not tonight. Too many people here care for her and will protect her at all costs. So for once, I am relaxed when it comes to her safety.

"That's not the problem, princess."

"What is then?" I grab her hips and pull her against my lap tighter so she can feel just how much I want her. Her eyes widen and she grins at me. Why should I be the only one turned on and left hanging? Might as well show her what she can have later when we get home.

"Do you feel what you do to me? I'm gonna have a difficult time watching you all night without taking that sexy little ass of yours into my office and bending you over my desk," I whisper in her ear so only she hears me and gently bite her earlobe. Goose bumps form along her arms and her breathing picks up. She grinds her ass harder against my already painful erection and I suck in a harsh breath. There's no way in hell I'm going to survive tonight. Maybe I can convince her to come into my office for just a few minutes.

"No. I'm not going to your office with you."

"How did you know that's what I was thinking?"

"Just a... feeling," she says as she rubs her ass against my cock again. Damn. This woman is going to kill me. At least I'll die with a smile on my face. Slowly, she slides off my lap, looking over her shoulder to make sure Paul isn't watching. Before moving away, she reaches down and tightly grips my cock in her hand as she puts her lips right up to my ear. "I promise it will be worth the wait." She moves her hands so that they are resting on my shoulders and places a sweet kiss on my lips then smiles up at me. "Don't get yourself too worked up tonight. Before you know it, it will be time to take me home." With a sly grin and a kiss on the cheek, she's gone. I watch her walk to the booth in the back where her friends are waiting with a little extra sway in her hips, just enough to tease me.

"Looks like the two of you have gotten a lot closer over the last week," Paul says as he slides a beer in front of me.

"Let's just say that I'm no longer sleeping in a chair." I give him a wink.

"Good for you both. I'm happy to hear things are getting back to normal."

"You and me both."

"Not as happy as I am. It's about time you get your ass back in here and work," Clark says as he sits down next to me. Paul and I both look at him with shocked expressions on our faces. Clark is usually very quiet and serious. He looks between the two of us, smiles, and shrugs his shoulders. Paul hands him a beer.

The three of us sit there for a while talking about the bar. My eyes keep wandering over to Amber's booth. I wonder if there will ever come a time when I won't think she is absolutely the most beautiful woman I have ever laid my eyes on. She looks so happy, laughing and talking with her friends. I wasn't sure if I would ever see her like this again. It makes me happy and gives me hope that we are finally going to be able to have the life we've dreamed of.

"Who is that with Amber, Taryn, and Holly?" Clark asks as his eyes study Becky from top to bottom. All the years I've known him, I don't think he's ever shown interest in a woman. His time away from work is devoted to his two sons, Mason who's nine and Skylar who's six. He love's those boys with everything he has. His girlfriend took off five years ago and hasn't tried to contact him at all since. Not even to see how the boys are doing.

"That would be Becky. Amber met her while she was in the hospital. She was her nurse and I'm pretty sure she's single," I tell Clark as I notice a smile spread across his face. She's very pretty; I can see how she's caught his eye. Paul places a tray of drinks on the bar in front of Clark.

"Why don't you bring these over to the girls for me?" Paul asks Clark, giving him a reason to go over there. He smiles as he grabs the tray and walks over to their table. Becky looks up and smiles at Clark.

"Looks like there might be a little love connection starting up over there," I say to Paul before taking a pull of my beer.

"It's about damn time that guy finds a woman and has a little fun."

"I agree. Well, guess I'll go take care of some of the paperwork that's piling up on my desk." Grabbing my beer, I turn toward Amber. She looks over and waves. I give her a little nod and walk back to my office. I need to give her some space and I've been neglecting my duties here. I don't know what I would do without Paul and Holly. They've been running everything for me while I take care of Amber, but it's time for me to take back over.

Concentrating on paperwork, I don't notice Marcus walk into the room. Standing in front of the desk, he clears his throat to get my attention.

"You have got to come see this," he says, trying not to laugh.

"What's going on?"

"You have to see for yourself. You wouldn't believe me otherwise." It must not be anything bad. He is laughing, after all. I get up and follow him out. The music is blasting from the speakers, yet I can still hear people cheering and whistling. What in the hell is going on out there? I look over at Marcus, hoping to get some kind of idea, but he's laughing so hard, tears are running down his cheeks. I recognize the song that's playing, it's *Country Girl (Shake it For Me)* by Luke Bryan. When the bar comes into view, I come to a dead stop and Marcus plows into the back of me.

"Damn! A little warning would be nice," Marcus whines. Ignoring him, I make my way closer to what has everyone else's attention. Every eye in this bar is captivated by the show Amber, Holly, Taryn, and Becky are putting on. Amber's eyes are closed, arms raised above her head, and she's swinging her hips to the beat. Watching her dance like this has me thinking of her in some sexy lingerie and high heels in front of a pole. However, if I'm thinking like this, so are ninety-percent of the males in here. Now I don't know whether to be pissed or turned on. Then, I notice the smile on her face and how much fun she's having. Amber doesn't do things like this. She doesn't like people watching her; always afraid they are judging her. I can't believe she's out there. So, turned on it is. At least with the girls out there dancing no one will notice the erection I'm now sporting. I take a quick look around, just in case, before I adjust myself. I see Paul and Clark watching with a puddle of drool at their feet. I quickly pull out my cell phone and take a quick video. I have a feeling Amber may not remember this tomorrow and it'll be fun to tease her with. Plus, it's just plain hot. I wouldn't mind being able to see it any time I want to.

"You realize we're not the only guys drooling over them, don't you?" I say as I come up to stand beside the guys. Coming out of their daze, they start to look around. Every male eye in the bar is on our girls. Luckily, the song comes to an end. Paul tends to be a little on the jealous side and I can tell he wasn't too thrilled with the way people were looking at the girls.

"It's nice to see Amber having so much fun. She really deserves to let loose a little bit," Clark says to me.

"Yeah. For a while there, I was worried I'd never see her smile again." Honestly, I didn't think she was ever going to wake up. I was so close to giving up, I didn't think any of this would be possible again. "I'm one lucky guy," I tell him, noticing his eyes haven't left Becky since I walked out here.

"I hope someday I'll find the kind of love the two of you have," he says, a sad smile playing on his lips. I hope he does, too. If anyone deserves it, he does. Who knows, the way he keeps eyeing Becky, there may be something there.

"Hey, handsome! Enjoying the show?" Amber slurs as she throws her arms around my waist. I have a feeling my plans for later tonight are shot, but it's worth it to see the smile on her face.

"Eh...it was okay," I tease, earning myself a slap on the chest. I lean down slowly and whisper in her ear, "It was the hottest thing I have ever fucking seen." Goose bumps immediately break out across her skin. The other two giggling girls come over and pull her back to their booth before either one of us can say anything else. It's probably a good thing. Last thing I need is to go on stage with a huge boner.

The guys and I head up to play our set. It really feels good to be playing again. I didn't realize how much I've missed it lately. I wouldn't change anything I've been doing, though. Amber needed me, and she will always be my first priority. The entire hour we are up there, the only person I can focus on is Amber. Every song I sing is to her. This night is something we've both desperately needed. For the first time in a while, there's no dark cloud hanging over my head. I am one hundred percent happy.

CHAPTER
Six

Amber

ꙮT'S BEEN two months since I've been back working at the center and luckily, I've been able to come in and pick up where I left off. It's almost like I was never away at all. There's only one thing that's different, and that's Jax. He's been acting really strange toward me. Most of the time he seems to be avoiding me, and when he isn't, he seems cold and distant. I don't understand what's gotten into him. All the years we've been friends, he's never acted this way.

I had mentioned seeing him and Leena at the fair. Maybe that's what upset him. He told me he didn't have the heart to send her back home. There was nothing there for her and he is the only family she has. I just don't buy it though. There's something else going on. I know in my gut the two of them are up to something. I just wish I knew what it was. I never would have believed before the accident that Jax could be capable of hurting me. Now, I'm not so sure. Since the accident, I see things a lot differently than I did before. I can see the things in Jax that everyone else did from day one — all of those mannerisms that made them so suspicious of him.

Beasley is checking into Jax and Leena's backgrounds. I feel a little bad at times for doing it, as if I'm betraying him by going behind his back, but too much has happened to me over the last year, and I can't afford to take any more chances. It's time that I worry about my family and myself. Better safe than sorry.

For the last few hours, I've been sitting at my desk, attempting to work, but concentrating has been a little difficult today. Standing up to go the file cabinet, I instantly fall back into my chair, feeling lightheaded. I close my eyes, hoping it will stop the room from spinning. Sweat beads along my forehead and my mouth begins to water. *Oh no!* I quickly jump up from my desk and run into to the hallway, almost plowing Holly over in the process. Damn, I forgot I was meeting her for lunch. The thought of food only makes me feel worse. Holly must know I am going to be sick because she is opens the door to the bathroom for me. I hear the door close behind me and feel her pull my hair away from my face as I empty the contents of my stomach. She lays a damp paper towel on the back of my neck and my body instantly becomes cooler.

Finally, after what seems like forever, there's nothing left. Holly reaches around and pulls the lever to flush the toilet. A new damp paper towel is pressed to the back of my neck as Holly helps me to my feet.

"Are you okay, sweetie? Do you have the flu?" Holly asks, concern clear in her voice.

"I'm fine now. I haven't felt sick at all. This just came out of nowhere."

"Why don't I take you home? Kyle and Paul can come get your car later. You may be coming down with something and the last thing you want to do is spread it around the center." Holly doesn't wait for my reply before gathering my things to go. She's right. If I'm getting the flu, I don't want to get all of the kids and the rest of the staff sick. Giving in, I let her take me home.

As soon as we get in the car, I call Kyle to let him know I'm going home to rest. After a few minutes, I'm able to convince him to stay at work, that I'm fine and Holly is with me. I know he worries. Truly, I understand why he does, but he needs to relax or he is going to drive us both crazy. No matter who you are, what you do, or how much you try to stop it, bad things happen. I refuse to live my life in fear every day, wondering if today is the day that something bad happens to us. I'm not foolish enough to think that the rest of my life with Kyle will be without any pain or heartache. That's life. We can't enjoy the sun without first experiencing the rain.

Maybe I should have gone home alone. Holly is about as bad as Kyle. She insists on tucking me into bed, taking my shoes off, and even tries to change my clothes for me.

"Holly...I love you but if you don't stop hovering and treating me like a toddler, I'm gonna have to kick your ass." I was trying to keep the smile from creeping across my face, but as soon as the words were out of my mouth, she burst out laughing. Yeah, I suppose me trying to be a badass is pretty hilarious. She finally stops laughing enough to talk.

"You poor thing, having the flu by itself is bad enough but PMS on top of it must really suck."

"What makes you think I have PMS?"

"You've been a little on the cranky side lately." She's totally right. I have been a bit bitchy recently. And it hits me. Like a baseball bat to the face. I'm late. Really late. What is Kyle going to think? We talked about this before the accident, but it hasn't really been discussed much since. That feeling I had earlier is coming back full force. I jump up out of bed, pushing Holly out of my way as I race to the bathroom. I barely make it to the toilet before I'm heaving.

With the help of Holly, I once again get cleaned up and back into bed. The need to know if my suspicions are correct is imminent. This is something I know we both want. The question is, do we want it now? Is it the right time just when we are getting our life back to normal?

"Holly, I need you to do me a favor."

"Of course. Anything, you know that."

"Can you run to the store and buy me a couple pregnancy tests?" She starts squealing like a teenage girl, until she sees the uncertain look on my face.

"This wouldn't be something you would be happy about?" Concern is evident in her voice.

"I am. I've always wanted this. *We* have always wanted this. I just don't know if now is the right time." She sits down on the bed and smiles warmly at me.

"Is there ever really a right time? Maybe this is the universe or God saying you've had enough heartache and it's time to be happy. It's time for the life you both have always dreamed of." I want so much to believe that's true. Deep down, there is still something telling me that Kyle and I haven't been through our toughest time yet. I just can't shake that feeling and I've tried to for months now.

My nerves get the best of me as I wait for Holly to get back with the tests. I'm afraid to let myself get too excited in case I'm wrong. Then

I think again of Kyle. How is he really going to take this news? What if he's upset? He may have changed his mind about starting a family right after we got married. Why would he though? Nothing has really changed between us. If anything, it's more important for us not to take a single day we have for granted. We never know what tomorrow holds.

Just before I completely lose my mind, a panting, out of breathe Holly comes barreling through the door. The sight of her has me in a fit of giggles. She looks like she ran a freaking marathon. Sweat is running down the sides of her face and she's having such a hard time catching her breathe, she's actually wheezing. She gives me a glare that has me throwing my hand over my mouth to suppress the giggles.

"Wh... what…" she holds up her finger, telling me to give her a minute, "What is that you find so fucking amusing?" She tries to keep a straight face but I can see the corners of her mouth raise.

"I really don't know. I think I'm slowly losing my mind. I'm sorry." With a shrug of her shoulders, she hands over the bag. All of a sudden, I'm not so confident any longer. In a few minutes, my whole life could change forever. *Our* whole life. Noticing the anxiety raising up within me, Holly sits next to me and puts an arm around me.

"Are you more worried about being pregnant or not being pregnant?" Hmm. Good question. I really don't know. "The way I see it, if you are, you will both be over-the-moon happy. If you're not, you know you are ready to discuss starting a family." This is why I love this woman. She is absolutely right. It's not as if we were trying and I'm getting bad news. If it's negative, it's time to bring the subject up to Kyle. If I am, we will both be thrilled. Feeling resolved and slightly better, I look in the bag.

"Do I really need six? I figured two would be enough."

"I didn't know what kind to buy and really, how do we know how accurate they are? With six different ones, we'll know for sure." She is so serious in her explanation that I can't argue with her logic. She tells me to stay put and leaves the room.

When she comes back a few minutes later, she's holding a large bottle of apple juice. She opens it and hands it to me. It probably would help to pee on all those sticks if I actually had to pee. I start to drink it as she begins to set up the tests in the bathroom. I finish the juice then read the instructions for the tests. Pretty simple really. Pee on the stick, wait a few minutes, and read the results. Simple. Yeah not so simple, especially when I have Holly standing there watching, waiting to take the peed on stick and hand me a new one. As odd as this is though, I couldn't do it without her here to support me.

We both sit on the edge of the tub waiting for the timer to go off. I am afraid to look. There's a lump in my throat and knots in my stomach. If there weren't a possibility of being pregnant, I would seriously need a drink right now. And with that, the timer Holly set on her phone buzzes. We both look at each other. I can't look. Without having to say a word, Holly stands and walks over to the counter. Watching closely, I look for any signs in her expression of what the results are. Nothing. Her face is like a statue. Silently, I plead for her to show me something, some emotion.

"Well...they are all the same. So I think it's safe to say that it's unanimous." She looks at me. "Ready?" I nod my head yes. Here goes. "Sweetie, you definitely are pregnant!" Holly hugs me tightly and I can't help the tears that fall to my cheeks.

"I'm gonna be a mom." My hand goes to rest on my flat stomach. This is something I have always wanted. To be a mom, that is. I always thought it would be a little more planned out, but that doesn't that matter. I have to get Kyle home so that I can tell him now. I don't want to wait. I leave all of the tests on the counter for him to see when he comes home, grab my phone from the bedroom, and call him.

"Hey, princess. How are ya feeling?"

"A little better. I need you to come home."

"Are you okay? What's wrong?"

"I'm okay. I just need you to come home now, can you do that?"

"Of course I can, but you're scaring me. Are you really okay?"

"Babe, I promise. I'm fine. Actually, I'm great." After a little more convincing, I finally get him to hang up. Holly sits with me as I nervously wait for Kyle to get home. As worried as I am about how he might react, I still can't wipe the stupid grin from my face. We are going to have a baby. We hear Kyle's truck pull up and Holly quickly hugs me, saying she'll send Kyle up on her way out. I watch her leave. *Deep breathe.* This is it. The moment of truth.

Kyle

I HANG up the phone with Amber and try to quickly put everything away in my office, but the more I think about our conversation, the longer it takes and the more I worry. I can't help all of the scenarios that run through my head or the fact that they are all negative. My nerves are out of control and I have to remind myself that she said she's fine. I'm so lost in thought that I don't notice Paul talking to me until he snaps his fingers in front of my face.

"Earth to, Kyle. What's going on? You were a million miles away there."

"Amber called and asked me… no, told me to come home now. She says she's okay, but something's up." When I look at him, he looks amused. What the hell?

"You have got to stop getting yourself wound so damn tight man. One of these days you're going to over think things so much that head of yours is gonna explode." He laughs. He actually stands there and fucking laughs at me. I should dot him right between his eyes. The guy is lucky he's my best friend. He finally stops and holds his hands up in surrender. "If she says she's okay then she's probably okay. Maybe she just misses you. Why? I have no idea," Paul teases. With that, I flip him off and I'm out the door.

On the drive home, I can't shake the feeling that something is up. Why else would Amber call and have me drop everything to come right home? As I pull in front of the house, I see Holly's car is still here. I don't know if that eases my nerves some or makes them worse. When I walk through the front door, Holly is coming down the stairs.

"She's waiting for you up in the bedroom," Holly says with a beaming smile.

"Is she really okay? Nothing is wrong with her?"

"I wish you both would save the worrying until there is actually something to worry about." She stops and hugs me tight. It almost looks like she's a little teary eyed. "I am so happy that you both are finally getting the life you deserve. I love you guys"

"What are you two up to?"

"Go find your wife and ask her. See ya later." With a kiss on the cheek, she bounces down the stairs and out the door. Confused, I head up the stairs to Amber.

Walking into our room, I see Amber sitting on the edge of our bed. She's smiling at me but she looks nervous. Smiling back, I walk over and place a sweet kiss on her lips.

"Hey there, princess. What's so urgent?"

"There's something you need to see in the bathroom." Now, I'm confused. She called me home to look at something in the bathroom? "Go on," she urges. I walk to the bathroom, my curiosity getting the best of me.

As I step into the bathroom, I look around and notice a bunch of things lined up on the counter. I get closer to try to figure out what they are. It takes me only a second to realize what I'm looking at. The moment it hits me, I have to grab hold of the counter to hold myself up. My heart is beating so fast and hard, I'd be surprised if Amber can't hear it from the other room. I let my eyes examine each and every test for confirmation. Six. Six positive pregnancy tests.

I can't believe she's pregnant. We talked about this before we got married — about wanting to start a family right away. After the accident though, I haven't given it a whole lot of thought. We've been too busy just trying to get our lives back; trying to heal. Now that it's actually happening, I'm not exactly sure what I'm feeling. We both love kids. I can't think of anything better than a child that's part Amber and part me. I want this. There's no doubt in my mind about that. I'm just a little concerned that it may be too soon. She's only been back at work for a couple months. The excitement hits me full force. Everything happens for a reason, so we can do this.

I turn around and almost slam right into her. She looks up at me with a smile on her face and tears in her eyes.

"Are you okay with this?" I ask as I hold her face in my hands.

"More than okay. I was scared at first, but it was because I was worried about how you would feel."

"I am so happy, this is amazing." I kiss her, gentle and slow. Swiping my tongue tenderly across her lower lip, she moans, parting her lips enough for me to swipe my tongue against hers. Just a slight touch, a tease, hoping my kiss tells her everything I need her to know, to understand… to feel. She moves her hands to my hair and grips on, pulling my face to hers roughly, turning the kiss into something much more erotic, needy, frantic. Pulling back, I catch my breath before kissing her nose and whispering my lips along her cheeks to her ear, slowing down the moment. As much as I need her, I don't want to fuck her. I want to show her how happy this makes me, how excited I am to take this journey with her. How much I love her. I need her to feel it all, everything I can't explain.

I breathe deep, taking in her scent of coconut before resting my forehead against hers. I look her in the eyes, trying to convey everything that I'm feeling but I notice the flash of hurt in her own. Knowing she feels like I'm rejecting her, I move to bend down, claiming her lips with my own again before reaching my hand under her legs and picking her up bridal style. I never break our kiss, just pull her closer to me as I move her to the bed. Laying her down gently, I move on top of her. Slowly brushing her hair away from her face, I look into her eyes and say, "You've made me so happy, princess. Let me show you how much." She nods her head slowly and closes her eyes. Sweeping my fingers ever so slowly across her lower belly, I lift her shirt in small increments, gracing her soft skin as I go. I bend down, kissing each closed eyelid, her nose, her cheeks, before settling back on her lips. She inhales sharply as I graze my fingers up over her bra and move to lift her arms. Sweeping my tongue into her mouth once more, I softly glide it along hers, tasting her. With a soft kiss, I break apart and lift her shirt over her head, tossing it to the floor. My eyes connect with hers once more and I can't help but gasp at how much love shines through. The emotion wafting off her hits me straight in the heart and I give back everything I can, showing her how much she means to me, how much this baby will mean to me.

Slowly, I move down her body, placing soft kisses in a path from her breasts, down her stomach, and stopping to swirl my tongue in her belly button. She undulates her hips and moans and the sound goes straight to my cock, making me painfully hard. I push back the need to rush, to take her hard, rough, and fast. Instead, I slowly unbutton her pants and pull the fabric down her legs, using my fingertips to wisp across her skin. I kiss my way back up, slip her panties down, and move to her bra, never breaking eye contact. "You're so beautiful, baby. So fucking beautiful, it hurts in the most delicious ways."

"Kyle, I need you. I need to feel you, please don't make me wait," she says, barely above a whisper, her voice husky with desire. I take one nipple into my mouth, swirling my tongue around it slowly as she moans, her breath quickening with every swipe. Moving to her other breast, I give it the same treatment as I reach down, unbuttoning my jeans. Her moans become louder, raspier, needier, and I can't wait any longer. I need to make her mine, need to have us connected. I need to feel her gripping me, our bodies bringing each half of our hearts together.

I move up and begin to ease my jeans down my hips as I take in the sight before me. Her skin a deeper pink, flushed with desire. Her eyes big and round, shining with need. Her lips swollen from my kisses. Her hard, rosy nipples beckoning me. Before I can move to stand, Amber lifts up, removing my hands from their task and taking over. I lean down over her once more, taking her lips with mine as she glides my pants down my legs with her feet, gripping my head in her hands. She tugs gently at the strands in her grasp and I moan, my cock twitching in anticipation. Her motions start to become frantic again and I slow her movements by breaking our kiss once more. I lean up, stroking my cock while moving my fingers to her entrance. She so hot, so wet. I groan as she undulates, forcing my fingers into her dripping pussy. The action has my cock rock hard, pleading with me to bury myself within her. Ignoring the desire once again, I move forward, touch my forehead to hers, and stare into her eyes as I thrust slightly forward.

The moment I breach her entrance, I'm lost. I pull back out slowly, swirling my length in her wetness before pushing forward once more. I never break eye contact as I move in and out of her, giving her everything I have. I'm hers, completely. The mewling sounds coming from deep within her throat have me grasping at every ounce of control I have.

I lean over, brushing my lips to hers once before burying my head in hair.

"You are so perfect, baby. So amazing," I whisper into her ear, setting a gentle pace.

Her low moans and fluid movements push me to the edge. I can't think. I only feel, hoping she feels everything as much. I move my hand to her clit and stroke slowly, needing to build her up further. Her breathing accelerates as I continue to tell her how in awe I am of her, how much I love her, how I can't wait to start our family together, how she's my one and only, my other half. There's a hitch in her breath as she gasps.

"I love you, too...so much," she says, almost breathless, as her muscles tense and clench around me. In that moment, I move to her lips, kissing her passionately as I let go, giving her everything I am, everything I aspire to be.

I lay with my head resting on Amber's belly. She's been sound asleep for about thirty minutes. I'm trying to imagine what she's going to look like when her belly gets big and round. I bet she'll be even more beautiful than she is now, if that's even possible. I wonder if Amber wants a boy or a girl. It doesn't matter to me, but the thought of a son makes me happy. A son to play sports with, to teach how to play the guitar.

"What are you smiling about?" Amber asks. I didn't even realize she was awake.

"I was thinking about how you are going to look with a big round belly." That earned me a slap in the head. "What? I think it will make you even more beautiful because you'll be carrying our baby." She starts to rub the spot on my head she just slapped.

"Good save. I think I would like our first child to be a boy. Do you have a preference?"

"I think I would like a boy first also. That way if we have a girl next, she'll have a big brother to watch over her."

"That sounds perfect." I thought that the happiest I've ever been was the moment we said, "I do." I think I was wrong. And, I know exactly how we can celebrate.

As I drive up I-75 to Venice Beach, I look over at Amber who is looking out her window with a peaceful smile plastered to her face. It didn't take much to convince Amber that we should take the trip. When we were in high school, we went to Venice once on a weekend. It's a popular place to find shark's teeth and absolutely gorgeous. Amber always said she wanted to go back, so what better way to celebrate? She let Jax know she'd be gone for four or five days, and Holly and Paul are watching the bar for me. I did, however, ask Holly not to say anything about the baby to anyone but Paul. We want to make the announcement ourselves. She agreed, but on one condition. Holly is now planning a party for when we get back and that's when we'll announce our news. Holly and her parties. I shake my head and laugh to myself at the thought. That woman looks for any excuse to throw a party.

"What's so funny over there?" Amber asks as she takes my hand and interlaces our fingers.

"Just thinking about how Holly will find any excuse to throw a party."

"Yes, she does, but what would we do without her? She has become my best friend. I feel very blessed to have met the people I have since I came back to Oakville. This baby is going to be so loved. I just wish my grandparents could be here to share this with us." There's a tear in her eye and a hint of sadness in her voice. My poor girl. I know she misses her grandparent. I understand because I miss them too. Time to lighten the mood back up.

"So, princess, would you like to hear about where we'll be staying?" Ah, that brought my girls' beautiful smile back.

"Yes I would." Perfect. The sadness I heard in her voice is replaced with pure excitement. At first, I had planned to get us a room at the same hotel on the beach that we stayed at the last time we were here, but the more I thought about it, the more I realized that we're not seventeen any longer and Amber deserves the royal treatment.

"I found us a beautiful house that is totally secluded. There's a heated pool and it sits on a private beach. I think you are going to love it."

"I can't wait to see it."

Turning onto the tree-lined driveway, a beautiful two-story house comes into view. The vision before us is nothing short of a tropical paradise. The entire front yard is covered in Palm trees, Hibiscus, Bird of Paradise, and many other plants and flowers I don't recognize. I glance over at Amber and the look of awe on her face makes me so happy that I brought her here. Once I get the car parked, we get out and instantly smell the salty ocean air. I love that smell. I go to grab our bags from the trunk. As I'm getting my bag situated on my shoulder, Amber reaches for hers.

"What do you think you're doing, princess?" I ask, trying my damnedest to look stern, but I don't do a very good job. She always makes me smile without even trying.

"What does it look like? I'm getting my bag."

"I'll get it. You shouldn't be lifting anything heavy in your condition." She starts to laugh, but I don't get the joke.

"First, thank you for taking my bag and looking out for me and our baby. Second, I don't have a condition. It's not a disease." She starts giggling again. She looks up at me with such a bright smile. I love seeing her this happy. It's true when people say pregnant women glow; there is this radiance about her I've never seen before. I wrap her in my arms and hold her tight.

"This is going to be absolutely amazing," I tell her as I breathe in the scent of her hair. The smell of coconut that always makes me feel like a hormone crazed teenager. I wonder if I will always feel like this with her. Thirty years from now when I hold her like this and smell the coconut in her hair, will I still get hard as a rock? God, I hope so.

"What will be amazing? This vacation?"

"Yes, the vacation will be great, but I was talking about our life. This journey we are on together is going to be amazing. What we have together is a once in a lifetime thing. We have proven to the world and to ourselves that nothing is stronger than the love and bond we share. Together, we can overcome any obstacle, and we have been thrown every obstacle I can think of and then some. Now it's our time to just live and be happy." Reaching down, I take her face in my hands and kiss her. It starts out gentle and sweet. Our tongues lightly dancing together, but our bodies take control and it becomes something hungrier, needier. As much as it pains me, I pull away. She doesn't look any happier about it than I feel. I grab the bags and close the trunk.

Entering the code into the lock box at the door, I retrieve the key and unlock the door. The inside is beautiful. With all white walls and light beige tile flooring throughout the house, it definitely looks like a beach house. There are paintings all over of different types of sea life and birds. I don't get a chance to really look at everything because Amber passes right by me and makes a beeline right for the back deck. The back is just as tropical as the front. The deck is done in sand colored stone pavers, which are surrounded by various tropical trees and flowers. A lagoon shaped pool sits off to the side with a raised Jacuzzi that overflows into the pool like a waterfall. There are lounge chairs and side tables all around the pool. Under the covered part of the patio, there is a huge built in kitchen with a grille and a nice patio table that seats twelve. This would be a great place to have a vacation with a group.

"Do you feel up to checking out the beach, princess?"

"I can't wait! Let's go." She takes my hand and leads me to a path that we assume will take us to the beach. The path isn't very long and at the end is a beautiful white sandy beach. We walk down to the double lounger just at the water's edge. I sit first and pull Amber down to sit between my legs with her head resting on my chest. We lay there silent for a long time just enjoying each other and the beauty that surrounds us. If someone asked me right now what I thought heaven is like, I would have to say it's exactly like this.

CHAPTER
Seven

Amber

TODAY WE leave our paradise and it has been nothing less than perfect. This is definitely my idea of heaven. We've spent our days laying by the pool or on the beach relaxing and drinking virgin frozen appletini's or doing a little shopping. Breakfast and dinner are spent out in a quaint little beach front restaurant down the street. Our nights are spent making love anywhere and everywhere we can think of. So far, my favorite has been on the beach in the moonlight. Even though I am having so much fun, I'm anxious to get home to our friends. I can't wait to share our wonderful news with them all. We've decided to wait until after our first doctor's appointment just so we know everything's okay. Kyle insisted on packing our bags while I relax by the pool. I'm seriously thinking about having one of these put in at home. I really could get used to this.

"Amber, sweetie, wake up. It's time to head out. We have a big day tomorrow," Kyle says just above a whisper in my ear.

"Sorry, I fell asleep. I'm so tired lately."

"Don't be sorry. Our little guy takes a lot of energy from you. You rest whenever you need to and never apologize for it," he says as he kisses my forehead and helps me up. This is one of the reasons I am so in love with this man. He's sweet and considerate. I have a feeling I am going to be one very pampered woman for the next eight months or so. Sadly, we say goodbye to our paradise, but promise to come back again before the baby comes. I spend most of our drive home sleeping. No matter how hard I try to stay awake and keep Kyle company, I just can't do it. As soon as we pull into the drive, I wake up noticing Paul's truck is here.

As soon as Kyle turns the car off, I see Paul and Holly come out of the house. My door flies open and I am being pulled out of the car and hugged tightly by Paul. I can't help but to laugh. All of these big bad tough guys are all a bunch of softies.

"I'm so happy for you guys! I can't believe I'm gonna be Uncle Paul!" he says excitedly.

"What are you doing to my girl, dude? Put her down now before you hurt her," Kyle yells playfully at a laughing Paul. Paul gently puts me back on my feet and takes off toward Kyle. He picks Kyle up the same way he did Holly and me and I start to laugh so hard, we're crying. Kyle is trying to get down but the more he fights, the tighter Paul holds him.

"You better put me down before I have to kick your ass and embarrass you in front of the ladies."

"Okay. Okay. Congratulations. I'm really happy for you. I know this is something you have always wanted."

"If you boys are done with all the mushy shit, we'd like to eat," Holly says as she puts her arm around me. "Oh, and grab the bags on your way in," she tells the guys before guiding me into the house.

Just like I thought there would be, a feast is laid out on the counter. All of my favorites from the bar, including the scallops I love so much. After I got out of the hospital, Clark and Marty learned how to make the scallops the way I like them. They are now a menu item. It is so thoughtful of Holly and Paul to do this. They are both such wonderful friends. Without them, we wouldn't have gotten through half of the shit we have.

"I thought it would be nice for the four of us to celebrate the newest Connor. Plus, I really missed you guys," Holly says with teary eyes.

"Isn't it me that's supposed to be emotional with all of the hormones?"

"Real funny. I am just so happy for you. And I am excited to be an aunt and godmother."

"What makes you so sure you'd be our baby's Godmother?" I ask her teasingly. Of course we would ask Paul and Holly to be our child's Godparents. That's a no brainer. I just like to give her shit. By the look on her face, she knows this is one of those times.

"Amber Lewis Connor, don't you dare joke about something as serious as this."

"Sorry, of course we would chose the two of you. I just like to tease you. Especially when you are a pushy bitch and you don't wait to be asked," I tell her as I laugh. She smiles as she sits me in a chair at the counter. She then starts to make me a plate of food. Even though to most everything would look just fine, I can see a sadness in her eyes as well as hear it in her voice. Something we were talking about hit a nerve with her. She won't talk about her past before she came to Oakville. When I asked her, she said she wasn't ready to dig it up enough to explain it. I can respect that. She'll tell me in her own time. I just worry about her. I also asked Paul if he knew anything about it. Not so he'd tell me, but so she had someone to go to that knew about whatever haunts her sometimes. Luckily, she has confided in him.

I've been a nervous wreck all day long. We are on our way to our first doctor appointment and I should have made the appointment for first thing this morning. I just want everything to be okay with the baby.

"Stop worrying, princess. It's not healthy for you or the baby," Kyle says for the hundredth time. I know he's right, but so many bad things have happened to us it's hard to believe that we will finally have our happy ever after this easily.

"I know it isn't. I'm trying not to. I really am." He squeezes my hand.

"Don't you think if something were wrong with our baby you would feel it? You are the one he's connected to. If something is wrong, you will know before anyone. Now, do you have any bad feelings or truly think there is something wrong with our baby?" I never looked at things that way. He's right, though. I would have some sort of mother's instinct right? Honestly, I have felt great aside from the bouts of morning sickness. I smile over at him. How does he always know exactly what I need him to say?

Sitting on the examination table in only a paper gown, I glance over at Kyle. Looks like the tables have turned and he's the one who's nervous now. When the door opens and Dr. Monty walks through, I see why Becky recommended him. As if this weren't uncomfortable enough, I'll now have a gorgeous man inspecting my vagina. I quickly glance over at Kyle and he has a look on his face that says, "This guy is not touching you down there!" This should be a very interesting appointment.

"Good afternoon, Mr. and Mrs. Connor. I'm Dr. Monty." Even his voice is hot. He keeps eye contact with Kyle as he introduces himself and moves to shake his hand first. Kyle visibly relaxes a little bit.

"Let's get the unpleasant part over with first. After we finish, I'll send you over to have an ultrasound so you can both get a glimpse of your baby," he says with a smile while he puts on a pair of gloves. And just like that, the tension is right back in the room. Kyle holds my hand through the entire exam and only growls twice. I'm very proud of him. During the breast exam, I really thought he was going to lose it, but he didn't.

"Okay. Go ahead and get dressed, Amber. A nurse will come and get you both in a few minutes. After the ultrasound we'll all meet back up in my office." He smiles at me and walks over to Kyle to shake his hand before he leaves. I quickly get dressed and impatiently wait for the nurse. When the door opens, we both jump up, ready to see our baby. It makes the young, bubbly nurse giggle.

"I guess I don't need to ask if you're both ready. Follow me," she said with an amused smile on her face. We follow her down the hall and into a huge room. There's an exam table next to what I assume is the ultrasound machine. On the wall is a gigantic TV screen. There are two other women in the room waiting. One slides a chair next to the exam table.

"Mr. Connor, you can sit here. Mrs. Connor, hop up on the table and lay back," Nurse Bubbly says. We do as we're told. One of the other nurses comes over to lift my shirt up and unbutton my shorts. She squirts a generous amount of warm gel on my stomach and begins to move the wand around. Our eyes immediately focus on the large screen in front of us, waiting to see our baby. When it appears, we are in complete awe. I can't stop the tears that start to flow down my face. It's the most amazing thing I've ever seen. At first, it was like looking at a fuzzy black and white television. But then the image became clearer. I can make out feet, legs, hands, and arms. He or she is wiggling around as if it's doing a little dance for the camera. We are so focused on the image in front of us, we don't realize one of the women hurrying from the room as the other two whisper to each other.

When I see something is going on, the nurse that left is back with two more women in tow. Immediately, I start to panic. I look at Kyle and see the worry in his eyes too. All of the nurses are still huddled together, speaking in very hushed tones. If they don't start talking to us, I'm going to lose it.

"Is there something wrong?" I ask, my voice laced with fear.

"Just a moment, Mrs. Connor. We just need to be sure of something." They continue their whispered conversation while looking at the screen and I can't help the anger and frustration bubbling up inside of me. I start to open my mouth to let these women have a piece of my mind when Nurse Bubbly appears. She places her hand on my shoulder and smiles down to me.

"Amber, there's nothing wrong. But there is something you need to see," she says, pointing to the screen. "This is baby A, this is baby B, and this here, is baby C." She looks at me warmly, allowing it to all sink in. As soon as it does, I look over at Kyle. He's as white as a ghost and looks like he's about to pass out. Three. Three babies. Triplets. Holy shit! What the hell are we going to do with triplets? I'm scared to death about having one, now we are going to have three. Three at once.

We are led down the hall to Dr. Monty's office. As soon as we walk in, he stands from behind his desk.

"Have a seat," he says, motioning to two chairs opposite himself. "Congratulations. This is the first set of triplets we've had in this office," he begins. He continues speaking, but I can't seem to focus on anything that's being said. I'm still in shock. Dr. Monty must realize that neither of us are paying attention.

"I suppose this must all be shocking and probably needs to sink in. We can schedule another appointment when you've had time to get used to all of this," he says while looking at us with an amused grin. Nodding is all either of us seems to be able to manage for a response.

We finally get out of the office and into Kyle's truck. After a while, I notice that we still haven't said one word to each other. I glance over and see that the color hasn't returned to his face yet. What if he's upset? Maybe he doesn't want three babies at once. It is a lot to handle.

"I'm sorry, Kyle. I had no idea." He still hasn't said a word since the news. He pulls the truck into KC's — where Holly has planned our announcement party — parks, and removes his seatbelt. Slowly, he turns in his seat and stares at me. My heart is racing because I have no idea what he's going to say.

"Why are you apologizing? This is a shock, I won't lie about that. Not because I'm not thrilled to death, though. I want to be the perfect dad. I was scared when I knew it was one. Scared because it's my first time at this and I don't want to mess anything up. We are at the beginner level, princess, and triplets...triplets are for people who are experts." He shakes his head and chuckles. "I'm not upset in any way. We always said we wanted three kids. We are just gonna have them all at once. Maybe it will turn out to be easier this way in the long run. I didn't mean to scare you. It just took a while for it to sink in and the shock to wear off. How do you feel about it all?"

"About the same. I'm definitely shocked but excited and scared all at the same time. I do know one thing...we aren't alone. We will have so much help from our wonderful friends. These babies will be spoiled, no doubt. For once, I'm not going to worry. I'm going to enjoy being happy."

"I say we both do that. No more worrying until we have a reason to worry. Now, let's go shock the shit out of all of our friends."

Kyle

"Oh this is going to be fun," Amber says with a mischievous grin on her face. She is so beautiful. Even more beautiful now that she's carrying our baby...babies. That's still going to take some getting used to. I help her out of the truck and we make our way into the bar.

When we walk through the doorway, all eyes are on us. Everyone looks very anxious to hear why they're here. Poor Beasley looks the most nervous. Holly looks like the cat that ate the canary because she thinks she knows what everyone else doesn't. She's going to be surprised when the little triplet bomb is dropped in her lap. Paul quiets everyone and I look over at Amber, silently questioning. She shakes her head and gestures for me to tell the news.

"Okay, well we wanted you all here today so we can share some pretty big news with you. Amber is pregnant!" The room explodes — people are yelling congratulations, women are teary eyed. It's wild, to say the least. I lift my hand and try to quiet everyone down again. "We had an ultrasound today. They found something we weren't expecting."

I pause for a moment, letting the suspense build. Yeah, it's an asshole thing to do, but it is going to be so funny when I see the look on their faces. "There were three little blobs on the ultrasound instead of one." I wait for it to register. I think Beasley puts it together first by the beaming smile that spreads across his face. Then Holly is next. No one can miss when it sinks in for her. She comes running to us and wraps us both in a hug.

"Triplets! Are you serious! I can't believe it. You're gonna get huge!" Poor Amber pales. I bet it hadn't crossed her mind that she'll be three times bigger than normal. I'll have to reassure her later. Beasley squeezes his way through the crowd to get to his daughter. He looks so excited. Amber pulls out the ultrasound photos and begins to show them. I'm finally able to make my way to the side of the bar where things are a little calmer. Paul is waiting for me with a beer.

"You don't do anything half ass do you? Can't just produce one baby, can you? Do you have some kind of super sperm?" Paul says in between laughs and me flipping him off.

"Don't be jealous. Not everyone can be as awesome as I am."

"I hope you're awesome at changing diapers, 'cause there are going to be a whole lot of them." He's laughing again. I pale at the thought. Triple the diapers. Triple the feeding. Triple the crying. They are all going to be driving at the same time and going to college all at once. "Here, you look like you need this," Paul says as he slides the shot of whiskey in front of me. I give him a nod and throw it back.

"Better give me one more. Actually, two more. One for each baby. I think I'm still in shock." I'm only half teasing. This is going to take some time to fully sink in. I sit and talk to all of the guys for a while and let all of the women "ooh" and "awe" over Amber and the ultrasound photos. Of course, Holly is already planning the baby shower.

Beasley finally pulls himself away from Amber and makes his ways to the bar. He sits down on the stool next to me, his smile still running from ear to ear. I'm so glad Amber will get to share this with him. I look over at Beasley who raises his beer for a toast.

"To my daughter and son-in-law. Thank you for making me a very happy man. Not only have I gotten the chance to be the father I've always wanted to be, but now I'll get to be a grandpa," he says with so much pride and excitement in his voice, it starts to choke me up.

"I'm sure it was all Kyle's pleasure. Ya know, knocking up your daughter," Angel says with a wink in my direction. Leave it to Angel to tank a nice heartfelt moment. Paul spits his beer out and sprays Marcus and Clark. I just stare at Angel. It's typical for him. Only thinking about the sex and not thinking about the fact that Beasley doesn't want to hear about how his daughter got pregnant. After what seems like an eternity of silence, Beasley starts laughing. Not a chuckle, but a full-blown belly laugh. That's not what I expected.

"What's so funny? Please don't encourage Angel, he has no filter," I say him.

"It's not what Angel said, it's the looks on the faces of the four of you. It's not like I don't know where babies come from. I'm not some old prude. That doesn't mean I want to hear any of the specifics, though," he says with a chuckle and a glare to Angel telling him the subject is closed.

"Congrats, KC. I'm off to go make a lovely lady a very happy lady," Angel says before emptying his beer. He gives Amber a kiss on the cheek before walking out the door. I wish he would settle down. He's the only one of us four that I think would love the rocker lifestyle. I'm so glad I didn't follow that path any further. If we would have hit it big, I think leaving it behind would have been very difficult. I love playing music, but I also love my privacy. I like that I don't have to be traveling and away from Amber. I never wanted to be famous and play huge stadiums. That's just not me. I like my quiet, normal life, especially now that I'm gonna be a dad.

"Kyle, I've got my friend digging into Jax and Leena. He said he'll get back to me as soon as he finds something," Beasley says, pulling me out of my thoughts.

"You sound confident that there's gonna be something to find."

"I am. I've never trusted the guy. I just have a gut feeling he's not the friend to Amber he pretends to be."

"Is it your cop or fatherly gut that tells you he's up to something no good?"

"A little of both. We need to keep a close eye on him. Nobody is hurting my daughter again on my watch."

"I'm right there with you. Not only do we have to protect her, but we have the babies to think of now too. Do you think he is a physical threat like Beau was?" A pained look flashes across Beasley's face. It matches the stabbing feeling I get in my chest every time the name Beau comes up.

"I'm not sure. I don't think so, but look where that got us before.

We just have to pay close attention to everything he says and does." Just thinking about this makes my stomach turn. I have wanted to punch that fucker in the face since the first day I met him. The slightest reason is all I'm gonna need to kick his ass right back to Georgia.

I hear Paul whistle. When I look up at him, there's a smile a mile wide on his face. I turn and look behind me to see what he's smiling about. Amber, Holly, and Taryn are all out on the dance floor. The way these girls are moving to *Bottoms Up* by Brantley Gilbert makes me very happy that this is my bar and the only people in here know not to mess with these girls. There's something sensual about the beat of this song. Top it off with Amber out there moving her hips to the beat with her arms raised makes me hard as a rock. She's looking right at me. She knows exactly what she's doing to me. This woman is gonna kill me. Guess we had better get it out of our system, 'cause once these babies come, I don't see a whole lot of sex or sleep in our futures. I'm in awe of her as I watch her move around the dance floor. I cannot believe she's carrying our babies. I didn't think it was possible to love her more than I already did. Since finding out she's pregnant, I have fallen for her even more.

When the song ends, Amber hugs and says goodbye to the girls and a few of the guys. The closer she gets to me, the more I think I may not be able to wait until I get home.

"Take me home, cowboy," she whispers against my ear. I wasn't going to argue. I yell bye to Paul and lead her out the door.

CHAPTER
Eight

Amber

"Ow! Not so hard. I don't think it's going to work this way," I tell Kyle.

"Maybe if you lay flat it will work better." I lay back. I'm already sweating and out of breath. This is a lot more work than I thought it would be. He carefully tries again. I think this time he's got it. Oh, that's it. It just might work now.

"Just like that. Keep going. Don't. Stop." Just when it looks like it's going to work, it doesn't. He's so close, but it just won't go all the way in. "It's too tight. I don't think it'll fit," I snap. Poor Kyle, it's not his fault. We have been at this for over forty minutes now and I still can't get these damn jeans zipped or buttoned. It's just not going to happen. I can't believe this! Nothing fits. Not one damn thing! What the hell is going on? I shouldn't be out growing out my clothes already. I have a little bit of a baby bump, but it's only noticeable without clothes, or if you look really hard. I guess with triplets you grow three times faster also. *Ugh!*

"Princess, why don't you throw on some yoga pants and we can go shopping before you go to the center," he says somewhat hesitantly, like I'm gonna snap his head off for the suggestion. I haven't been that bitchy lately. Have I? Maybe I have been a little hormonal. Okay, a lot hormonal. I have good reasons for being the mega bitch though. I have morning sickness twenty-four seven, my boobs hurt, I'm exhausted all of the time, and now I can't fit into any of my clothes. I'm only twelve weeks along, so it's only just beginning. What do the next six months hold? Being a snapping bitch doesn't suit me well. I need to relax and try to focus on the happy and exciting things. Not look at this like I am getting fat, but that our babies are healthy and growing. That's it. That's what I'll do from now on. That and try to curb my attitude toward Kyle when he's only trying to help.

"I'm sorry. I don't mean to be a hormonal bitch. I just can't seem to control it or anything else that's happening lately. I promise to try not to be so moody. Shopping sounds perfect and at this point, I think it's a necessity." We both laugh as Kyle helps me stand up. Probably a good thing I didn't get these things buttoned. If the button popped, I could have really hurt someone.

"You don't have to be sorry. This can't be easy on you. Hell, the all-day morning sickness would kill me alone. I can take it, so if you have to dish it out to make yourself feel better, that's fine with me. I'm here for you, whatever you need," he says as he wraps his arms around me. Just when I think there isn't any possible way to fall harder for this man, I do. He's always so considerate of my needs. How did I get so lucky?

Kyle insists on cooking me an egg white omelet before we can leave. While I eat, he goes to call Jax to let him know I'll be in a little later. He makes sure I eat three times a day no matter what. Even when I'm a nauseous wreck, he's shoving crackers in my face. It really is sweet though, the way he always takes such good care of me. After I've eaten enough to satisfy him, we head out to the mall. While we're driving, he confesses that he told Jax I wouldn't be in at all today. I should be mad but I'm not. He's trying to do something nice for me and it's something I need to do. Besides, most men would be complaining about going to the mall shopping, but not my Kyle. It's his idea and I should be happy about that, so I will be. I'm going to sit back and enjoy whatever the day has to offer.

He's been wonderful. Helping me pick out outfits he says look great on me. On top of my overall bitchy mood, I've been feeling fat and undesirable lately. Without even realizing he was doing it, he totally changed that for me. I've been noticing lots of women, and even a few men checking him out today. Subtlety is definitely not the theme for today. They aren't even trying to hide it. Not once did he even notice. The whole time, all of his attention has been on me, and it's just what I needed.

There's one salesgirl in particular that really pisses me off. I'm not overly jealous. I know my man is hot. I don't blame other women for looking. That doesn't bother me at all. I can appreciate a nice looking man. It's the people that don't respect the fact that he's with another woman or that he's wearing a ring. The ones that think they are entitled to whatever they want and screw whomever gets in their way. And this woman is one of those types. She's not a woman that's going to be unnoticed. Tall with long straight blonde hair and a perfect tan, I can admit she's beautiful, but it's all fake. From the bleached hair, all the way down to her fake toenails. A Barbie doll is made with less plastic. She doesn't realize she couldn't be any farther from Kyle's type. In her mind, she's perfect and every man wants what she has to offer. She's had her eye on us, or I should say Kyle, since we walked through the front doors. We're looking through a rack of dresses when she slithers up behind us.

"Is there anything I can help you find?" she asks in a sugary sweet voice. I can tell her question is directed to me even though her eyes haven't left Kyle. My blood pressure rises. I'm still polite even though I really want to punch her in the throat.

"No, thank you. We're doing just fine." Kyle's eyes never leave mine and that doesn't sit well with blondey. I can see the wheels turning in her head. She's trying to figure out how to up her game. Then, she does something that absolutely infuriates me. Thinking she's being sneaky, she tries slipping her number to him. I mean, really! He's in a maternity store, shopping for clothes with his pregnant wife, and this woman is bold enough to hit on him with me standing right there watching? She's smiling at him as if this is acceptable behavior. Maybe for some men it is. Not for this one, though. Before I can tear into this bitch, Kyle gives me a wink.

"Let me get this straight. I don't want a misunderstanding." He has a mischievous look on his face. What is he up to? "You're hitting on me? That's why you're passing me the phone number, correct?"

"Yes."

"And exactly who do you think this is?" he asks, motioning to me.

"Does it really matter? I mean look at her and look at me. It's a no brainer," she says, matter of fact. Kyle's jaw starts twitching. He's pissed.

"You're right, it's most definitely a no brainer." She's smiling. "You're no match for my wife. I don't find you the least bit attractive." She looks at him completely stunned. I'm sure that's not something she's ever heard before. "The fact that you would disrespect my wife so blatantly makes you downright ugly. Can't you find any single men? You should know better than to try to take something that's not yours. That just makes you look desperate." She gasps like someone slugged her right in the gut. "Princess, did I cover it all? There's ugly and desperate. I know there was something else I was thinking of. What was it? Oh, yeah, I remember. Fake, that's it. Most guys don't like ugly, desperate, and fake women." He turns to me, kisses my forehead, grabs my hand, and leads me out of the store. Just before we get to the door, I turn to look at blondey. She's still standing in the same place, totally dumbfounded with her mouth gaping open. I can't stop the giggle that escapes me.

When we reach the courtyard, I am in hysterics. That was amazing. He knocked her right off her pedestal onto her ass.

"I'm sorry that was probably a little harsh, but she really pissed me off. Acting like you weren't even there. If she were a man, I would've kicked her ass." If this were a cartoon, he'd have smoke billowing out of his ears. Picturing that makes me laugh even harder. "What's so funny?" he asks, trying to stop his own laughter.

"The look on her face. I bet if you go back, she's in the same spot trying to figure out how *she* got rejected. She was a bitch. Harsh is what she needed, so don't apologize. That's the best smack down I've witnessed in a long time." He could no longer hold his laughter.

The rest of the afternoon is hassle free. We buy my entire pregnancy wardrobe and then some. Kyle also manages to pull me into a couple baby stores. He finds three matching fluffy frog stuffed animals and three onesies that say 'My dad rocks'. It's adorable seeing him picking out tiny little baby clothes. If I didn't tell him no, he would have bought three of everything in the whole store. I don't want to jinx anything. I know I'm probably being a little ridiculous, but things are just too perfect and that scares me. There's this nagging feeling I have that something bad is going to happen. The more I try to push it away, the worse it gets. So, I'm just taking everything one day at a time. Enjoying every happy moment I'm given. If something does happen, at least I didn't waste all of the good times being miserable.

Kyle

"So, HOW's it going, daddy?" Paul asks as he walks into my office.

"Pretty good. How were things around here yesterday?"

"The usual. A little slow. What were you up to all day?"

"I took Amber to the mall. None of her clothes fit any more, it was time for maternity clothes." Holly walks in then. Actually, it's perfect timing. I have a plan but I am going to need help from Holly, Paul, and the rest of the guys too. The idea came to me yesterday when we got home from the mall. We'd been reading about multiple pregnancies. Something we read said it's common for a woman carrying triplets to be put on bed rest at some point during her pregnancy. I want to surprise Amber by completing the nursery for her. I know she's worried about jinxing things, but that's just her nerves talking. She'll really love this once it's finished, plus it will get her more excited. "I'm gonna need some help and it's the type of thing that's right up your alley." I explain everything I want to do to Holly and how I want it to be a surprise.

"This is going to be so much fun! Just leave it all to me. I'll take care of everything." She's so excited she's almost jumping out of her skin. Within seconds, she's texting everyone we know and my idea is no longer mine. Oh well. If anyone can make it perfect, Holly can. Becky and Taryn will take Amber to the spa for the weekend. Clark and Marcus are going to paint the nursery the second Amber leaves. Holly, Angel, and I are going to pick out all of the furniture and accessories, then put them all together once we get home. Paul, the lucky bastard, gets to take care of the bar. Once we have everything set up, Paul and Holly go out to open the bar and I start on my mountain of paper work.

"Hey, babe!" I look up and see Amber coming through my office door. Is it two already?

"Hi, princess. How's your day been?" I ask as she makes herself comfortable on my lap. When I say she makes herself comfortable, I mean she grinds her ass against my cock. Whether or not she did it on purpose, I don't know. What I do know is that it's going to be a very long weekend by myself.

"Good. A little strange...Jax brought something up that got me thinking. He thinks with all the time I've been taking off and with the babies coming that I should give someone Power of Attorney. Just in case something needs to be done at the center." It makes sense, but I also get the feeling that Jax is hoping to be the one to get that responsibility. Is that what his end game is? Does he want control of the center? It's not like it makes a bundle of money.

"Let me guess, he wants you to sign it over to him."

"It was implied. I had my lawyer draw up the papers for you to have control. If you aren't available, Holly will be next. It continues down the line of all our friends but Jax is not named. I'm worried he wants my center."

"I don't think you're wrong. Choosing to be careful is a good idea."

"Are you sure you can't let Holly out of work this weekend so she can go with us?" she asks with a pout. I feel bad lying to her.

"I wish I could, princess, but you know what it's like on the weekends." She sticks out her lower lip. If this wasn't all for her, I would give in. I always do.

"Okay. The girls are waiting for me. Try not to miss me too much," she says with a smile and one hell of a kiss.

"How can I not miss you after a kiss like that?" I ask as she gets up from my lap. I quickly catch her and pull her back to me so that she is standing between my legs. I take my hand and rub her belly. I'm anxious for the day that I can feel the babies move. "I love you, princess." I lower my face to her belly, placing a kiss on it. "I love you guys too. Take care of your mamma. You girls have a good time this weekend."

"We will. We love you too, babe. See you in a couple days." After another hot kiss, I walk her out to meet the girls.

As soon as they leave the parking lot, Holly is giving orders. Clark and Marcus are out the door and on the way to paint the nursery. Seeing that we have no idea what sex the babies are, Holly and I chose a pale blue with an off-white trim. That will match the Winnie the Pooh design Amber has her eyes on for the bedding. I figure Holly knows what she's talking about, I know I don't have a fucking clue.

"Earth to, Kyle. Let's get going. The shit's not gonna put itself together," Angel jokes.

"Am I keeping you from a hot date or something?"

"Not anymore. Holly made me cancel that already," he whines.

"Okay McWhiney Ass. I'm ready," I tease, quickly dodging his fist. Before I can get to the door, Paul stops me. Holly says they'll wait for me in the truck as I toss her my keys.

"Hey, make sure Holly doesn't get too crazy, will ya? This baby stuff is a little rough for her," he says, his voice laced with sadness. It's none of my business, but they are both my friends and I don't want to see either of them hurting. Maybe I shouldn't have Holly helping with this.

"Did I do something wrong by asking her to help me out?"

"She doesn't like to talk about it. Please don't let her know you know anything about this. The only reason I'm saying anything is because I'm worried about how she's gonna handle all of this." He looks around nervously.

"You don't have to tell me anything. Don't break her trust. I'll keep an eye on her. I don't need details to do that. If she starts acting unlike her usual bossy, pushy, and in charge self..." before I can finish, Miss Bossy herself sticks her head in the door.

"Let's go, Connor!" Holly shouts before going back outside.

"I'll take care of her. That is, if I don't strangle her first," I say to Paul as I head for the door.

"Thanks, Kyle," he says through his laughter.

During the ride to the store, Holly goes over her list of what we need. I can handle shopping with Amber. Holly, on the other hand, is a totally different story. She really would've made a good drill sergeant for marine boot camp. Actually, she scares me a little. I think even Angel is a little scared of her. It's gotta be the red hair. Red heads can be pretty damn mean when they want to be.

"Angel, what the hell are those?" Holly barks.

"The car seats you told me to get."

"*Those* are not what I told you to get. I said to get the ones that match these strollers," Holly says, pointing to three boxes on a flatbed cart. "See, the car seat part snaps in here when they are small. Then, when they are bigger, they sit in the stroller part." She's explaining this shit to Angel like he really cares. He looks at me, his eyes begging me to help him. As fun as it is to watch him squirm, I'll put him out of his misery.

"Holly, why don't you start looking at the cribs and I'll help Angel get the right car seats? We'll meet you over there when we finish."

"Fine. Don't take forever, though. We have a ton of things to get still," she states before hurrying off in the opposite direction. I hope she's not having a meltdown. I'm gonna feel like a pile of dog shit if asking her to help me causes problems for her.

"What the hell is up with her? She's normally a little bossy but today she's over the fucking top," Angel whispers. He's probably afraid she'll hear him. Chicken shit.

"She's just trying to make everything perfect for Amber. You know how Holly gets." We finish our task of getting the correct car seats and Holly is pleased when we meet her in the crib aisle. She's also calmed down quite a bit. The rest of our shopping expedition is uneventful. We find everything on Holly's list. Car seats, strollers, swings, cribs, dressers, and changing tables. All the big stuff that needs to be assembled. It's going to be a very long weekend.

Saturday is spent building baby furniture. There are men, tools, and parts spread throughout the house. Four letter words are flying around left and right but the furniture is going together rather well. There is just a lot of it. Overall, it's been a fun day. We've all been laughing and joking with each other. Clark and Marcus finished painting last night so it finished drying today. They even put up a border to match the bedding sets. Amber is going to love it.

Sunday we have just enough time to put everything in its place. I have to admit, the room looks great. Everyone is in the kitchen waiting for the girls to get back and Holly has food set up for a little make shift party. Holly and her parties. We hear car doors slam and all of a sudden, I'm a little nervous. I hope she likes her surprise. As Amber walks into the kitchen, she glances around, and she strolls over to me, greeting me with a kiss.

"Okay, what's going on? What are you up to, Kyle?" Amber questions.

"We have something to show you. Everyone worked all weekend to do this for you." She looks around the room and smiles. I grab her hand and take her up the stairs. Everyone follows behind us. "Close your eyes, princess." Slowly, I open the door to the nursery and lead her into the room. "Open them," I whisper in her ear. Her hands cover her mouth and she gasps as tears begin to well in her eyes. *Oh no. She doesn't like it.*

"It's...it's so beautiful," she stutters as she turns and faces our friends. "You all did this for me? Thank you so much! I love you all. This is the best gift ever." She starts hugging everyone one at a time. *Thank God, she likes it.* We spend the rest of the afternoon and evening eating and enjoying time with friends. Beasley even stops by for a while. It turns out to be a great day.

CHAPTER Nine

Amber

FINALLY, I'VE started to relax. Things at the center are going smoothly and I hired a few new people. One of the new hires, Chelsie, stands out from the rest. I see a lot of potential there and know that she will eventually be more than just a counselor. Not only is she wonderful with the kids, but they all love her as well. You can tell she really enjoys being around them and it's not just a paycheck to her. That's the kind of person I want running this place someday. Don't get me wrong, Jax has done a great job and he seems to be acting normal again, but there's still a nagging feeling I have that tells me he can't be completely trusted. I haven't seen Leena around again and that in itself is cause to celebrate. Maybe she finally got the hint and is off stalking someone else's husband.

I'm also allowing myself to relax and get excited about the babies. One more week until our next appointment with Dr. Monty. I'm in week twelve and the morning sickness has pretty much gone away. There are a few times here and there that it will still hit me but not as often. My belly is protruding quite a bit now. I look more like twenty weeks along than twelve. The internet has become my newest addiction to research everything I can on multiple pregnancies. I want to make sure I know everything I can. You can never be too prepared, right?

After sitting at my desk for hours, it's time to stretch my legs and check on things downstairs. When I reach the bottom step, I see Angel talking to Chelsie. I love Angel like a brother but he is not going to pull his shit with my staff. As I get closer, I'm shocked by what I hear. Shocked and amused. I might have been way off on my assessment of Chelsie. I know it's wrong on so many levels, but I hide around the corner and listen.

"If you think you can sweet talk yourself into my pants you've got another thing coming. I'm not some naive little farm girl. I know this must be hard for you to comprehend, but not every women wants you. Some of us actually have some self-respect," Chelsie states calmly. The whole time she speaks, her eyes never leave his. I swear I can see the sparks flying between them. When Chelsie turns on her heal and walks away, Angel starts to smirk. The shit head. He fully enjoyed being put in his place by her.

"You can come out now, ya little eavesdropper," Angel chuckles. *Oops. Busted.*

"Can you not run her off? I really like her and she has a lot of potential," I say as I come out of hiding. Angel just smiles down at me. "What's the deal, anyway? She's not exactly the type of girl you normally hit on. You know, groupie skank." Chelsie is a beautiful girl. She's tall about five foot six or seven, and her hair rests on her shoulders in sandy blonde waves, perfectly framing her round face and bright hazel eyes. She is the total opposite of what Angel usually goes for. If you look up groupie or skank in the dictionary, the picture next to those definitions is his usual type.

"Ouch. I think I should be offended by that remark."

"Angel, you know I love you, but I know how you are with women. Chelsie is not a fuck 'em and chuck 'em kinda girl. Do not mess with her unless you're looking for more. Please don't give me a reason to bury you in my back yard." He starts laughing so hard his face is red.

"Ya know, for a tiny little thing, you scare the shit out of me," he jokes as he kisses my cheek and walks into his classroom. The fact that he didn't promise to stay away from Chelsie doesn't go unnoticed. I'm gonna have to keep my eye on him. I turn, surprised to see Becky walking through the front doors.

"Hey there, momma! I thought maybe we could have some lunch together," she says holding up a bag from the deli at the hospital. She knows I love their grilled veggie subs. I love this woman.

"Let's go up to my office." We go up to my office and enjoy the awesome subs she brought. I tell her all about Chelsie and Angel.

"I want to meet the girl that can resist the advances of that man," she says, giggling.

"It was a sight to see. She put him right in his place. He never even said a word to her. I think he was stunned stupid." We both laugh. Angel always has something to say.

I get up to go pee. I swear I pee about twenty times an hour. I sit but before I do my business, a sense that something's not right washes over me. What it is exactly, I'm not sure. The palms of my hands are moist and my stomach is rolling. I turn to look down into the toilet and instantly panic.

"Becky!" I scream as my body begins to shake. Becky comes flying through the bathroom door.

"What's the matter? Are you okay?" I can't speak; I can't seem to do anything but point to the toilet. Slowly, she looks down and gasps.

"Oh shit!" She pulls out her cell phone and immediately starts dialing a number before flushing the toilet. She grabs my hand and guides me to the couch in my office. "Lay down and put your feet up." I do as she says, knowing I shouldn't argue. I watch as she paces back and forth, the motions slightly calming my nerves and giving me something to concentrate on. *Stay calm, stay calm*, I repeat over and over in my head. *Calm.* At the words 'mucus plug' and 'preterm labor', I snap out of my daze. Labor! How can I be in labor? It's way too early for that. Either not noticing the small panic attack I'm having, or ignoring it, she walks over to the door, points to me, and whispers, "Stay." She moves into the hallway and starts speaking in hushed tones, but I still make out 'hospital', and 'as soon as possible'. What's happening? What's wrong with my babies?

"Amber I know you're scared, but I need you to try to stay calm. I think you're in pre-term labor. We need to get you to the hospital so they can get it stopped," she says calmly. Thank God, she's the one here with me. I nod my head okay, still too scared to speak. Angel walks into the room, his face pale. Becky must have went to find him. "Angel, I need you to carry Amber to your SUV and lay her in the backseat."

Angel comes over and scoops me up into his arms as gently as he can. I'm still shaking, my nerves getting the better of me and Angel notices it the second he picks me up. When he speaks, the fear in his voice shocks me. He's always so together and in control.

"It's okay, baby girl. We're gonna get you taken care of. I promise. I called Paul and he's bringing Kyle to the hospital to meet us. They should be there the same time as us." To hear him break his cool guy facade is too much and my emotions finally come to the surface. Angel holds me closer as I sob quietly into his chest and carries me to his car. "I know you're scared. I'm sure everything will be okay. We have to believe that."

"Okay, I'll try," I squeak out between sobs.

"That's my brave girl," he says with a smile as he places me in the backseat of his large SUV. The ride to the hospital feels like it takes forever even though we make it in half the time it would normally take. Rubbing my belly to soothe and relax the babies, I pray to God that he will keep them safe. Becky was trying to keep my mind busy by explaining what was going to happen when we get to the hospital. The way Becky is talking, this is fairly common, and it can be stopped. At her words, I finally begin to relax a little bit.

At least, until we pull up to the hospital and I see Kyle. As soon as he notices Angel's SUV, he races through the parking lot and has the back door open before the vehicle comes to a stop. The look of terror on his handsome face is enough to break me.

"Princess, are you okay?"

"I'm okay. Becky thinks I'm in labor, but it can be stopped."

"Let's get you in there so they can check you out." He starts to pull me out of the car until Becky stops him.

"We need to put her in a wheel chair. That way there's no additional pressure on her cervix," Becky says to him. Again, I'm so thankful to have her here with me. Kyle lifts me out of the car and carries me into the hospital. When they try to give us a wheel chair, he waves it away.

Becky helps us find our way to the OB floor. As soon as we get there, Dr. Monty is waiting. From that moment on, everything is utter chaos. They get me into a gown and have me lay in the bed as they strap a monitor around my belly to test for contractions. Who would've thought you could have contractions and not feel them?

Now that they have determined that I am, in fact, having contractions, they start an IV. Then I'm given the most vial medication ever invented.

"I'm going to have the nurse give you Magnesium. It will help to slow the contractions. Sorry, but it's a little unpleasant. You'll feel like you have a mild case of the flu while it gets into your system. Hang in there, I'll be back to check on you in a bit," Dr. Monty explains. He instructs the nurse on what he wants then leaves her to it. I can handle a little unpleasantness if it means my babies will be okay. Really, how bad can it be?

The nurse quickly goes to work, setting up the IV. After several painful attempts at finding a vein in my arm, she finally places the needle in the top of my hand. Once it's secure, she pushes a few buttons on the IV machine and I can see the liquid from the bad start to drip into the clear tube. Within seconds, there is a slight burning sensation. A minute later, my veins are on fire. Not long after that, my body begins to ache all over. A few more minutes pass and sweat begins to form on my brow. When the waves of nausea start, I want to be put out of my misery. *A little unpleasant my ass!* "I-I'm gonna be sick," I say to the nurse. She quickly runs over with a trashcan, reaching me just in time. As soon as I finally feel like I'm done, Dr. Monty comes in with a portable ultrasound machine.

"I want to take some measurements of your cervix so I can see what we're dealing with," he explains. Poor Kyle's eyes widen when he sees the wand for the transvaginal ultrasound. If I weren't so sick, I'd be laughing. The look on his face is priceless. I grab his hand and hold tight when the doctor inserts the wand. I'm nervous, waiting to see what he finds.

"I've found the problem," Dr. Monty says as he slowly puts everything away and washes his hands. Is this man trying to add heart attack to the list of medical conditions?

"Do you plan on filling us in, Doc?" Kyle asks a little impatiently.

"Yes. Sorry. Amber you have what is called an Incompetent Cervix." He pauses and looks at us. I don't know what he's waiting for. I'm sure he can tell by the looks on our faces that we don't have a clue what that means and there are so many questions going through my head that it's making me dizzy. I close my eyes, take a deep breath, and try to calm myself. Kyle's hand grips mine. I can feel him tremble and know that he's as scared as I am. I can also tell his patience is wearing thin with the doctor. If he doesn't start explaining, Kyle might explode.

"What this means is...when pressure from the weight of the baby, or, in your case, babies, is put on your cervix, it starts to open. This condition usually leads to miscarriage or premature delivery." He stops again, giving us a chance to let what was said sink in for a minute.

What does this mean? Are we going to lose our babies? If the weight of the babies is a problem, it will only get worse, right?

"What can we do to keep our babies safe?" Kyle asks with a shaky voice. Please let him keep it together. If he can't keep it together, there is no way in hell I'll be able to.

"There are two steps we will take. First, there is a procedure called a cerclage, where we sew the cervix closed. Then we will put you on bed rest until the babies are born."

My concentration waivers, going back and forth and only allowing me to catch bits and pieces of what he's saying. Apparently, there's still no guarantee that the cerclage will keep the cervix closed. The only thought running through my head is there isn't a guarantee that my babies will survive. I don't think I could survive that. Losing them would crush me.

This is what women are made for...to have babies, except I can't even do that right. There's no Beau to blame for the problems we're faced with this time. It's me. I'm defective. Why? If something happens, Kyle will never forgive me. I wish my grandmother were here with me right now. She would know what to say to help me deal with all of this a little better.

"Princess, did you hear what Dr. Monty just said?" Kyle asks, pulling me out of my own head. I look at him but can't seem to form words, so I just shake my head no. He gets that look on his face that he usually does when he starts to worry about me.

"He said they are going to do the operation first thing in the morning. They want to make sure they stop the contractions," he says softly and slowly, like I'm a bomb he's trying to not detonate. Does he really think I'm that fragile? Maybe I am. I never thought I was before. I don't know if it's this particular situation or all the shit that has been thrown at me over this past year, but this might be the final crisis in my life that totally breaks me.

All of our friends have stopped by to check on me, but I ask Kyle to tell them I'm not feeling up to seeing anyone. I appreciate it, I really do, I just can't handle hearing people tell me everything will be fine and not to worry. How the hell can they know that? They can't. I know they're just trying to be good friends and keep me thinking positively, but I'm just not up for it right now. I just need to let this all sink in. Kyle refuses to go home, but I did convince him to go and eat with everyone.

What a miserable night. I swear someone has been in here every hour on the hour to draw blood. Kyle, true to his word, wouldn't leave. He's sleeping in the chair next to my bed. He was also awake most of the night worrying about me. I feel bad I really haven't had a whole lot to say to him. The thoughts and fears have taken over, completely consuming me. There's a knock on the door and my stomach flip-flops, nervous over the surgery. Then I notice the red hair.

"You really didn't think you were going to surgery without seeing me, did you?" Holly scolds as she enters the room. I should've known better. For the first time in twenty-four hours, I actually smile. For once, I'm thankful that Holly is so damn pushy.

"I'm sorry about not seeing anyone last night. I just...I was just overwhelmed with everything and needed my own little pity party."

"Don't worry about it. We all understand. We let you have yesterday...but you don't have a choice today," she informs me as my door opens. In walks everyone — Paul, Angel, Marcus, Clark, Taryn, Becky, and Beasley. Though, Jax is missing. We were such good friends — best friends, even — for so long, how did it all change so quickly? Better yet, why? They all have somber looks on their faces. The smile that spreads across my face must be contagious because they are all suddenly smiling. As much as I needed to be alone yesterday, I need this now.

I look over to see the smile I know will be on Kyle's face, but he's still sleeping! How can he still be sleeping? Angel notices me looking at Kyle and an evil grin appears. He walks quietly over to my sleeping husband and bends down like he's going to whisper something in his ear.

"WAKE UP, FUCKER!" he yells. Kyle flies straight up from the chair like he has a rocket up his ass and everyone erupts into laughter. Even me, I can't control it. This is definitely what I needed this morning. Kyle is about to retaliate but Dr. Monty walks in. Just like that, I'm slapped in the face with reality. The laughter-filled room goes dead silent in an instant. With the laughter, go the smiles. The worried looks are once again all I see staring back at me.

After they all say their goodbyes and wish me luck, our friends go to the waiting room. I should've known they wouldn't leave. Stubborn asses. Dr. Monty explains the procedure to us one more time. It really doesn't sound that bad. I'll be given a spinal anesthesia to numb me from the waist down and the rest will be similar to a pelvic exam. They will go in and place stitches around the outside of the cervix to keep it from opening. The procedure itself should only take about fifteen minutes. I'll be kept a couple hours for observation and the anesthesia to wear off, and then I'll be able to go home. I'm ready. It's something that will help keep my babies safe and I will do whatever is necessary to protect my babies. No matter how much it scares me.

"I love you, princess. I'll be right here when you get out," Kyle says as he leans down and places a sweet kiss on my lips. I know he's scared and worried but I just don't have it in me to comfort us all right now. I need him to be the strong one, the one that will hold us together through this because I don't have the strength to do it.

"I love you, too. I'll see you in a bit." I give him my best smile, but we both know it's forced. He kisses me one more time on the lips, then the forehead, and rests there for a moment.

"Hang in there, baby. I got you. I promise. I can carry the weight of it all. The only thing you need to do is let me." Before I can respond, the nurse says it's time to go. I knew I'd be able to count on him. I hope he realizes what he's doing. This is a lot of weight to carry even for his strong arms.

Kyle

SHE LOOKS so damn fragile as they wheel her out of the room. The Amber I know is strong and tough — a fighter. When she described to me the way she was when she first moved to Atlanta, I didn't believe her. She's not a weak woman. I guess we all have a breaking point. There are only so many emotions we can handle at one time. Knowing her the way I do, she's blaming all of this on herself — thinking it's her body that's causing the problem; therefore she's at fault for the danger our babies are in. Like she has any control over this. None of this is her fault, but how do you make someone as stubborn as her believe that? I'm determined to do everything I can to keep her and our babies safe. The four of them are my life and my number one priority.

I slowly make my way down the hall to the waiting room. Everyone refused to leave. I can't blame them. They all love Amber and want to be here for her. I have a feeling we are gonna need them quite a bit over the next several months. When I talked to the doctor, he told me she'd be on complete bed rest. No sitting at all, limited showers, no baths, and when she had a doctor's appointment, we needed a wheelchair to take her from the car to the office. This is not going to be easy on her, but I know she can do it. She loves our babies and will do anything to protect them. I just pray we can.

"You doing okay, Son?" Beasley questions, nervously. I know he's worried about his daughter and grandbabies.

"Yeah, I'm fine, Just worried about Amber."

"I know you are. I am too. Who worries about you though? Don't get me wrong, I'm proud to call you my son-in-law, you take excellent care of my daughter and make her happy, but you also need to take care of yourself. Don't get too overwhelmed or worn down taking everything on by yourself. We're all here and are happy to help in any way we can," he states as he looks around. They are all nodding their heads in agreement. I can't ask them all to put their lives on hold to help us out for the next six months. This is something we will have to figure out on our own.

"Thank you all. Believe me, we are going to need your help over the next several months. We have a long road ahead of us." I listen as the girls start right in on making schedules up for who'll do what and when. I have to laugh. To think I thought I actually had a choice in whether or not they'd be helping. Even the guys are getting in on it. What did I ever do to end up with this group of amazing friends?

After a while, I glance at the clock and realize it's been over forty minutes since they wheeled Amber from her room. The procedure was only supposed to take fifteen minutes. Why haven't they come to take me to see her yet? Dread creeps into my veins, consuming me with the thought that something went wrong. Dr. Monty appears only a few moments later with a somber look on his face. My heart stops and my breath whooshes out of my lungs. Beasley comes up and puts his hand on my shoulder, not missing the doctor's expression.

"Kyle, we had a complication during the procedure. The amniotic sac surrounding baby A was ruptured. The baby had moved further down due to Amber being in preterm labor yesterday. When I was suturing the cervix, the needle hit the sac and put a pinhole in it. Unfortunately, once that happens, there's nothing we can do to correct it," he informs us. Fear turns my veins into ice.

"What does all of this mean?" I ask, unsure of whether or not I want an answer.

"It puts Amber at a greater risk for infection. It also puts baby A at risk. The baby can't survive once the fluid is gone. I'm sorry, but it's very unlikely that baby A will make it."

"Does Amber know yet?" The question barely makes its way past my lips before I fall back into the chair. My head is spinning and my heart…my heart is broken. I knew I loved our babies, but until now, I had no idea just how much.

"Yes, she was awake during the procedure so she was aware of what was happening. I also discussed it with her in more detail after she was brought to the recovery room."

"I need to see her." He nods. I look back at everyone. The girls are crying while the guys try to console them. What do I say to Amber? She's gonna be heartbroken. Hell, I'm heartbroken. How do I hold us both together when I'm not sure how to hold myself together? I follow the doctor to the recovery room. There are about ten beds separated by curtains. Most of the curtains are open and the beds empty. That's when I see the closed curtain and I hear her. She's crying. My heart shatters into a million pieces at the sound. My poor girl. I have to get myself under control. I need to be strong for her. If she sees my pain, it will cause her more. I pull back the curtain and see her body shaking from her sobs.

I walk over to her and rub her back. She looks up at me and her sobs become harder. She slides over in the bed, allowing me to slide in next to her. I wrap her in my arms and hold her as tight as I can, trying to give her the security she needs while she lets it all out. Luckily, she doesn't notice the tears streaming steadily down my face.

CHAPTER
Ten

Amber

SEVEN WEEKS. It's been the longest and scariest seven weeks of my life. At the same time, it's also been amazing. I go to the doctor every week to have my cervix measured and to check the fluid levels for baby A. Who, by the way, is still hanging in there nice and strong. When we went to our appointment at my sixteen-week mark, we found out the sex of the babies. Baby A, my little fighter, is a girl, baby B is a boy, and baby C is a girl. Poor Kyle almost passed out at the thought of two daughters starting to date the same time. I told him not to worry; I have my grandpa's shotgun in the attic. Now, we are trying to figure out names. We thought trying to decide on one was hard; three are going to kill me. I want the names to be perfect and special, just like the babies they are going to be.

At eighteen weeks, I went into preterm labor again. Luckily, I was in the doctor's office for my weekly appointment when the contractions started. I was rushed across the street to the hospital. We spent hours in pure agony, not knowing what was going to happen. Neither one of us was naive enough to think everything would be okay. Finally, the contractions stopped, but I spent a week in the hospital. Not only was I confined to bed with a catheter, but my bed was also placed in

Trendelenburg position, where the head of the bed is lower than the foot. Talk about awful, it feels like you're standing on your head. The doctor wanted to keep me in the hospital for the remainder of my pregnancy. Thank God for Becky. She spoke to him and convinced him to let me go home. She promised to keep an eye on me and make sure I stay on complete bed rest.

Bed rest is absolute torture. Really, the military should start using this as one of their interrogation techniques. You start this whole bed rest thing out thinking this might not be so bad — people waiting on me all the time, plenty of time to read and catch up on the shows I love to watch. It wasn't bad, for about the first three days. I'm as big as a house. I imagine most normal women wouldn't be too uncomfortable at this stage of pregnancy, but with triplets, it looks like I reached forty weeks about two months ago. It's even more uncomfortable when you're only allowed to lay down. Of course, laying down is even a chore. When I lay down on my right side, the baby on that side starts to kick and wiggle until I move. So, I roll to my left side, but the baby resting on that side kicks and wiggles until I move. My only option is to lay on my back. This isn't comfortable for me to begin with but it's my only option. Then there's my sweet little girl Baby A, she doesn't like this position. She usually gives me a little more time than her brother and sister do, but eventually she starts to kick and wiggle until I move. This is how most of my day and night are spent — rolling around like a rotisserie chicken.

All of our friends have been great. They take turns coming over and keeping me company or bringing me food. Not that I can eat a whole lot lately. There's not much room in my stomach these days and if I eat too much, it just makes me sick. Even Jax has been coming over, acting like he's my best friend again. Kyle tries to cook, but he's been working a lot at the bar. At first, I thought maybe he's staying away more because he's too tempted when he's near me. The doctor told us we couldn't have sex after the cerclage was put in, but I think there's more to Kyle's absence. Something just feels off between us lately. It's almost as if he's trying to put distance between himself and the babies. He used to talk about what things might be like in the future, but that has completely stopped. Something is definitely bothering him and I need to know what it is.

"Morning, princess. I'll make you some breakfast before Holly gets here. I have to get to the bar early today," he says as he quickly makes his way to the kitchen. This just isn't like him. I don't understand why he's being so distant. When he comes back in thirty minutes later, he has my omelet and juice. He places it on the tray next to me, kisses my forehead, and starts to walk away.

"Kyle! Wait, can we talk about something?" I ask before he can make it out of the room. Instead of the smile that he usually has when he sees me, he looks like he wants to be anywhere but here with me.

"It will have to wait until later when I get home. I don't have time this morning," he states. He gives me a chaste kiss on the lips and walks out of the living room, leaving me alone and hurt. He didn't even tell me he loves me. He always says he loves be before leaving for work. My heart breaks when I hear the front door open then slam closed. A minute later, his truck roars to life and drives away. The tears start to flow and I don't even try to stop them. Maybe all of the drama and stress that comes along with this pregnancy is too much and he wants out. What am I gonna do if he leaves me? I'm so lost in my own head that I don't even realize Holly is here until her arms are wrapped around me.

"Hey there, what's this all about?" she asks, concern in her voice. How do I explain my fears to her? She's gonna think I'm crazy. Hell, maybe I am.

"Kyle seems so distant ever since I came home from the hospital this last time. It's really starting to worry me. I'm afraid he doesn't want to be here anymore."

"There's gotta be an explanation. Kyle loves you, nothing is going to change that. You just need to talk to him."

"I tried this morning. He told me he didn't have time then left without saying I love you. Holly, he always tells me he loves me." I sob harder and she holds me tighter.

"We'll figure it out. I guarantee it's some stupid damn male insecurity that he doesn't know how to deal with. Right now though, I think we need a pamper Amber day." Who am I to argue? She's on her phone calling Becky and Taryn before I have time to object.

A little while later, I'm sprawled out on the couch with Holly painting my toenails and Becky painting my fingernails. Taryn is in the kitchen making banana split milkshakes. That has been my one and only pregnancy craving.

"Here you go, momma! One tasty milkshake just the way you like it!" Taryn exclaims. I take a long sip through the straw and immediately feel so much better. A little girl talk, painted nails, and a milkshake, the perfect combination. What would I do without these girls? For a few hours, I actually feel normal. I forget that I've been living on bed rest the last several months, spending every second fearing that I might lose my babies. My earlier worries about Kyle have even left my mind for now. The girls have decided our girl's day isn't enough and have now turned it into a slumber party. Taryn can't stay because she needs to get home to the kids and Holly leaves for a little while to get some clothes and go by the bar to tell Paul what her plans are. I also have a feeling she's going to have a talk with Kyle. Normally, I wouldn't be too thrilled with that idea but in this instance, I don't mind. I need to know what's going on with him and Holly may be able to get the answers I need.

"So, what's the story with Clark? Is he as nice as he seems?" Becky asks.

"Yes, he's as nice as he seems and he loves his boys more than anything."

"Why'd his wife leave?"

"He wasn't married as far as I know, but the boys' mom left because she didn't want to be a mom anymore."

"Tell me you're kidding. No woman could be that cold."

"Believe me, I wish I were kidding. She wanted a life for herself. It almost destroyed Clark from what I've been told. He seemed very interested in getting to know you."

"I would like to get to know him a lot better" She giggles. I knew it. I could tell she had the hots for him. The night they met at the bar there was this chemistry between them. I can't even explain it, but it just being there, watching them, made you feel like you were intruding on a very private moment.

"Enough about me and my possible but still non-existent love life, tell me about you? How are you doing?"

"How am I doing? How do you think I'm doing? I lay here day after day, scared out of my mind, praying that my babies will survive!" I snap. *Wow! Where the hell did that come from?* "Becky, I'm so sorry. I didn't mean to snap. I don't know what came over me," I apologize, feeling awful for my reaction. Becky moves next to me and smiles.

"Sweetie, it's no big deal. You've been confined to this couch or your bed for months. That alone is enough to make you a little edgy. Factor in being terrified that you could lose something so precious and then the thing that probably eats at you the most, the thing I'm sure you haven't talked about to anyone." She just looks at me. Is she waiting for some sort of answer from me? If she is, she'll be waiting a long time because I have no idea what she's talking about. The rest of what she said, I can see. I am going crazy. I have to lay down twenty-four seven, only allowed one five minute shower per week, if I need to go to the bathroom more than three times a day, I have to crawl on my hands and knees so I don't put any more pressure than is necessary on my cervix.

"Okay, I'll bite. What is this thing that eats at me the most?" I ask with a little too much bite in my voice.

"I bet you are blaming yourself for all of this. Thinking your body is defective so you are to blame for your babies being in danger," she states, matter of fact. "Am I wrong? I don't think I am. I've been there. Not in the exact position, but very similar. I have blamed myself for something that I know isn't my fault in my head, but my heart doesn't follow the same logic. I'm not going to tell you to stop blaming yourself because it's useless right now; however, I will tell you that no one else, and by no one I mean Kyle, blames you for what's happening." I want to believe her about Kyle, but I can't. The way he's been acting lately tells me something's wrong. What else can it be?

"You haven't seen the way he's been toward me lately. Something is wrong with him. He just isn't the same with me as he always has been."

"That sucks. You both are under more stress than any couple should be. The two of you are always trying to protect each other and in doing so, you keep how you really feel from each other. Maybe you guys need to really talk about how you're feeling. No holding back." I know that's what needs to be done, if only I can get him to talk to me and stop avoiding me like he did this morning.

Kyle

I SLAM the front door behind me and quickly jump in my truck, racing as fast as I can down the driveway before I change my mind and go back inside. I really acted like a Dick. The last thing I want to do is hurt her, but I panicked when she asked to talk. I knew it was coming because of the distance I've been keeping lately. How do I explain what

I'm feeling to her when I don't even really know myself? There are so many emotions that I'm feeling all at once. Every time I start to let myself feel happiness and excitement about this pregnancy, something bad happens again. I'm afraid to get too attached to the idea of having these babies just to end up losing them.

I feel like a total shit, but I have a terrible feeling eating away at me and it's telling me that this isn't going to end well. How can I tell her that? I can't. The only thing she has is hope that what she is doing will keep our babies safe long enough to be born healthy. More than anything, I want our babies to be born safe and healthy. I just don't think that's possible. She will hate me if she knows that I don't have the faith that she does.

I pull my truck into my spot at the bar and slam my hands against the wheel. Damn it! I should be home with Amber. I'm such a fuck up! I've got to figure out how to make this right. I need to explain to her how I'm feeling without upsetting her more than I already have. Hopefully by the end of the day I can find the right words. For now, I need to work and clear my head. Walking into the bar, I'm greeted by a very angry Paul. This can only mean one thing. Amber is a lot more upset than I thought and Holly is with her.

"What the fuck is wrong with you, douchebag!" Paul roars as he rushes toward me and shoves me hard. I stumble backwards, the hard tabletop slamming into my back as the only thing stopping me from going any further. Before I can regain my footing, he's standing in front of me, fuming. His eyes are bulging and his nostrils are flaring. I don't think I've ever seen him this pissed. "Would you care to explain what the hell that was for?"

"It was for the simple fact that you are an asshole. What did you do to Amber this morning?"

"What are you talking about? I didn't *do* anything to Amber."

"Holly called. Said when she got to your house Amber was crying her eyes out. When Holly asked her what was wrong, she said it's the way you've been acting toward her." Taking a deep breath, he sits down at the table. He looks a little calmer, so I sit across from him and wait for the rest of his inevitable lecture. "We've all noticed it lately and it's not like you. You would never treat Amber badly. Why now?" He's right, I can't deny that. Still, I can't help but get defensive. I know he's only trying to watch out for Amber and me, but he'll be asking questions. Questions I haven't figured out the answers to yet. "Maybe you and

Holly should mind your own damn business," I snap and stand. Paul grabs my arm and pushes me back into my chair.

"We're your friends, dumbass. Things can't be easy for either of you right now and I'm here if you need to talk shit out. No matter what it is. If you all don't talk about what you're feeling, it will eat at you. So, do you want to tell me what your deal is?"

"I don't know what I'm feeling half the time. I'm always either so fucking confused or guilty."

"Why would you feel guilty? None of this is your fault," he asks with concern in his voice rather than the anger that's been there. I try to explain to him the way I've been feeling. How I really don't think this pregnancy is going to end happily. I try to make him see that I can't exactly tell this to Amber.

"She has enough to deal with right now. I just can't let her see that I have the doubts I have. I can't lie to her so what do I do when she wants to talk?"

"Honestly, I think it's time you learn to lie. You tell her what she needs to hear to get her through this. No one knows what the outcome is gonna be. You may be wrong. I know why you don't want to get your hopes up, I get it, but she needs to believe. There's no way in hell she'll give up."

She's not going to give up. That's what I'm afraid of. The more time that goes by, the more she believes we'll have a happy ending. I've been reading up on her condition until I think my eyes will bleed. I've also listened to the doctors and watched their body language as they spoke to us. They don't think this will end well either. I can't build her up just to allow her to fall harder. This is tearing me up inside. I want this just as badly as she does. Acceptance of what is coming our way is something I'm finding now instead of later. I can't allow myself to get anymore attached than I already have. It will break me if I do.

I try to concentrate on the piles of paperwork in front of me, but there's no use. Amber is the only thing on my mind. At least, she was until Holly comes barreling through my door. It's bad enough I had Paul on my ass earlier, now I'm gonna have to listen to her run her mouth. I am really not in the mood for this right now. She slams the door closed behind her so hard it shakes the pictures hanging on the wall. She's even more pissed than Paul was. Great. I'm never gonna get her out of here.

"Paul says he talked to you but won't tell me what was said. Spill it. Now. Amber is a wreck. She thinks you're going to leave her." She demands, her arms crossed.

"Why the fuck would she think I'm gonna leave her?"

"Gee, I don't know. You barely talk to her. You leave the house without telling her you love her. She has herself convinced all that's happening is her fault and you blame her. She thinks you're ready to bail," Holly says, her eyes pleading with me to give her answers. I didn't realize how upset Amber was this morning. I can't believe I left without telling her I love her. I wanted to avoid a conversation about my feelings so bad that I rushed out as fast as I could.

"First of all, I don't blame her for anything. She has no control over what's happening any more than you or I do. Second, I would never leave her. Ever. Not for anything."

"Then what's your problem? Why are you keeping this distance between the two of you?"

"Holly, I appreciate that you're looking out for Amber, but I'm dealing with this shit too. I need to be allowed to do that in my own way. I'm doing my best to hold myself together and take care of Amber. Sometimes I need some space to figure things out without everybody jumping all over my shit." I'm trying not to sound like an ass. I love the fact that they are all so protective of Amber, but sometimes it's a little much.

"I'm sorry. I know this hasn't been easy for you either. I guess we've all been so worried about Amber that we've neglected you."

"Amber is always the most important thing. I just need to get my head together."

"Well, it's your lucky day. Becky and I are having a little slumber party with Amber tonight, so why don't you stay with Paul and have a boy's night?" That does sound like a good idea. It will give me a little time to try to clear my head, plus Amber will have a night of fun that will keep her mind occupied.

"Okay, but can you do me a favor?" Holly nods yes. "Make sure she knows I'm not going anywhere and that I don't blame her for anything. I'm just as scared as she is. The only difference is that she's handling it a hell of a lot better." Holly smiles and agrees to talk to Amber. Hopefully tonight will give me the time I need to figure out how to be there for her the way she needs me to be.

CHAPTER
Eleven

Amber

As I cross another day off my calendar, I'm so thankful. Today I hit twenty-two weeks. I'm so close now. Getting to thirty-two weeks would be ideal with triplets. Though, my main goal is to get to twenty-five weeks. The babies have the greatest chance for survival after that time. *Three more weeks*, I keep saying to myself, over and over again. For the first time, I really think everything will turn out okay.

Kyle and I had a talk after the girls and I had our slumber party. I wasn't able to get a whole hell of a lot out of him. He says he's just trying to deal with the stress of everything, but I have a feeling there's something more to it. I just wish he would tell me what's really bothering him. He shouldn't have to go through this alone. Unfortunately, by not talking to me, it feels like I'm all alone in this. Once we get past the danger point, he can relax and get back to normal. At least, I hope he can.

Paul, Holly, and Becky have been here for a few hours. I was craving pizza earlier so, like the awesome friends they are, they brought one over. The five of us are sitting in the bedroom eating and watching movies. I've been laying in my bed all day because I haven't felt like moving to the couch. I'm paying for it now though because my back is killing me. No matter which way I turn, it doesn't seem to ease up.

"Amber, sweetie, are you okay?" Becky asks. Standing up from the chair, she comes and sits next to me on the bed. Paul pauses the movie and everyone's attention is on me. The concerned looks they are all giving me has me very uneasy.

"Yeah, my back is just bothering me. I've been in this bed too long," I explain, but Becky still looks concerned.

"It's just your back? Do you have pain anywhere else?" She's in nurse mode. Sometimes a backache is just a backache. Right? Apparently not. Becky and Kyle share a worried look.

"No, just my back. It's from being in here all day. It wouldn't feel like this if I'd have spent time on the couch some today." She gives me a smile that I'm guessing is meant to keep me calm. Everyone's looking at her now and wondering why she is so worried. I'm curious too. What's the big deal about a backache? I have them all the time because of laying down so much and the fact that my belly is the size of a Volkswagen.

"I think maybe you should call your doctor," Becky says, way too calmly. A way that has me scared to death. My body starts to tremble and I can't seem to catch my breath.

"Why? What's wrong?" Kyle blurts as he pulls his phone out, ready to dial our doctor.

"It's possible you could be in labor. I don't want to scare you, but better safe than sorry." Before she can finish, Kyle is on the phone with the doctor's answering service. He gives all the info then hangs up. Immediately, he begins pacing the floor. He looks like a caged animal. It's really not helping my already frazzled nerves. To make matters worse, it's so quiet in this room, you could hear a pin drop.

How could I have been so stupid? I've read about back labor, I just thought it would feel different. If something's wrong, it's all my fault. My back has been hurting for hours and I'm too fucking stupid to know something's wrong.

"Amber, please stop crying. Don't get so worked up until we know something for sure," Holly says as she wipes tears from my eyes that I didn't realize were falling.

Even in the state I'm in right now, I still notice something that only adds to my distress. Holly is on one side of me, Becky on the other, and Paul is on the end of the bed rubbing my feet. But Kyle... Kyle is nowhere near me. He's on the other side of the room with his back is turned to us as he stares out the window. The one person who should be comforting me is the farthest away. Deep down, he does blame me for all of the hell we've been going through. What other explanation is there? I can't think about this now. The most important thing is the babies. Whatever is going on with Kyle will have to wait until later. The phone rings, it's Dr. Monty. Kyle explains that I have been having lower back pain for several hours.

"On our way," he says and quickly ends the call. All of a sudden, Kyle is scooping me up in his arms. "Dr. Monty will meet us at the hospital. Paul, can you please drive?" Paul nods yes. Kyle carries me all the way to Paul's SUV and lays me down in the back seat. As soon as everyone else piles in, we're on our way.

The usual twenty-minute drive feels like it's taking much longer. I only had three more weeks to go. If they can stop it again like before, then maybe I can hold on for three short weeks. *Please God! Let me hold on a little longer.*

Once we get to the hospital, it's the same routine as before. I'm hooked to IV's and monitors. By the time they finish hooking everything up, I know without a doubt that I'm in labor. With each contraction, it's as if my insides are being twisted in knots. If I would have felt like this earlier, I'd have known without a doubt I was in labor. I'm trying to stay calm and think positive, but this is the worse it's been. They put pain meds in my IV to help me relax. I wake up slightly disoriented, not realizing I fell asleep. Kyle is in a chair across the room, staring into space.

"Hey, is everyone still here?" I squeak out, my throat dry.

"No. Paul and Holly took Becky home a while ago. They brought my truck up and dropped it off in case I needed it." He sounds so tired and doesn't look much better either. I look at the clock again and see that it's after midnight.

"Maybe you should go home and get some sleep too. I'm gonna keep falling asleep anyway." There's no point in us both being uncomfortable all night long.

"I don't want to leave you alone. What if something happens? I need to be here with you." Before I can argue, the doctor comes in. He tells us that the contractions have slowed down but haven't completely stopped. They are going to keep giving me the magnesium and hope by morning they've stopped completely.

"Kyle, why don't you go home and get some sleep? If anything changes tonight, we will call you right away. We'll have Amber sleeping most of the night anyway," he says to Kyle, encouragingly. Who the hell is he trying to fool? Oh... then it dawns on me. He's trying to help me get Kyle home. He knows I won't be sleeping for more than forty-five minutes at a time. They have to come in to draw blood every hour to check the Magnesium levels. It's going to be a miserable night.

"I'll be leaving for the night myself. Dr. Jarrett will be the doctor on the floor if you need anything. They'll call me if there are any changes. I'll see you in the morning." With his usual comforting smile, he shakes Kyle's hand, pats my shoulder, and walks out the door.

"You should go home and get some rest. I'll call if anything happens. One of us needs to be one hundred percent."

"Only if you promise to call me if anything changes or you need me."

"I will. I'll be okay, you don't have to worry."

"I love you and our babies more than anything, princess. You know that, right?" He looks like he's lost his best friend. There's sadness and regret in his eyes. The sadness I understand completely, I feel it too. The regret I see scares me. What is it he regrets? Is it being with me or having the babies? I wish he would talk to me and tell me what's been bothering him.

"Of course I know that. I love you, too. Now, go home and get some rest. I'll see you in the morning." I give him my best reassuring smile as he leans down and kisses me. There's so much passion and love in his kiss, it contradicts what I see in his eyes. When it's over, I'm left breathless. I'm so confused.

"See you first thing in the morning," he says. With one last chaste kiss on my lips, he walks toward the door. Before walking out, he looks back at me with a look I can only describe as sympathetic. Maybe he really does hate leaving me here alone.

The mixture of pain meds and sleeplessness are making me slow. I try to roll onto my side to get comfortable. The thin white sheet slides against my protruding belly as I begin to roll over and immediately stop. Just that slight movement causes a stabbing pain to shoot through my body. Moving my hand to my belly, I slowly and gently move it around and wince at the pain. *Why is my belly so tender to touch?* I pull my legs up in an attempt to get more comfortable and feel wetness between my legs. *Something's wrong. Something's very wrong.* Trying not to panic, I feel around for the call button. When I find it, I press it several times. The longer it takes the nurse to come in, the more freaked out I get. Every time I move, it hurts. It's not the same pain I've been feeling with the contractions.

"What do you need, honey?" The nurse assigned to me asks in her forced concerned voice. She's been a bitch to me since she came on duty tonight.

"Can you please get the doctor for me? Something's wrong. I'm in pain and I feel a lot of wetness between my legs." She eyes me like I'm a nut job.

"Sweetie, calm down, all of that is normal. You're still having contractions, there's going to be pain. The wetness you're feeling is the amniotic fluid that's been leaking since you had the cerclage," she says in her usual condescending voice. What is it with this bitch?

"Please, just call the doctor. I know my body, it's not the same pain as the contractions. As far as the wetness, it's not amniotic fluid. This hasn't happened before."

"I'll give you something more for the pain. Dr. Jarrett will be back in at four. He can check you over then," she states as she walks out the door, not waiting for a response from me. What the hell? I know something is wrong. I know my own body. I'm helpless here. I can hardly move from the excruciating pain I'm in, along with all of the crap they have me hooked to. It's only two-thirty, so I have another hour and a half before a doctor will look at me. The door opens and a different nurse comes in. She's been really nice, but I can tell she takes her orders from Nurse Ratchet. I try anyway, my babies' lives are at stake.

"Can you please call the doctor for me? Something is wrong and Nurse Ratchet out there doesn't want to listen to me," I plead. She gives me that look that says, 'I'm sorry, but you're on your own'. This place sucks. She puts more pain medication into the IV before she walks out the door. Somehow, I manage to fall asleep.

My sleep is anything but restful. Even with all of the pain meds, the slightest touch across my belly has me in complete agony. To make matters worse, I feel like I'm lying in a puddle of water. Four o'clock came and went without a visit from Dr. Jarrett as Nurse Ratchet had promised. I have begged and pleaded with anyone and everyone who has walked into this room to please get me a doctor, but no one will listen. For hours, I have been laying here sobbing quietly to myself and praying someone would come help me and my babies. I have a terrible feeling that it's too late. Whatever this is, it's bad. I can feel it.

"Hey there, are you okay? I'm Dr. Courtney, the floor doctor for the day," she introduces herself, sounding concerned. I didn't even hear her come in. I try to roll over so that I'm lying flat and can see her.

"Please, just humor me, I have begged all night for someone to just look at me. Something isn't right. The slightest touch to my belly feels like I'm being stabbed and I've been laying in what feels like a puddle all night. No one will even lift the damn sheet to see what it is! So, please, if nothing more than to shut me the fuck up, look under the sheet!" I yell, my frustration and fear reaching its limit. I know she just got here, but someone needs to fucking listen to me. She begins putting on a pair of gloves and I feel slightly relieved. Walking to the foot of the bed, she sets the chart down. She grabs the corner of the sheet, lifts it just barely off the bed, and gasps. Fear races through my veins once more, paralyzing me to the unknown of what she's going to say. She pulls a phone out of her lab coat pocket.

"Get Dr. Monty here now," she barks into the phone before walking over to me and sliding the thermometer across my forehead. "Amber, you have an infection. That's why you hurt so badly and it's the wetness you feel. I'll call your husband for you then I'm going to take care of the night staff that should have caught this. I'm so sorry you went through this all night."

"What does this mean? What about the babies?" Deep down, I know what the answer is, but part of me is hoping that by some miracle, I'm wrong. By the expression on her face, I know my miracle isn't going to happen.

"Dr. Monty can tell you more, but the babies will need to be delivered." That one little sentence shatters my entire world. Still trying to grasp any little thread of hope I can find, I think maybe, just maybe, they could still be okay. I can't let myself give up.

Kyle

CLOSING THE door to her room and walking away makes me feel like such a dick. What kind of husband am I? I left her there in that hospital bed terrified and in pain. And why? Because I'm a coward who can't deal with what is going to happen. I can't seem to find the faith and hope that Amber has. This chapter in our life is not going to end well. I don't know how to deal with the emotions swirling around inside of myself, let alone the ones that will hit her. She's going to hate me. I know she senses how I feel. That I've already given up any ounce of hope that our babies will be okay. Who can blame her? She's doing what a mother should. She's fighting tooth and nail for her children. So what does that say about me as a father? As a husband? Shouldn't I be doing the same? Why can't I? I just know the more I hope now, the more it will hurt later when we lose them. This is what I've been struggling with. As her husband, I should be fighting right alongside her, but I can't. If I'm going to hold us both together when this falls apart, I need to prepare myself now.

I pull up at the bar, get out of my truck, and walk up to the door, needing a drink. Before I can get the door unlocked, my cell phone rings. My thoughts immediately shift to Amber. I fish my phone out of my pocket with shaky hands, my heart beating so hard it feels like it's going to rip out of my chest. When I see the name on the screen, I breathe a sigh of relief. Then suspicion takes over. What the fuck is Jax calling me for at one o'clock in the morning?

"Hello."

"Kyle, its Jax. Sorry it's so late. Holly sent me a text to let me know about Amber. I just wanted to see if you needed anything... if there's anything I can do?"

Though I don't trust him or his intentions, I do need someone to talk to. Paul and the guys have been great but I'm afraid they will look at me differently if I tell them how I really feel. I don't give a damn what Jax thinks of me.

"I just got to the bar. Want to come by for a drink? I could use some company."

"Sure, be right over."

It doesn't take long for Jax to get here; long enough for me to have a couple shots of whiskey and a beer, though. I'm sitting on a stool at the bar, feeling much better than before, when he walks in.

"Hey. You okay?"

"No, Jax, I'm not." Maybe it's the fact that I hardly know him, or maybe it's just simply that the alcohol is beginning to take effect, I have no idea, but I start to tell him everything, every feeling that I've been too ashamed to share with my wife and friends. I tell him how I've given up hope that we will ever be able to bring home our babies.

I even tell him something that I haven't been able to really admit to myself, how I'm not sure if Amber's going to be able to handle a loss this big. He just sits and listens to it all. Not one ounce of judgment anywhere on his face. I've needed this, to unload all of these concerns without worrying about being judged. Hell, I judge myself enough; I don't need it from everyone else too.

"I can see why you haven't wanted to discuss any of this with Amber. I totally understand why you feel this way. I agree, Amber will never understand it," Jax says.

"That's an understatement. She'll hate me if she knows I gave up hope weeks ago."

"I won't say a word, but at some point you'll probably need to talk to her."

"Yeah, I suppose I will. Tonight though, I'm drinking until I pass out." Jax stayed for one more drink before leaving. I keep drinking long after he leaves.

"Wake up, asshole!" Holly screeches as she shakes me. *Damn! My head hurts.*

"What was that for Holly?"

"Where's your phone, dipshit? The hospital's been trying to reach you for an hour." I search my pockets, looking for my cell phone. Damn it! I see it laying on the floor and pick it up. I look at the screen. Ten missed calls.

"What's going on? Is Amber okay?" I'm starting to panic. What could have happened? Again, here I am, fucking everything up. Sitting here passed out in the bar when I should be at the hospital with my wife.

"I'll explain on the way to the hospital. Let's go." Holly grabs my arm and drags me out to my truck. As soon as we start driving, she better start talking. I need to know what the hell is going on. I start to walk around to the driver's side but Holly pushes me toward the passenger side and gives me a nasty look. I guess that means she wants to drive. Once we're in the truck, she peels out of the parking lot like a bat out of hell.

"Are you going to tell me what's going on?"

"I should've let Paul come so he could kick your ass. Everyone is at the hospital with your wife, even Angel who you can't drag out of bed for anything before noon. Everyone but you!"

"Damn it, Holly! Tell me what's going on!" I roar, panic and fear taking over. Holly jumps a bit, startled by my tone. She recovers quickly, and finally begins to explain what's happening with Amber.

"Amber developed an infection called Chorioamnionitis. They have to deliver the babies as soon as possible. We're having a hard time getting it through to Amber that this is the only option. She won't do anything without you there, but she also says she's going to wait until the babies have a better chance of survival." She looks over at me, realizing I need a minute to let this all sink in. I never should have left the hospital last night. I should've stayed with my wife. Instead, I go and drink until I pass out and don't hear my phone. Amber needed me and I wasn't there. I have promised her, over and over again, that I'll always be there when she needs me. Now, that promise looks like a lie. Holly squeezes my hand to pull me out of my head.

"Can't they give her something to get rid of the infection?"

"I wish they could. The only way to stop it is to deliver the babies."

"And what happens if she won't agree to it?"

"She'll die, Kyle," Holly says, tears streaming down her face. "I know you love your babies, but they aren't going to make it no matter what we do. Amber can, though. We have to make her see that she's done everything she can."

That's the problem, making Amber see it. She's not going to do anything knowing it will harm those babies. This is going to destroy her. Hopefully, I can hold us both together.

CHAPTER
Twelve

Amber

I THROW MY cell phone to the foot of the bed. Why isn't he answering his phone? If things were reversed, I'd have that damn phone glued to me. There's no way in hell I would miss a call from him. I'd be too worried something would be wrong.

Dr. Courtney called Kyle but it went to voicemail. She found my cell phone for me so I could keep trying. After a couple more tries without luck, I call Holly. I explain everything that's happening and that I can't get in touch with Kyle. If she was standing in front of me, I bet there would be smoke coming out of her ears. She's pissed. I can hear her telling Paul what's going on. He's furious, too.

"I'm sending Paul and Angel right down. I will go find Kyle. If I let Paul do it, Kyle may end up in a bed next to you," she says with a touch of laughter in her voice. "Hang in there. The boys will be there in a few minutes." With that, she hangs up. At least I now know that it's not just me — that I'm not overreacting.

The pain is becoming unbearable. Every move I make, no matter how big or small is excruciating. Flat on my back is the only position I can lay in. The cocktail of pain medication they've been giving me is doing absolutely nothing. I'm not sure how much more I can take.

Please, God, help me make it through this day. Give me the strength I need to make the right choice, whatever that may be. Between the fear and pain, the floodgates open and I can't stop them. I lay there sobbing uncontrollably. It's not until Angel is by my side, wiping the tears from my eyes, that I even notice Paul and Angel are here.

"Oh, baby girl. Please don't cry. We're here with you now. Everything is gonna be okay," Angel soothes.

I wish I could believe him. Paul looks at me with those big green eyes full of sadness and sympathy. It's so hard to see a look like that on the face of such a big strong man. Why is it that these two men can rush to my side and be here to comfort me, but my husband can't even be reached? If I didn't need him so badly right now, I'd tell him to take a flying leap when he does get here. *If he ever gets here.*

It doesn't take long before my room starts to fill up with people. Becky, Taryn, and Marcus are here with me, but still no Kyle. Becky says she called Beasley on the way over and he is on his way. I forgot he went to a conference in North Carolina. Nurses are coming in and out, checking vitals, and pumping me full of more pain meds. Not that they are doing any good. I have such a major decision to make, but I can't...I won't make it alone. I need Kyle here with me to help me. Just then, Dr. Monty walks in and panic sets in. He's here to explain everything to us. There is no way I can take all of this information in right now, not by myself. Thankfully, I won't have to. Behind Dr. Monty is Kyle and Holly. I'm not sure if I want to kiss him or punch him. By the sheepish look on his face as he approaches my side, he knows I'm conflicted.

"Princess, I'm so—" I cut him off before he can finish. Right now is not the time. I don't want to hear his apology or excuse or whatever he is going to spew from his mouth. There are more important issues that we need to deal with.

"Not now. Please. Dr. Monty is here to explain to us what's going on." He nods his head sadly, but I'm still too pissed to feel sorry for him.

"The infection is spreading faster than I've ever seen. We have to deliver the babies now."

"What are the babies' chances of survival if they are born now?" I ask, hopeful that by some slim chance something has changed since earlier.

"I know this is hard to hear, but they won't survive," Dr. Monty states, his voice brittle.

"Can't I just wait until I'm closer to twenty-five weeks? You can just give me more antibiotics," I plead, trying to grasp at any possibility.

"That's not possible. The babies have been infected for too long already and so have you. If we don't deliver them soon, the infection will kill you. There's nothing we can do for the babies, but we can help you," he presses, his voice turning stern. I'm on a one-way street without exits and turning around isn't possible. Can I really keep moving straight ahead, knowing what awaits me could very well destroy me?

"Can you at least put me to sleep when you take them?" He looks at me strangely. "You are doing a C-section, right?"

"We can't do a C-section because of the infection. You're going to have to deliver them normally. I know this is a lot to take in all at once. I'll give you guys a little time to talk it over. We don't have too much time to waste, though. I'll be back soon." With that, he turns and walks out of the room. I can't do it. There's no way I can deliver my babies knowing I'll be killing them. What am I going to do? I gaze around the room at all of the faces watching me intently. What are they all thinking?

"I can't do this. If I deliver the babies, it's like I'm killing them. I won't do it!" I'm starting to get a little frantic now, crying hysterically. How can they expect me to do this? Holly and Becky come and sit on each side of me. Becky holds my hand, comforting me without words. Holly's a different story.

"Now, you listen and you listen good. I know you want to protect your babies, but you heard the doctor. There is nothing more you or the doctors can do. You have fought harder than most people ever could. You are not killing them. But if you don't go through with it, you'll be killing yourself. That's not something I'm willing to let happen. There are too many people in this room who love and need you. We'll help you get through this," she says in her no nonsense voice. As much as I know she's right, it's still difficult. I'm their mother. My job is to protect them. Doing this goes against every instinct in me to do anything necessary to keep them safe. Even if that means dying for them. I finally gather the courage to look at Kyle and I immediately wish I didn't. He's so pale. The expression on his face can only be described as lost. He's frozen, just staring into space like he'd rather be anywhere but here.

Paul notices me watching, waiting for Kyle to snap out of it. He walks up to him and slaps him in the back of the head. Kyle turns around, trying to figure out what brought that on and Paul nods in my direction. That seems to snap him back into reality. Holly and Becky move to the other side of the room with everyone else as Kyle kneels on the floor next to me. He looks into my eyes, almost like he's searching for something. For what, I have no clue. For the first time, I see just how much this is hurting him too. He takes my face in his hands and smiles sadly.

"Princess, I love you and our babies. I don't want to lose them either, but we can get through that and deal with it together. There's no way in hell I could ever get over losing you. I need you too much. Please, baby, you need to do this."

No one understands what this is like for me. A mother is supposed to protect her children no matter the consequences. How can I let them die to save myself? I don't know if I can. A huge part of me will die along with my babies, but will I ever be able to go a day without feeling like I'm to blame? Will Kyle ever look at me the same again? Or will he blame me, too? I will never be fine again. There's nothing that will make this situation okay. I know the time is coming because the contractions are becoming stronger and more frequent. I need to make a decision. "Fine," is the only response I can manage. I need this to be over quickly. As if on cue, Dr. Monty walks in with a parade of medical staff behind him. There are six or seven nurses, three of them wheeling in those big baby incubator things. Then there are two Neonatologists. For a second, as Dr. Monty tells me who all of these people are, I get another wave of hope. Why would they have the incubators and Neonatologists if there weren't a chance? I quickly squash that little glimmer of hope when it's explained to me that our babies could live up to several hours and will need to be kept comfortable. I pray that they won't suffer in any way. I just couldn't handle watching that.

I feel like I'm trapped inside my own body, like I have no control over myself. It has to be all of the different drugs they've pumped into me since I've been here. On the outside, I look calm, like I'm handling this perfectly. But, on the inside, my heart is being ripped from my chest.

My feet are in the air and there are a dozen or so people in this room, but I could care less. Normally, I would be mortified. I look around to see how everyone else is. Of course, Holly, Becky, and Taryn all have tears streaming down their faces. They all must think I'm a cold-hearted bitch. I want to cry. I need to cry, but I can't. No matter how hard I try, I can't shed a single tear. Before I know it, Dr. Monty is ready to get started. As soon as he starts speaking, I find it difficult to breathe.

"Okay, Amber. I need you to push as hard as you can until I tell you to stop," Dr. Monty instructs.

I open my mouth to answer him, but nothing comes out, so I nod in confirmation. I push with everything I have, while Holly, Becky, and the nurses encourage me along. Kyle looks like he's completely checked out. *Must be nice.* When Holly gasps, my attention is directed back to what's important.

That's when I see her. My heart hurts so badly when there are no cries from her. If I weren't listening so intently, I would've missed the barely audible whimper that comes from her tiny little body. Everything going on around me totally fades away, she is the only thing I can see. The Neonatologist looks her over, then a nurse cleans her and wraps her in a pink blanket and brings her to me. I'm not sure what I was expecting them to look like, but it wasn't like this. She's so tiny. The top of her head rests at the tips of my fingers while her tiny little toes touch my wrist. I can't help the smile that escapes when I notice the head full of dark hair. Her skin is paper thin, so much so, you can almost see through it. Her poor little face is black and blue. She's had it the roughest over the last several weeks and it shows all over her face. No matter though, she is still the most beautiful baby I have ever seen. For a moment, I let myself pretend that I don't notice how difficult every breath is for her. I pretend that she can open her eyes and they are a beautiful blue just like her daddy's. Holding her as close to me as I can, I gently kiss her face.

"I love you, sweet girl. I'm so sorry I couldn't protect you." Before I can say anything else, a nurse takes the baby. I feel another contraction and know it's time to push again. Out of the corner of my eye, I see the nurse try to hand the baby to Kyle. He won't even look at our baby girl. He hightails it away from the nurse like our baby has a disease he doesn't want to catch. Paul and Angel both stare daggers at his retreating back. Then, Paul takes the baby from the nurse. I'm so thankful at that moment for him. He's doing what I can't and what Kyle won't. He's comforting our daughter in what are probably her last moments. He looks over, sees me watching him, and winks. I mouth, "Thank you," and he smiles.

It doesn't take long before they are handing me my son. He's as tiny as his sister, but doesn't seem as fragile. His face isn't black and blue, but is still paper thin. I touch his little hand and he grabs a hold of my finger tightly. He's strong like his daddy. He has the same dark hair. I have only a few short minutes to tell him how much I love him and to kiss him before it's time to deliver our second daughter. The nurse tries to hand the baby to Kyle, but he just moves away again. I can't help the hurt and disappointment that washes through me. Again, another man is doing Kyle's job. Angel holds onto my son, talking to him in a soft, gentle voice. I don't think he and Paul realize the gift they've just given me.

The third baby is delivered and the nurse puts her in my hands. She is just as beautiful as her brother and sister. As I hold my daughter and tell her how much I love her, I notice the medical staff speaking in hushed tones at the foot of my bed. I start to feel lightheaded and my eyelids are suddenly very heavy. When a nurse quickly takes the baby from me and another starts to unhook wires and monitors, I know something is wrong. But, I can only think of my babies. *Why are they taking them from me?* I'm just about to demand for them to give me my babies back when I notice the look of panic on everyone's face and quick movements. My head spins as my eyes roll. All of the sounds from the people around me become muffled. What the hell is going on? My eyes keep closing and I'm fighting with what little strength I have left to keep them open. I need to know what's happening.

"Amber," Dr. Monty says loudly. He's right in front of my face, trying to get me to focus on him, but I'm so dizzy, everything becomes blurry. "We can't get the last placenta to come out on its own. It's causing you to hemorrhage. We need to take you down to surgery so we can remove it." I know this is serious, but I can't leave my babies, they need me. I try to open my mouth and express this, but I'm too weak. I manage to turn my head enough to look for my babies. Paul and Angel are still each holding one, while Holly hold my other daughter. The rest of our friends are looking over their shoulders, waiting for their turn to hold our precious babies. My body relaxes at the sight. If they can't be with me, at least I know they are being loved and protected. I don't, however, see Kyle. I turn to look as best I can around the room. Confusion sets in when my eyes spot him. He's at the opposite end of the room, sitting in a chair with his head bowed, staring at the floor. I don't have time to analyze him because they quickly start to wheel me out of the room. I notice Beasley in the hall as they wheel me by.

"Hey is that my daughter? What's happening? Is she okay?" He sounds so scared. I manage to grab ahold of his hand for only a second as they race my bed by him.

Kyle

I watch them wheel her out of the room and realize I never told her I love her. I am such a mess and it's making me screw up royally. Everyone looks at me like they want to rip my head off. Sitting in this room, surrounded by my friends, I feel like an outsider. They are all taking turns holding the babies and I can't even bring myself to look at them. I want to, but I can't. It hurts too much. So much more than I thought it would. I have no idea how Amber is as strong as she is. I should be holding her and making sure she knows I'm here for her.

"Mr. Connor, we're going to have to take the babies soon. Are you sure you don't want some time with them before we do?" a nurse asks me. She's very nice and I know she is only trying to help.

"I can't. It's too hard to deal with as it is. It will be even worse if I see them and hold them. I'm sorry. I just can't." I put my head down because I can't stand to look at her or anyone else. I'm so ashamed of myself for feeling like this. What's wrong with me? I fell in love with them the second Amber and I knew about them. I wanted these babies so much. The idea of losing them was hard enough when I couldn't see or touch them. Holding them in my arms and seeing their faces, it would break me. There's no way I could come back from that kind of heartache. Amber has proven to be the strongest person I know. I was expecting her to need me to take charge and hold her together; however, she was the most together person in the whole room. That left me without something to occupy my mind and breaking heart. I was lost. I'm still lost.

"It's okay, Mr. Connor. There's no right or wrong way to deal with this. How ever you're feeling is okay. You have to deal with these things the best way you can." I wish I could say she makes me feel better, but I still feel like I've failed as a husband and a father. "We will take pictures in case you change your mind later on," she says as she and the other nurses take the babies and leave the room.

"What is with you, man? Why are Paul and I the ones doing your job? You stood there like a statue the whole fucking time. You wouldn't hold your own babies. Hell, you wouldn't even look at them," Angel snaps in my face, looking like he's ready to beat my sorry ass.

"I'm doing the best I can! When you're in my shoes, you can tell me if I'm handling things the right way. Until then, mind your own fucking business!" These guys are supposed to be my friends; don't they see the amount of pain I'm in too? "Do you honestly think any of this is easy for me or that I know what the right or wrong thing to do is? I'm just trying to do what hurts the least. I'm trying to keep from falling apart so much that I can't pull myself back together." The tears start to fall and I can't stop them. For the first time today, I don't feel like such a fuck up. I finally feel normal, that my reaction is the right one. "I couldn't have gotten through today without all of you. I will never be able to thank any of you enough, especially you and Paul. You both held and comforted my babies when I couldn't. I wanted to so bad, but I couldn't. I don't expect you to understand why, because I don't. As my friends though, I would hope you at least trust me and know that I'm not just flaking out on my family for the hell of it." Neither of them need to say a word. I can see by the look on their faces that they get it now. They both come at me and wrap me in a group hug. If this were any other time, I would've knocked 'em on their ass. Before I know what's happening, everyone has joined in.

Beasley comes rushing into the room. Normally he looks very young for his age, but right now, he looks ancient.

"What's going on? Where are they taking my girl in such a damn hurry?" he questions. Paul brings a chair over to him but he refuses to sit. He wants answers. I can't say that I blame him. I would, too. I just don't know if I can explain it all. I start to walk over but Holly stops me. *Oh. Thank. God.* She walks up to Beasley and points to the chair, but he shakes his head no.

"Now, you listen to me. I'm not telling you a damn thing until you sit your ass down in that chair," she informs him. Beasley being the smart man that he is, sits his ass right down in the chair. I hear Angel chuckle, but it stops instantly from the death glare that he gets from Holly. She would make one hell of a drill instructor. She starts from the beginning and explains everything to him. Good ol' Holly doesn't leave out a single detail, not even me being M.I.A this morning. At first Beasley shoots me a look filled with daggers, but by the time she gets to the end, something has changed. He looks at me now with some sort of understanding. I wish he'd fill me in so maybe I could fully understand my actions.

After a little while, Beasley convinces everyone to head out, telling them we will wait for Amber to wake up and we'll call if she needs anything. The doctor told us he was going to keep her medicated a little so she would rest through the night, but he wants her to wake from the anesthesia first and they would bring her up from recovery as soon as she does.

"I understand in a roundabout way how you're feeling. When I first found out I was Amber's dad, but couldn't be with her as her dad, I stayed away. I thought it would be easier that way. Out of sight, out of mind. I know the situations are completely different, but the reasoning behind what we both did is pretty much the same. I want you to know that I get it. I know how much you love my daughter. You have always been right there by her side and strong for her no matter how you were feeling and I admire you for that, son. You don't always have to be the strong one though, you can grieve, and you can fall apart a little. It's okay to hold each other up, it doesn't have to be one or the other," Beasley says sincerely.

"Thanks. I was starting to think everyone was turning against me today. You know I'll always put Amber's needs before my own. That's my job as her husband. Sometimes, though, it all just builds up to a point and if I don't get time to think and sort it out, I'll explode." He nods his head in understanding. At least I have one person who gets it — gets me. Its times like this I really miss my dad. He would know just what to say to make me feel a little better. I'm glad I have Beasley as my father-in-law; I couldn't have picked a better one if I tried.

The door opens and a nurse walks in. She smiles at us and clears a few things out of the way. I can see the end of a bed in the hall and my palms start to sweat with nerves. I don't know what to expect. I picture an inconsolable, crying Amber in my head. I wouldn't blame her. If that's how I feel on the inside, it has to be worse for her. She carried and took care of our babies for twenty-two weeks. She felt them moving and growing inside her. This has to be slicing her apart. Out of all the pictures popping up in my head, what comes through that door isn't one that I would ever have imagined in a million years.

CHAPTER
Thirteen

Amber

A s THE nurses wheel my bed down the hall, I realize that I'm still in the maternity ward, just a different section. This is the section for women who come in pregnant thinking they'll be leaving with a baby only to have something go wrong. It's to keep us separated from the happy new mothers and their babies, so that we aren't reminded of our loss. Like that's really going to make any difference.

When they push my bed into the room, I see Kyle and my dad sitting together. The two most important men in my life look so tired, sad, and nervous. Nervous because of me. They're afraid of how I'm holding up, they have no idea what to expect. Even though I want so badly to fall to pieces right now, I won't. I can't. For these two men who have been so strong for me more than once, I can be strong for them this time. I have to do this for them. They did nothing but worry about me throughout the whole Beau mess. I can't put them through that again. It's my turn to take care of them. The best way to do that is by not letting them see how broken I am. So, as I'm pushed farther into the room, I smile as brightly as I can and pray they can't see right through me.

After a little while of them asking me constantly if I need this or that, I finally convince them both to go home. It isn't an easy task. I fake drifting off to sleep and tell them all I'm going to do is sleep. When the door closes behind them, the damn I've built comes crashing down. Without all of the drugs in my system, I'm able to let all of the emotions out. Pulling the pillow over my face, I scream into it as loud as I can. Over and over again. This pain is unbearable. I think I could break every bone in my body right now and it wouldn't hurt as bad. Why is this happening to me? What did I do to deserve to be punished like this? Someone touches my arm and I jump, completely unaware that the nurse had come in.

"I'm so sorry, Mrs. Connor. I didn't mean to startle you," she says softly. "I want to make sure you're okay. Is there anything I can do? Call someone or get something to help you sleep?"

"Something to help me sleep, please," I manage to squeak out between sobs.

"I'll be right back with that," she says with an understanding smile. There's something about her that says she has been through pain like mine. Maybe that's why she works in this area. If I can sleep, then I can stop hurting for a little while. I know it's only a temporary fix, but right now, I'll take whatever I can get. She's back quickly, handing me two small pills and a little cup of water. I swallow them as fast as I can, hoping they take affect right away.

"They will work quickly. If you need anything tonight, I'm only a button push away," she says as she puts the call button within my reach, "even if you just need someone to sit with you, okay?"

"Thank you. I appreciate that." I give her the best smile I can. I'm sure it's a lame excuse for a smile, but it's the best I've got for now. It doesn't feel like I'll ever be truly able to smile again. Rolling to my side, I close my eyes. Waiting for sleep to take away the pain, I let the tears silently fall.

I wake up and glance at the clock. It's seven in the morning. I can't believe I slept the whole night without waking up. For just a few seconds, that agonizing pain in my heart is gone, but it doesn't take long to return. I wonder if they'll give me something so I can just sleep all day too. Probably not, but it sure would be nice. My door opens and in walks Dr. Jarrett. He has his nose in my chart as he walks in the door. Just being in the same room with this guy aggravates me. Not that I'm a big ball of laughs as it is, but he makes my mood worse. He smiles down at me as he sits at the foot of my bed. *Go right ahead.*

Make yourself at home.

"How are you feeling this morning?" he asks brightly. Is he for real? How does he think I'm feeling after yesterday?

"Okay...I guess." He's hardly looked up from that damn chart, let alone made eye contact with me. I wonder if he even knows whose room he's in.

"So, how are the babies this morning? Have you seen them yet?" he asks, still not looking at me. What the fuck is he talking about? He cannot be this incompetent and insensitive. He must know what part of the maternity ward we're in, plus he's had his nose in my damn chart since he walked in the door. Has he even been reading it? I don't know what comes over me, but I'm beyond livid. With every ounce of energy I have, I kick him as hard as I can. He goes flying off the end of the bed, landing on his face with a thud. My chart along with his glasses, slide across the slick floor.

"Get out! How dare you be so insensitive! Did you even read that fucking chart in front of you, you son of a bitch. No, I didn't see my babies today. Seeing that they died yesterday, I would guess they aren't doing too well!" He starts to pick himself up off the floor as I try to keep the tears at bay. I refuse to let this ass make me cry. It's hard to do when I see Holly standing in the doorway with a 'you go girl' look for me and an 'I'm gonna kick your ass, douche' for Dr. Jarrett. He finally composes himself. Before he can speak, I cut him off. I really don't want to hear a word he has to say. "I suggest if you have any other patients to see that you make sure you know everything before you open your trap. I do not want you in my room again while I'm here. You will not be treating me ever again." He nods his head and almost runs past Holly out the door. I picture her tripping him as he walks by her and it makes me giggle.

"You thought I was going to trip him, didn't you?"

"I could see you doing that. Did you hear everything?"

"Yeah, I heard it all. He got off pretty easy, if you ask me. Although, it did look like that kick to the floor hurt quite a bit."

"I wish I could've reached his face."

"Oh yeah, that would have been awesome. You really doing okay? Well, as okay as you can be anyway?"

"I'll be okay. It will just take some time," I tell her, hoping if I say it enough, I might actually believe it.

"I know you will. Is there anything I can do for you?" I know she'll do anything for me, but can I really ask her to do this for me? It's an awful lot to ask of her. I don't think I can do it myself though. "What is it, Amber? You can ask me anything."

"There's one thing, but I will totally understand if you don't want to do it. I don't think I can."

"Jesus, woman, spit it out already."

"Can you go down to the funeral home and find out what needs to be done to plan the funeral?" I ask as I look out the window. I can't bear to see the pity that I'm sure is all over her face. I haven't got a clue as to what needs to be done to plan a funeral. When my grandparents passed away, they had everything already set up and paid for. I just had to make a phone call. Aside from that, I'm just not strong enough to handle it right now. Falling apart in front of my family and friends is not an option so doing it in front of strangers is definitely a no go. I have to keep up the strong front so that no one is left picking up the pieces of poor Amber's messed up life again. They have all done it enough lately. It's my turn to be strong for them. This loss hasn't affected only Kyle and me, all of our friends are feeling it just as much as we are.

"Of course. Becky and I talked about that last night, actually. We planned on asking if you wanted us to set it up for you. We thought we could set everything up then you and Kyle can just look it over and approve it or make whatever changes you want." As always, these girls are taking care of me.

FOUR DAYS. I've been stuck in this damn hospital for four days. I'm ready to get the hell out of here. Dr. Monty came in this morning and after my exam, said I was okay to go home. He told the nurse to discharge me. That was three hours ago. What could possibly be taking so long? I called Kyle after I spoke with the doctor to tell him to come get me. To my surprise, he's too busy with inventory at the bar. He can't leave to come get me so he's sending Angel instead. I'm not sure what to make of the distance he's putting between us, or how to deal with it. On one hand, I want to scream, throw punches at him, and ask him what he's done with my loving husband. On the other hand, I understand that people grieve in their own way and this may possibly be his. If that is the case, how can I fault him for it? I do know he's hurting just as badly as I am. I can see the pain every time our eyes meet. It would be so much easier for us both if he could let me comfort him instead of pushing me away.

"Hey there, baby girl! You ready to blow this joint?" Angel's carefree voice tears me from my thoughts. I love Angel, but I really wish Kyle were the one standing in front of me, wanting to make me smile and ready to break me out of this place.

"Yes, I am. As soon as these asshats bring my discharge papers." I'm already dressed and ready to go.

"Leave that to me," he says with a wink as he walks out the door. I have no doubt he's out there sweet-talking some poor, unsuspecting nurse right now. I shake my head and smile at the thought. Poor girl won't know what hit her.

Fifteen minutes later, I'm being wheeled out the door to Angel waiting outside his SUV. I should have called him hours ago. After we've been driving a little while, I get the feeling that Angel has something to say. Even though I've been staring out the window, I've felt him glancing my way.

"I'm not gonna pretend that I have a clue as to what is going on in Kyle's head right now. The way he's acting isn't right, though. He's got all of us pretty damned pissed at him for it. I do know that he loves you more than anything and whatever has got him being an ass is all him . We are all here for you if you need anything. Eventually, he will get his head out of his ass and realize he's been a complete dickhead." Sounds like he is fighting the same dilemma I am. I know there's a reason he's acting the way he is, but it also doesn't excuse his behavior toward me.

"Thank you. I appreciate everything. He'll come around. He just needs some time." At least, I hope he'll come around.

Pulling up the driveway to the house, I'm both happy and nervous to be home. I am hoping to see Kyle's truck, but it doesn't surprise me that it's not here. Angel helps me out of the car and grabs my bag. I unlock the front door and we go inside. Everything looks the same as it did when I left. Why I was thinking it would be different when I walked in, I'm not sure. Maybe because I'm different. I've changed. I always pictured the day I would come home from the hospital after giving birth to my babies. I imagined Kyle by my side, both of us smiling because we are so happy, with three beautiful bundles of joy in tow to introduce to the world. This is not the beautiful, happy picture I had in my head. No Kyle by my side. No smiles. And worst of all, no babies.

"Let me help you upstairs. Holly will be by in a little while with some lunch." He stops and looks at the clock. "I guess we missed lunch. She'll be bringing dinner." Angel's trying so hard to make everything as normal as possible for me, even though he knows there's nothing that is normal in my life right now. I allow him to help me upstairs and into my bed. I have really missed my comfy bed.

"Can I get you anything?"

"No, thank you. I might take a nap. I'll be okay. I'm sure you have better things to do than babysit me."

"I'm not babysitting you. I'm just here to make sure you relax and follow doctor's orders. Take your nap, I have a ton of texts to return from some female...ah...friends," he says as he wiggles his eyebrows. I can't help but laugh.

"Then go ahead and make yourself at home. I'm just gonna try to rest a little." He kisses the top of my head before walking out of the room. Closing my eyes, I try to fall asleep.

Thirty minutes later, I'm still not able to sleep. *I might as well go keep Angel company.* Slowly, I get out of bed. As I start walking down the hall, I get to the nursery and stop. Knowing this is not a good idea, I still can't help it. I push open the door and walk in. Looking around, my heart breaks. Why is this happening to me? To us? Falling to my knees in the middle of the room, I cry. I cry for the pain I feel in my chest that fills the space where my heart used to beat. It was once overflowing with happiness, now there's nothing but this sharp stabbing pain. I cry for the three beautiful babies that will never take their first steps or say their first words. I cry for the canyon that seems to be between Kyle and me right now. There's no stopping the tears or the river of emotions flowing through me. I'm sad at all we've lost and all we'll never get to experience. I'm angry, really angry. Angry at myself, my body for failing to do the one thing it was made for. I'm angry at God for allowing this to happen after I prayed and begged for him to help keep them safe. And most of all, I'm angry at Kyle for not being here when I need him the most.

Strong arms wrap around me from behind and pull me back against a rock hard chest. I assume its Angel and don't bother to open my eyes. I just let out all that I've been holding in the last four days and let him hold me. I've tried to be strong, to hide my emotions, but I just can't do it any longer. It hurts too badly.

"It's okay. Let it all out. I've got you," Jax says in a calming voice. I ignore the small part of me that has been suspicious of him for so long now. At one time, he was my best friend. The only one I could confide in. Right now, I need the friend he used to be. I allow him to hold and comfort me.

"I don't know if I can take this. I wanted them so much, Jax. Why did this have to happen?" Thankfully, Jax knows I don't need him to answer. I just need to get all of these feelings out. Keeping all of this inside in order to be strong for everyone else is building up like a pressure cooker. I have no idea how long we sit there on the floor, me crying while Jax comforts me, but I start to feel a little relief.

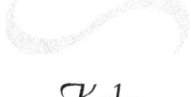

Kyle

MY HEART hurts so badly. It's not like I've never had to deal with death. I've lost my father and Amber's grandparents, but this is just so different. These were my children, my babies who never had a chance to grow. It hurts so much worse than anything I have ever experienced before. Unfair is the only word that seems to play over and over in my head. This whole thing is unfair to me, to Amber, but most of all, to our babies. I don't know how to handle this. To say I'm doing a terrible job is an understatement. Facing Amber, seeing the hurt and fear in her eyes, kills me. I can't seem to face her. Husband of the year is not coming my way any time soon, but for the life of me, I can't bring myself to be the man I need to be for her. She has always been my first priority, she still is, only this time I'm not able to set aside my own pain, grief, and guilt long enough to take care of hers.

The thing I'm most scared of, the thing that eats away at me every waking minute, is that I'm to blame for all of this. She is going to hate me and that's the one thing I really can't bear to see in her eyes. What kind of man, husband, and father am I? I'm supposed to care for and protect my family. That's my job. My purpose. I failed at that miserably. I was helpless to stop any of this from happening. My children are gone and I didn't protect them, didn't save them. I can't protect Amber from the pain and heartache she's feeling. What good am I if I can't do the things I am supposed to be doing?

Angry with myself and the whole situation in general, I throw the glass in my hand across the room. I watch as it hits the wall and shatters. Feeling slightly better, I throw the bottle of whiskey. Before I know it, I'm destroying my entire office. Pictures are broken, papers are all over the floor, and there are several holes in the walls. I fall to my knees and cry. The rage is gone and now all I'm left with this overwhelming sadness.

"What the fu...?" Paul says as he comes into my office.

I really don't need this right now. It's bad enough I'm acting like this to begin with, but I don't need anyone to see me. It could be worse though, at least it's not Angel. He would never let me live it down. I sit back against my desk, take a deep breath, and wait for the lecture I know is coming. They have all been pissed at me. Not that I blame them. I know I haven't been treating Amber right. I know I haven't been there like I should. Paul sits down next to me.

"There are better ways to redecorate, ya know?" he says with a chuckle.

"Probably is, but this made me feel a little better," I admit, relieved that he's not biting my head off.

"I wish I could make it all better for the both of you. I'm here if you need to talk about it."

"I know and I appreciate that. I do, but no one will understand how I'm feeling. I don't even understand it."

"There is one person who will understand. One person who knows exactly how you feel and what you're going through. Though, for some reason, that's the one person you keep avoiding." There's a frustrated tone to his voice. "I understand it's not easy, but you need to be together. None of us can truly understand what the two of you feel. That's why you need to hold on to each other and talk through those feelings together. I'm afraid if you stay on this path, it will tear you both so far apart there will be no way to put you back together."

He's right. I need to man up. I need to keep the promise I made to Amber to always be there for her, no matter what. We've already lost too much. I won't allow us to lose one another as well.

"Thanks. I'm going home to my girl," I tell him as we get up off the floor. He nods his head and smiles. I go out the back door and jump in my truck. I've been such an ass. I didn't even pick her up from the hospital today. She needed me there and I wasn't. I hope she can forgive me when I explain everything.

As I pull into the driveway, I notice Angel's car is here, but also Jax's. What is he doing here? When I get into the house, Angel is sitting in the kitchen.

"What's Jax doing here and where is he?" That came out a little harsher than I intended it to. I just don't like that guy around my wife.

"He came by to see how Amber was holding up. He seemed genuinely concerned about her, which is more than I can say for you lately. He went upstairs to check on her."

Yeah, I deserve that, but I'm not getting into this with him right now. I turn and go upstairs. When I reach the top, I can hear Amber crying. She's in the nursery. Why is she in there? I walk over and look through the partially open door. My heart instantly breaks at the sight of my sobbing wife, but my blood boils at the sight of Jax holding her. I know I should walk away, it's the rational thing to do, but rational is not the way my mind is working right now. I rush in before I can stop myself.

"What the fuck is going on in here?" Venom drips from each word. They both jump. Amber looks nervous and scared. I trust Amber, she's not the one I'm angry with. But for some reason, I can't break my glare from her. Jax, as usual, looks cocky, like he's getting away with something. Jax stands up and grabs Amber's hand, helping her to stand.

"Relax. I came by to check on her and she was in here by herself, breaking down. Of course, you were nowhere around." He's right, I wasn't here when she needed me. I am pissed at myself, but seeing Jax's arms around my wife makes me snap. My fist connects with his nose before I can talk myself down. There's a sickening crack when the two connect, followed by a steady gush of blood. That feels a lot better than it should and I don't feel guilty at all.

"Oh. My. God. Jax are you okay?" Amber rushes past me to the bathroom. She comes back with a damp towel and hands it to Jax. "What is wrong with you? That was uncalled for!" she yells as she jams her finger into my chest. "I was upset and my friend was here. That's all this was. You're behaving like a child. You've been avoiding me like the plague and I've needed you! Maybe you should go stay with Paul and Holly until you can learn to grow up! It's not like you want to be around me lately anyway." She turns away from me and back to Jax. "Come on, Jax, let's get some ice on that." They both start out the door. Jax turns just before he gets through the door and smirks. The son of a bitch. He's enjoying this.

"Damn it!" I yell. What is wrong with me? I came here to explain myself and make things better. The only thing I've managed to do is make it ten times worse. There's nothing I can do now except what she has asked me too. I'll give her some time and try again.

CHAPTER
Fourteen

Amber

IT TURNED out to be a beautiful day. The sun is shining and sky is clear and blue. Holly and Becky did a great job planning the service. It's simple and perfect. I couldn't have planned it any better. Somehow, I've managed to not fall completely apart. When they look at me, they see the mother mourning her children — tears streaming down my face, a gentle hushed sob here and there. That's what I want them to see so they don't worry. I'm grieving like I should, but not falling to pieces in the process. Thankfully, they can't see inside. If they got even a glimpse of how I really feel, it would terrify them all. It scares the hell out of me. There are so many different emotions fighting to take control that I feel like I'm going crazy. How I'm able to contain the storm that rages inside me, I don't know.

The Pastor announces that the funeral home has a special gift for us. I'm trying so hard to keep up my "together" appearance that the statement doesn't even register as odd. We all stand and walk a few feet away from the rows of chairs. There's a table set up with a huge box shaped object on it. A sheet is covering it so I have no idea what's inside. I start to get a little nervous, hoping that whatever the hell this is it isn't the one thing that will tear down the wall that's keeping the storm inside. I cannot break down here. There's plenty of time for that when I'm alone. An older man and woman that I've never seen before walk up to the table. The woman gives me a smile. In that one smile and the pained look in her eyes are a thousand heartfelt words. I feel like she knows my pain and understands the war I'm fighting with myself. She's been in my shoes, I can feel it. I try to smile back. I have no idea if I actually accomplish a smile or not, it seems impossible to do that today.

The man pulls the sheet from the box and I'm in awe. There, in a cage, are three beautiful, snow white doves. It never crossed my mind to do this today. I look back at Holly and Becky and see that they never thought about it either.

"Mrs. Connor, we see death and grief daily and it's not something you ever get used to. However, there's something about you and your babies that really hit us a little harder. We all thought the doves would be a beautiful touch," the funeral director says, his voice is shaky and full of emotion.

"Thank you. It's very thoughtful and much appreciated." There is so much more I would like to say in order to express my thanks. That just doesn't seem to be enough, but right now, the words won't come to me. I hope they understand.

The man looks around to make sure everyone is ready. When his eyes land on me, I simply nod. He unlocks the lid of the cage and removes it. I expect the birds to take flight immediately, to seek freedom from the cage, but they don't. They each wait until they are lifted out of the cage. He raises each one above his head and let's go. One by one, these beautiful, white doves take flight. They look like angels flying against the pure blue sky. Again, I'm amazed by these majestic birds. They don't fly away from each other or us right away like I would expect, they gather together, side by side, as they fly. Just like my babies, three beautiful angels in the sky soaring above us. It is somehow peaceful for me to watch them soar back and forth above us together. Even though the tears are flowing much harder now, I'm still under control.

The service is over, but there is one thing left to do. I can't stay here for it, though. I can't watch them lower my babies into the ground and cover them. That will most definitely shatter that wall holding me together, but I hate the fact that they would be alone while they are put to rest.

"I'll stay and watch over them, baby girl. I won't leave them alone," Angel whispers in my ear. How does he always know? He's been my rock through all of this.

"Are you sure? I can't ask you to do that."

"You aren't asking, I offered. And yes, I'm sure. I'll do anything you need me to do. We're family and family watches out for each other. I know you can't watch this but you don't want them to be alone. I'll make sure they are not alone."

"Thank you, Angel. That means so much to me. You have been amazing, I couldn't have gotten through this without all of your support."

"I'm glad someone can be there for you at least." He glares over at Kyle as he says it. "Go ahead before they start. I'll come by later to check on you." He hugs me and kisses my cheek. I watch him walk back to the chairs and sit down in the front row.

I turn back and start to walk toward Kyle. I'm hoping we can go home together and put the last few weeks behind us. I just want to be in his arms, to feel safe and loved again like I used to. We haven't talked much since he punched Jax two days ago. He called me last night and asked if he could pick me up today and come with me to the service. Of course, I said yes. I needed and wanted him with me today. Every day, for that matter. Before I get to him, his phone rings and he doesn't look happy at all. As I get closer and hear his part of the conversation, I feel that familiar rage bubble up again.

"Can't I send my manager down? Why does it have to be me?" he bites into the phone. "Fine. I'm on my way." He gives me a pained look. "That was the security company. They responded to the alarm at the bar. Apparently, there was a break in and they need me there personally. I'm sorry, princess, this is the last thing in the world I wanted to do right now." I can see by the look in his eyes that he's being honest. He really doesn't want to leave me.

"It's okay. It's not like you planned this. I'll get a ride home with Holly. When you finish at the bar, come home. Okay?" I offer, silently praying he says yes.

"Of course. I don't care if the place has burnt to the ground, I'll be home in an hour. Tops." He softly kisses me before running to his truck.

Holly and Paul give me a ride home. They offer to come in and stay until Kyle comes home, but I tell them I'll be fine. Four hours and ten messages later, I'm not sure if I'm more worried or angry. I try his phone again and it goes straight to voicemail. Knowing that I can't keep sitting around, wondering what the hell is going on anymore, I grab my purse and phone and start out the front door. I'm looking down, digging through my purse for my keys, when I slam into someone. I jump back.

"Shit, Jax! You scared me. I didn't notice you there."

"Sorry. You should pay better attention. Where are you off to in such a hurry?"

I explain it all to him and he offers to drive me to the bar. I accept because I have a strange feeling I'm gonna need a friend. My stomach is in knots, as the dozens of different scenarios running through my mind just keep getting worse.

"Calm down. I'm sure there's nothing to worry about. After all, this is Mr. Perfect we're talking about," Jax jokes with a smile.

"Perfect, he's not. None of us are." I'm not convinced though that there's nothing to worry about. Even with the way Kyle's been acting lately, this isn't like him. Something is wrong. Either he's hurt or ignoring me on purpose, there's no other explanation.

Pulling up to the bar, the only vehicle I see is Kyle's truck. My stomach flip-flops as I slowly get out of the car and walk up to the front door. I pull on the handle, but it's locked. Looking through the window of the door, I notice a wine glass and half-empty whiskey glass sitting on the bar. Even from this far away, I can see lipstick on the rim of the wine glass. Suddenly, I feel sick. I grab my keys and unlock the door. I don't see or hear anyone. I go back to the kitchen and look to see if he's in there, but it's dark and empty. The poolroom and bathrooms are also empty. There are only two places left he could be — his office or the apartment upstairs. I look over at Jax who's sitting calmly at the bar. How can he be so calm right now? I take a deep breath, trying to slow my breathing down a little.

I go down the hallway toward Kyle's office, hoping that the scenario playing through my head doesn't come to fruition. As I open the door and flip on the light, I want to throw up. He's not in here either. This means he must be upstairs. Between the lipstick stained wine glass and the fact that he's probably in the apartment, my mind can only come to one conclusion and it's not a pleasant one. I gather my nerve and leave the office, taking my time walking up the stairs.

The apartment door is open just enough for me to hear the shower running. This is a little too familiar for my taste. I was wrong the last time, maybe I am again. I go to the bedroom first. The last time I found a naked girl in Kyle's bed while he was in the shower. Only he didn't know the girl was there. This time, I need to make sure I don't jump to conclusions. I gasp as my stomach plummets to my feet. Kyle's passed out in the bed, totally naked. Ignoring the array of emotions fighting to take precedence, I walk over and shake him. He doesn't budge. I look around, taking in the scene. Clothes are strewn all over the bedroom and an empty condom wrapper is laying on the floor. The panic builds in my chest, taking the air from my lungs. I want to run, but my feet are cemented to the floor. In horror, I stare at the unbelievable scene before me. Why? Why would he do this to me? To us? I have to get out of here. I just buried my babies today, I can't handle this too. It's all too much at once. I finally get my feet to move and start running from the room, crashing right into a towel wrapped Leena.

Without any thought, I grab her by her hair and slam her face into the wall before throwing her to the floor. *Damn, that felt good!* I don't say a word. I can't. If I do, I'll break down and I am not giving that bitch the pleasure of knowing she made me cry, let alone seeing it. Of course, she's not going to keep her trap shut. I should have known. She can't keep her legs closed, why would her mouth be any different?

"Would you like me to tell him you stopped by when he wakes up? I really wore him out, so he'll be sleeping for a while," she boasts with an evil grin on her face, like this is all some game and not my life. Like we're back in middle school, fighting over a crush. She has no idea. No fucking clue what she just helped destroy. The kind of love we have is something you're privileged to find once in a lifetime. We were able to have it twice and we blew it both times. I know how my luck runs; there won't be a chance for a third run. This bitch, however, has pushed me for the last time. She's not getting the satisfaction of thinking she's won.

"You can tell him to get his stuff from my house. I'm going away for a little while and when I get back, he better be cleared out." I take a deep breath because saying that out loud hurts like hell. "You should be happy to finally get what you've wanted since the day you laid eyes on him. Be careful though, a man who would cheat on his wife the same day they bury their infant triplets obviously isn't a good guy. I have a feeling that it's all about the chase with you, though. Once you get what you want, you're done. Am I right?" I know I am. Why am I even still standing here talking to this piece of trash?

"I told you both that I'd get him and I did. He was so good, I just might keep him around for a while and have a little more fun. Maybe this will knock you off that high horse of yours. You entitled rich bitches are all the same. You think you're better than everyone around you and you deserve everything. You'll see you didn't deserve half of what's been handed to you!" she rants. What the hell is she talking about?

"I've never thought I was better than anyone. But you, my dear, I am a better person than you. I would never take or even try to take what's not mine. I have self-respect, respect for others, morals, and most of all, I'm not a huge skank! As fun as our little chat has been, it's done. Enjoy my husband." With every single ounce of strength I can muster, I smile sweetly at her before turning away.

Walking down the stairs, I keep telling myself not to fall apart here, to wait to get home. I have to get away from here. At least this time I know I'm not running away. I just need some space to think, without distractions and reminders. Between the babies and now Kyle, I feel like my heart is in a million pieces.

"Let's go, I'll explain in the car," I order Jax as I storm by him. I have to get out of this bar before the damn breaks.

We get in the car and head to my house. In detail, I spill everything to Jax. I'm a little thrown that he's not more shocked to find out the girl is Leena. It's probably because he knows her so well. I get through the whole story without breaking down. I throw up in my mouth a little, but not I don't break down. I'm proud of myself. Maybe I'm stronger than I thought.

"Go ahead, say it," I encourage Jax.

"Say what?"

"Say I told you so. Even though he didn't do anything the first time, you said he'd hurt me. You were right. It doesn't get much worse than this."

"I wish I was wrong. I never liked the guy, but I want you happy. I get no pleasure out of being right if it means you're hurting." It's nice to have my old friend back again. "I know the perfect place for you to go to get away. There's this private island off the Keys. Not many people know about it. It has a house with a guest cottage in the center that's completely hidden."

"That sounds perfect."

"I can go with you, so you aren't all by yourself."

"What about the center? I need someone to take care of it. Besides, the whole point of going away is to think and sort through my mess. I have to do that alone."

"Chelsie is more than capable of running the center. I'm not going to get in your way. I know you need alone time. I'll stay in the cottage and just be there if you need me." It makes sense. I shouldn't be all alone on an island. It would be nice to have Jax close if I needed him. Chelsie is most definitely capable of running the center and this is the perfect opportunity to see how she does.

"Okay, but nobody knows where we are."

"Sounds good to me," Jax answers with a smile.

Jax drops me off so I can pack and goes home to do the same. He says he'll be back in an hour. I stay in my strong, no breaking down frame of mind even though that's all I want to do. Being in our house filled with all these happy memories is too much. Quickly, I throw everything I'll need into my suitcase and bolt down the stairs. I put the suitcase by the door and go to the kitchen. Sitting at the bar, I open the drawer and get a pen, some paper, and three envelopes. First, I write a letter to Beasley. I explain that I need some time away to clear my head. That I'm not running away, just taking some me time. I let him know that Jax is with me and I'll call and check in so he knows I'm okay. The next letter is for my friends. It basically says the same thing, but also thanks them for all they've done to help me through this rough time. The third letter is the hardest. It's Kyle's. By the time I'm done with it, I'm in tears. Just as I seal it up, I hear a car horn. Jax is here. I take one more look around. How did my perfect life turn into this? Where did I go wrong? Walking toward the door, I say goodbye to my marriage and my family. In one short week, I've lost the two most important things in my life.

Kyle

I RUN to my truck and haul ass to the bar. I can't believe I have to leave her. Of all days, why today? I planned on making this all right today. Explaining as best I could why I've been such a jackass lately and begging for her to forgive me. One hour. I don't care if the bar burns to the fucking ground. Nothing and no one is more important to me than Amber. She is my world and I haven't let her know that these last few weeks. That stops today.

When I pull up to the bar, I see two cars from the security company that monitors the alarm system. I park my truck and start inside. Before I can get inside, one of the officers meets me outside the doors.

"Mr. Connor?"

"Yes. I'm Kyle Connor. What's going on?"

"The alarm went off and when we responded, we found a woman inside. She has a key but not the code to shut down the alarm. She says she knows you, sir." He motions for me to go inside. When I see who's sitting at the bar, red tinges my vision. I've never hit a woman before, but this bitch just might be the first.

"What in the hell are you doing in my bar, Leena?"

"I need to talk to you. It's really important," she states.

"There's nothing you have to say that I want to hear. I told you before to never step foot in here again." I'm really starting to lose my temper. I should just let them arrest her ass and be done with it all.

"It's about Jax. I know what he's planning. I only want to help. To make up for my behavior from before," she blurts quickly, gaining my attention. "At least hear me out. I don't agree with what he's trying to do. If you don't believe me after I tell you, I'll leave. I promise." My curiosity getting the best of me, I decide to listen before kicking her ass to the curb.

"Fine. Thank you, guys, I'll take it from here. You can go." The security guys nod then leave. I'm in no mood to waste time or play games. "Okay, Leena, spit it out."

"Can I at least have a glass of wine? My nerves are shot. Those guys had guns drawn on me and I'm about to turn on my own family." This bitch is really pushing her luck. I could use a drink myself, though. Just to be an ass, I make mine first. I take a nice long sip of the whiskey before setting my glass on the bar then going to pour her glass of wine. I come back around the bar and put the glass in front of her. As I take a seat, I drink half of the whiskey in my glass. She's taking her sweet ass time sipping her wine while watching me a little too closely over the rim.

"Start talking. I'm in a..." I slur as my vision blurs. I squeeze my eyes shut for a moment, then open them again. The room sways as my vision goes in and out. My stomach roils and I shake my head, trying to clear the static buzzing in my brain.

"Kyle. Kyle, are you okay? You don't look so good," Leena says with amusement in her voice as she comes closer to me. *What the fuck did she do?*

Eyes still closed, I try to remember what may have happened to make me feel like I got hit by a truck and dragged for three miles. I flinch, my head pounding harder with each thought. Slowly, I open my eyes. Once they adjust to the dim light, I recognize the apartment above the bar. *What the fuck happened?* Amber. I need to get home to Amber. Jumping out of bed, way too quickly, I fall back against the wall, my head is spinning. I push back the nausea threatening to take hold and try to come up with some recollection. I know I didn't drink that much. Or did I? I can't remember anything. I look down and notice that I'm naked. Too afraid to look at the bed, I keep my eyes trained to the floor. Clothes are everywhere. Not only mine, but woman's clothing. None that I recognize as Amber's either. Bile rises to the back of my throat. I swallow it down just as I notice an empty condom wrapper on the floor. My head automatically snaps to the bed. Seeing Leena, naked in the bed, I rush to the bathroom and empty the contents of my stomach. *What have I done?*

When there's nothing left in my stomach, I rinse my mouth out. Throwing on a pair of gym shorts from the closet, I go back into the bedroom to get some answers. Something still isn't sitting well with me. There's no way I got so drunk I don't remember anything. When I get in the bedroom, I feel sick all over again. Leena is sitting up in the bed uncovered and smiling seductively at me. There is nothing about this woman that attracts me.

"Coming back for round three? I always knew you'd be amazing in bed, but you're even better than I imagined," she announces. Bile rises once more, threatening to send me back to the bathroom.

"There's no way in hell I slept with you once, let alone twice, and there definitely won't be a third!" I yell as I gather my clothes.

"Well, maybe you did...maybe you didn't, but good luck trying to convince Amber of the latter. She wanted me to tell you to get your things from her house before she gets back from her trip." I knew it. I didn't touch her, but if Amber was here and saw this, she's not going to believe that.

"Where's Amber going?" I snarl. This bitch is lucky I don't knock her into next week. I'll let Holly have the honors. She's been itching to get her hands on Leena again anyway.

"I have no idea. I didn't bother to ask. I do know that Jax is going with her, though. I'm sure he'll take good care of her." She chuckles as she gets herself dressed. With my clothes in hand, I go to the bathroom and quickly get myself dressed. How do I prove to Amber that I didn't do what she thinks I did? Between the way I've been acting and the scene she witnessed here, the only thing more convincing would be catching us in the act.

Once I know Leena is gone, I go downstairs. I see the wineglass covered in lipstick next to a half empty whiskey glass sitting on the bar. Suddenly, it hits me. That bitch drugged me. Thinking quickly, I find my phone on the bar and call Beasley. As calmly as I can, I explain all that I can remember and everything that has happened since I woke up, hoping he can run a test on the cup. After a few choice words, he says, "Stay put, son. I'm coming to get you."

"Okay. But what if I can't make her believe me? I love her, Beasley. I can't lose her again." He takes a long breath. I know he's just as worried as I am.

"Kyle, have you checked the security video? If she drugged you, she needed help getting you upstairs. You have cameras all over the place, they should prove that what you say is true."

"I'll check them now." I hang up the phone and run back to my office. I must still be drugged, I totally forgot about the videos. Once the computer is fired up, I open the recordings from today. Son of a bitch! I shouldn't be as shocked as I am. There's Leena, plain as day, dumping something into my glass when my back is turned, pouring her wine. When I pass out, she yells toward the kitchen and out comes Jax. He leans downs and kisses Leena with way too much tongue for them to be cousins. Once he finishes, he picks me up, throws me over his shoulder, and carries me out of the main bar. I click on the file for the camera in the stairway leading up to the apartment. There he is, carrying me up the stairs, and there's no doubt I'm out cold. Leena picks the lock to the apartment and they go inside. This is all the proof I need. I copy the files to a disk so I can show it to Amber.

Beasley gets there and I fill him in on the videos. His officers take the glass for testing and then we head to my house. *What if I'm too late?* This feels like six years ago all over again. When we pull up to the house, I breathe a sigh of relief. Her car is here and the light is on in the kitchen.

"Do you want me to wait here?" Beasley asks.

"No. I think you better come with me."

I unlock the front door. As soon as I walk through it, I know she's gone. Something catches my eye on the counter in the kitchen. I see three envelopes, one clearly marked for me. My hands shake as I open the envelope, terrified as to what I'll find inside.

Dear Kyle,

It's sad that we are in this place once again. This time, however, is different. I stuck around long enough to confront the situation and confirm that what I was seeing was real. I would have given you a chance to speak but as Leena put it, she wore you completely out. You wouldn't wake up, so she kindly filled me in. I know it looks like I'm running away, but I'm not. I need time to sort through all that's happened. Not only have I lost my babies, but now I've lost the love of my life. I trusted you, Kyle. I never thought you would hurt me like this, especially with the likes of Leena. Maybe you weren't ready for a family or maybe it was you're way of punishing me for losing our babies. Either way, you're free of me. I can't forgive this. As much as I want to, I just can't. So, please get your things together and move out before I get back. I'll be gone for at least two weeks. Don't try to find me because it won't do any good. You destroyed my heart in a way it won't ever be able to be fixed.

I will always love you.

Love,

Amber

I fall to my knees, my heart shattering. Broken is the only word that can describe how she sounds. She really thinks I've done this and she's gone god knows where with Jax. I have to find her and prove to her I didn't let her down. I have to do it before it's too late.

CHAPTER
Fifteen

Amber

I CAN'T GET the image of Kyle and Leena out of my head. It makes me want to vomit. However, there is a little satisfaction when the image of her face bouncing off the wall enters my mind. For a few seconds, the sadness that fills me is gone. I need to put that image on a constant loop in my head. Holly would be proud of me if she knew I didn't just lay down and take Leena's shit. Just like that, the sadness is back. All it takes is the thought of Holly and the rest of my friends. I miss them already. This situation is going to affect all of them. They are all already pissed at Kyle and this is going to push them over the edge. I need to call Angel and let him know I'm okay. He's been so protective of me recently, he'll worry the most. I reach into my purse for my phone and turn it on. Kyle and Beasley were calling it so often I had to shut it off.

"Who are you calling?" Jax questions.

"Angel. I don't want him to worry."

"I thought you weren't going to call anyone? You won't tell him where you are, will you?" he asks, sounding a little desperate. The hairs on the back of my neck stand up as an uneasy feeling washes over me. What's up with him all of a sudden? He's throwing off that vibe that makes me think he's up to something, but what the hell do I know? I thought Kyle loved me and would never cheat on me. I was wrong about that, so I could be wrong about this too.

"I'm not telling anyone where I'm going, but I want Angel to know I'm okay. He worries about me and this will freak him out."

"If you don't want Kyle finding you then I would keep that phone shut off. Beasley can use his connections and find you by your phone." He's right and I'm not ready to face anyone. I need some time to grieve the loss of my babies and now the loss of my marriage. I turn the phone back off and put it in my purse again. "Besides, you said you left them all notes explaining everything, so why would they be worried? You're an adult, not a child." Where's that coming from? They don't treat me like a child. They worry because they care. Too tired to argue with him right now, I lay my head back and close my eyes. Maybe I can sleep a little before we get there.

"Amber...wake up. We're here," Jax whispers as he gently shakes me. Reluctantly, I open my eyes. I was hoping this whole day was nothing more than a terrible nightmare. When I see where I am and who I'm with, I realize the nightmare is my reality. I wish I could just sleep until all of the pain goes away.

Jax hands me a cup of coffee — I must have really been out if I didn't even wake up when he stopped for coffee — and we both get out of the car. It feels good to stretch after the long drive. Jax explains that we will be meeting the caretaker here at the docks. He's going to take us to the island by boat and drop us off. I walk closer to the water and lean against the wooden rail. It's only eight in the morning, but already very hot. There's a slight breeze coming off the ocean. What a view. The sun is shining brightly against the clear blue water, making it look like there are thousands of diamonds sparkling on top. At least I chose a beautiful place to get my shit together.

"I'm going to bring our bags down to the boat," Jax informs me.

"Okay, I'll run into the store and grab a few groceries." He gives me an odd look before pulling out his wallet and handing me a few hundred-dollar bills. "I have money, but thanks anyway."

"Do you have cash? You don't want them to trace your credit cards, do you?" What is it with him? Once I call and tell Beasley I'm okay, he'll understand and won't be tracking me down. "I just want to make sure you have the time that you need to clear your head before Kyle comes begging for forgiveness." I don't think Kyle is stupid enough to come within ten feet of me right now. I take the money just to make him happy.

I buy enough food and essentials to last us two weeks. I'm not planning on staying much longer than that. I use Jax's cash to pay so he doesn't freak out on me. I'm starting to wish I came by myself. The bag boys offer to take all of the bags down to the boat for me and I tip them generously. As I'm following them out, I spot a cute purple sundress hanging in a shop window.

"Do you guys mind going ahead? I need to stop in here."

"Take your time, we've got this," the young boy says with a smile.

I go into the shop and head right to the dress that caught my eye. I find my size and bring it up to the register. I hand the woman my credit card. What Jax doesn't know won't hurt him. Nobody is going to be tracking me down and really, so what if they do? If Kyle really does have the balls to come find me right now, I'll just tell him to leave. Simple as that. I'm not running away like I did before. I think they'll respect the fact that I asked for some time to clear my head. Once I leave the shop, I look in my purse for my phone. I really do need to call Beasley. I don't want him or anyone else to worry. I can't seem to find it. Not that I'm really surprised, this purse is like a black hole. I'll look later when I can dump it out.

The boat ride out to the island only takes about ten minutes. It's breathtaking. There are white sandy beaches all the way around. Jax was right, the house and cottage are totally hidden by trees and bushes. There's a long, wooden dock with a gazebo that sits at the end. I bet that's a beautiful place to relax and watch the sunset. Once the boat is docked, Jax helps me off. The caretaker loads our grocery bags and luggage into a wagon. He leads us along a cement pathway through the tropical foliage. This place is beautiful. It makes me miss Kyle even more. This is the type of place I would've loved to have been with him.

The house comes into view and I'm not surprised to find that it looks like your typical beach house. It's very small, but cute. A hammock hangs between two large palm trees, partly shaded from the sun. It looks so inviting. Two lounge chairs sit side by side in a sandy clearing under a few trees. A few feet away, there's a round, wooden picnic table with a grille beside it. The so-called guesthouse is more like a bright yellow dollhouse. There is no way you could fit more than one person at a time in there. How is Jax going to be comfortable in that little box? I bet there isn't even a bathroom. *Not really my problem.*

This was his idea. All of it, even the little guest box for himself. He can't stay with me. The whole point was for me to have some time alone. I have too much to figure out and I can't do that with his anti-Kyle influence constantly in my ear.

"Well, what do ya think?" Jax asks.

"I like it. It looks so quiet and relaxing. Perfect for what I need right now." And it is. I don't need anything fancy to sort through my mess. Quiet and tranquil will do just fine. "I do need to call Beasley and let him know I'm okay, though. He's going to be worried out of his mind." Before I start digging in my purse for my phone, I notice a strange look pass across Jax's face. Irritation? Anger? I'm not sure exactly what it is, but I do know I don't like it. Why is he so against me having any contact with home?

Sitting down at the picnic table, I search through my purse. My phone is nowhere to be found. That's odd. I know I put it back in here earlier. Item by item, I pull everything out of my purse, hoping it's just hiding behind something else. No such luck.

"Can't find your phone?" Just like the look he had moments ago made me uneasy, so does the tone in his voice now. Maybe I'm just being paranoid. He is the one here with me trying to help me, after all.

"No. It must have fallen out in the car. Can I borrow yours?" He nods his head, reaches into his pocket, and hands me his phone. Once I turn it on, I notice there are no bars. I dial Beasley's number anyway, but it won't go through. *Just great!* Stuck on an island with no way to call for help if we need it. "No service out here. What happens if there's an emergency?"

"There should be a two-way radio in the guesthouse to call the marina," He says as he carries my bags into the house. *Oh, I feel so much better now.*

Again, something is gnawing at me, telling me something's not quite right. I just don't trust any feelings right now. Hell, I trusted Kyle and my feelings for him and look where that got me. Right here, more broken and damaged than I was before, if that's even possible. He should've been with me. We were supposed to be comforting each other over the loss of our children, not off screwing the town skank the very same day we bury them. It makes me sick to think about. How could he do that to me? I never saw this coming. He is not the type of man to be so cold. He stood by me after the accident, even when I couldn't remember who he was. Why is this so different? What would possibly make him do this now, when I need him the most? I shake the thoughts from my head for now. I have broken down enough in front of Jax, I don't want to do it again. I'm going to prove to everyone — including myself — that I'm not some weak little girl.

We walk inside. It's very different from the outside. The walls are painted in a light sea foam green with beige tile floors. There is a beige sofa and matching loveseat with a glass coffee table. The kitchen is small but beautiful. Bright white cabinets fill the room with black granite counter tops. All of the appliances are new, high-end stainless steel brands. The caretaker and one of the boys from the store carry in the grocery bags and place them on the counter. The boy goes back to the boat for the rest while I begin to put everything away. The caretaker and Jax go over the things that he will need to know. After a few minutes, they go outside to look at the electric panel or something. I get most of the groceries put away by the time the boy gets back with the rest of the bags. When I start to put those away, I hear a phone ring. I look over and the boy from the store is answering his phone. Why can he get a signal and we couldn't? I finish putting away the rest of the food. When he's through with his call, I ask.

"I didn't think there was any cell phone reception out here?"

"You're not that far from the mainland. You shouldn't have any problems using your cell phone here," he says as his phone rings again. He walks outside and I can't stop the fear that washes over me. *What the hell is Jax up to?* Keeping me from talking to anyone. Making sure I didn't tell anyone where I am. I bet I didn't drop my phone, he probably took it so I couldn't call Beasley. And that whole thing at the marina, insisting I pay with cash so my credit card couldn't be traced.

I used to think he was in love with me, but I don't think that's it any more. After seeing him that night with Leena, it looked like there was something between them. But what? And why would he lie about them being cousins? So much doesn't make sense to me. This is Jax, though. For a long time he was my best friend. The only one I truly trusted aside from Daniel. Unlike Daniel and now Kyle, Jax has never hurt or betrayed me. He's stood by me through what I thought was the toughest point in my life. I now know the pain and loss I was feeling after I left Kyle all those years ago couldn't come close to the feelings I have right now. I shake my head, as if it's going to clear all the confusion up. I need a drink and some time alone on the beach. Thankfully I bought so many bottles of wine while shopping, I have a feeling I'll need them for this little vacation.

Kyle

EVERY BONE in my body hurts. I realize it's because I fell asleep on the kitchen floor. I couldn't bring myself to move last night. I sat here and read her letter over and over again. I also tried calling her over a dozen times and left just as many messages. Beasley even tried, hoping she'd answer his calls. He had no luck either. I wouldn't be worried if it was just my calls she wouldn't answer. She thinks I cheated on her, I don't blame her for not wanting to talk to me. It's not like her to not let Beasley know she's okay, though.

Jax has been up to something from day one and I don't trust him with her at all. At first, I admit I was jealous, but that's not it anymore. He doesn't act like he wants her for more than a friend, but there's this look he gets that makes me uncomfortable. I've pushed it aside for Amber's sake. When she was in the accident, Jax came through and took care of the center until she was able to go back. He did it again when she was put on bed rest. I know it took a ton of pressure and worry off of her shoulders, so that alone was enough for me to push aside my dislike of the guy. If my girl is happy, so am I.

Slowly, I get off the floor. I feel as though I've aged fifteen years in the last few months. Beasley will be up any minute, so I start a pot of coffee. He refused to leave last night. I'm not sure if he was afraid I'd do something stupid or if maybe he just didn't want to be alone. This has taken a toll on him too. He was so excited to be a grandpa. Like the rest of us, he's trying to deal with his own pain as well as be there for Amber. Hearing a car coming up the drive, I rush to the window, hoping its Amber coming home so I can get on my hands and knees and beg for her forgiveness. I'm disappointed to see Paul's truck flying toward the house. Close behind him in a cloud of dust is Angel. Both vehicles look full, which means the whole gang is here. Just what I need, more people to be pissed at me.

"I called Paul this morning. Don't worry, I explained everything. They know you didn't do anything wrong," Beasley assures as he walks into the kitchen. "I have some interesting info on Jax. My friend from Atlanta got back to me this morning. You may want to add some whiskey to that coffee." *Well, that sounds promising.*

"When I get my hands on that skanky bitch, Leena, I'm gonna rip her head off her shoulders!" Holly roars as she storms into the house. She's followed by the whole gang just as I thought. Paul, Angel, Marcus, and Becky. I almost feel sorry for Leena. Almost. If Holly gets a hold of her, she won't walk away in one piece. Holly could probably beat the shit out of me. She comes over and hugs me so tightly I can't breathe. At least she's not going to rip me a new one and blame me for this whole fucked up mess.

"Her face was red and swollen when I woke up, I think Amber worked her over a bit." Everyone looks shocked. It's not like Amber to be physical. We all know she can hold her own — we saw it with Beau — but she's not the type to go looking for it. Angel bursts out laughing. I even see a smirk on Beasley's face. I can imagine him thinking, *That's my girl.*

"I would've loved to witness that. I bet Amber could kick her ass if she was mad enough," Angel says, still laughing. By the look on his face, I know he's picturing Amber beating the shit out of Leena. "All joking aside, how are you doing? This is the last thing the two of you need right now." Wow. Angel's not mad at me either. He and Paul have been in my face the most.

"I'll be a lot better when I find my wife and she knows the truth." I need her to know that I would never betray her like that, I love her too much. She's devastated from the loss of our babies and I've managed to make it worse and add more pain to it. I can't believe this is happening all over again. Losing her would destroy me. Six years without her was hell enough, I don't want to miss any more time.

"Okay, so my friend from Atlanta has finally gotten back to me with some information," Beasley says, in full sheriff mode now. This can only mean one thing, whatever he's about to say is serious. Is Amber in danger with Jax? I don't like or trust the guy, but I never thought he would hurt her. If we have another Beau on our hands, I might just lose it.

"Easy, Kyle, he's not a violent guy. There's no history with him like Beau." He pauses for a moment, almost like the thought of all that Beau did physically hurts him. "It looks like Charles had an affair with Jax's mom a year before Amber was born. Jax is Charlie's son." He pauses, letting what he just said sink in. *Holy shit!* That was the last thing I ever expected to hear.

"Charles never knew about Jax. His mother was a drug addict and when she heard that Charles died, she came looking for money from his parents, Amber's grandparents. They had a DNA test done and when it came back positive, they wanted Jax in their lives. His mother wanted no part of it, she wanted money and that was it. She never even let them see Jax. The Lewis' gave her the amount she wanted and never heard from her again." We are all stunned silent, not wanting to miss any part of this story. "Jax lived a very rough life. His mother died of an overdose when he was sixteen. Somehow, he found out about his father and the kind of money his grandparents had. He started digging into family histories and records. Then he up and moved to Atlanta right after Amber did. I think he was getting close to her in order to get to know his family or get more money. Amber inherited everything from both her parents and grandparents, Jax got nothing. Up until recently, he would've known she was his sister, so I don't think there were ever romantic feelings. Plus, Leena is not his cousin. She's his wife. I don't know details about any of it or what he's really after, I can only speculate. Jax is the only one who can give us the full story." Beasley gets up and grabs the whiskey from the cabinet. He must be pretty damn stressed in order to be drinking this early.

Jax must not really know Amber all that well. If he did, he'd know that she would gladly give him anything he wanted or needed if he's family. Now though, knowing that he's deceived her all these years, she's going to be pissed off.

"If Amber is off somewhere with Jax, then where is the skank bitch, Leena?" Becky asks.

"I'm not really sure. No one has seen her since she left Kyle last night. I've got my guys looking for her though," Beasley responds, sounding a little defeated. She probably knows where Jax and Amber are. I also imagine she knows what exactly it is he wants from Amber.

"When we find her, give us five minutes alone with her. We'll find out everything we need to know," Holly promises, gesturing between herself and Becky. These women scare me sometimes. She has an evil look on her face, as if she's imagining torturing Leena.

"Only if I have front row seats to the show, Red. I'd love to see the two of you beat some answers outta her. Cat fight!" Angel says as he quickly dodges a punch in the arm from Holly and a smack in the head from Becky. Paul, Marcus, and Beasley are shaking their heads and smiling. Even when the last thing I feel like doing is smiling, this group always knows how to put one on my face. The only thing missing is Amber. How did my life get so damn messed up?

CHAPTER
Sixteen

Amber

I OPEN MY eyes and quickly close them again. When the sunlight hits them, it makes my head feel like someone's in there banging around with a hammer. That much wine and crying yourself to sleep on the beach in direct sunlight, not a good idea. Now I feel worse than I did before, if that's at all possible. My heart can't decide what to feel. One minute, I'm devastated, my heart shattering into a million pieces all over again. How can I go on without my babies? Without Kyle? The next, I'm so pissed off I just want to beat on everything in sight. Pissed at myself for not being able to keep my babies safe. Pissed at my body for failing me. Pissed at the doctors for not being able to do more. In my head, I know there's nothing more I could've done to prevent what happened, but my heart just doesn't get it yet. Most of all, pissed at Kyle for leaving me here to deal with all of this by myself. He's supposed to be by my side, but he chose to be with her. That alone gets my blood boiling. I'm startled from my thoughts when someone touches my shoulder. I turn to look and see Jax looking sympathetically at me.

"You've been gone a long time. I was getting worried."

"Sorry."

"Are you getting hungry? I thought I would grill us some steaks."

"That sounds really good."

"I'll go back and get started. Come back when you feel like it," he says as he squeezes my shoulder before turning to walk back toward the path leading to the house. How could I doubt him? He's been nothing but sweet to me. I feel like such an ass for even considering his intentions were bad. Some friend I am.

I look at my surroundings before I get up and head back to the house. It's amazing here, so beautiful and peaceful. Paradise is the word that comes to my mind to describe it. The sand I sit in is clean and white, like something you'd see in a vacation brochure. Clear blue water is all I can see for miles in front of me. There's a slight breeze coming off the water that keeps me from getting too hot. Now that the sun is starting to set, it's even more beautiful. Being here makes me wish Kyle was here with me. Then I remember why he isn't and I am angry all over again. Before the tears start up again, I get up, brush the sand off my ass, and walk back to the house.

As I get closer to the house, I start to smell the steaks on the grill. It isn't until then that I realize how hungry I really am. Once I come to the end of the pathway, the back of the house comes into view. I gasp at the sight. The tiki torches scattered around the backyard are all lit, the table is covered with food with a bottle of wine chilling in the center. Jax turns and gives me a nervous smile.

"I hope it's not too much. I noticed you haven't eaten much since you left the hospital. I thought maybe the walk and the sun gave you an appetite." He has always been very perceptive.

"Thanks, Jax, I appreciate it. I am starving. It all looks so good."

"Check this out." He lifts the lid to the grill and my mouth starts to water. Not only do the filets look amazing but he's also grilling shrimp and scallop skewers. There's also something wrapped in aluminum foil. He sees me looking and carefully opens it a little so I can peek inside. Another one of my favorites, grilled mushrooms. This is really nice of him. Cooking all of my favorites and trying to cheer me up as much as he can.

"Do I have time to take a quick shower?"

"Yeah. It should all be ready in about fifteen minutes."

"Thank you for all of this and being such a good friend," I tell him before walking into the house.

While in the shower, I allow my tears to freely flow. If I didn't keep myself from crying, I honestly think I could do it all day long. It feels like the tears are endless. My heart wants me to lock myself away in a dark room and cry forever until I can't cry anymore. My head knows I can't do that. No good would come out of me giving up on life. My children wouldn't want that for me. I have children. I'm a mother. How do I answer when someone asks, "Do you have any kids?" If I say yes, they'll have more questions and I'll have to explain that they passed away. Then that's when I'll get that look. The one that's a cross between you poor woman and get me outta here before I have to talk anymore. Maybe it's because they aren't sure of exactly what to say and they're afraid to say the wrong thing and upset me. It could be that they don't want me to remind them that terrible things can happen to normal people. That life isn't always as perfect as we want it to be. I knew there was a chance that we could lose one, but never in a million years did I ever think I would leave the hospital childless. Why would God bless me with triplets and take them all away? One being taken, I may have been able to understand. He never gives us more than we can handle, right? Now, I'm not so sure of that. I've heard of a motherless child, but I'm a childless mother.

That thought puts me over the edge and I slide to the floor, sobbing with my face in my hands. I would rather feel the pain of my body smashing through the windshield of that truck over and over again than the pain I feel right now. The accident hurt so much less and I can explain why that happened, why I was in the pain I was in. This pain can't be explained. No one can tell me why this happened. The medical reasons only explain so much. I want to know why me? What did I do to deserve this? Why am I being punished?

"Amber. Are you okay in there?" Jax yells after he knocks on the bathroom door. I've probably been in here a lot longer than fifteen minutes. No doubt, he also heard me crying. He's going to think I'm a weak mess. Who am I trying to kid? I am a weak mess.

"I'm fine. I'll be out in just a minute," I yell back as steadily as I can. I pull myself together and get out of the shower. I quickly dry off and throw on a t-shirt, cargo shorts, and flip flops. I towel dry my hair, put it in a messy bun, and I'm good to go.

Dinner is wonderful. I had forgotten what a great cook Jax is. He keeps the conversation light and doesn't bring up whether or not he heard my breakdown in the shower. For that, I'm grateful. We talk about when I was a kid and my grandparents. He knows all of these things, but I suppose he's trying to keep my mind on happier things.

He's never talked to me about what his life was like growing up. I've always wondered. Every time I ever asked him, he'd change the subject. Feeling emboldened, I ask again, hopeful he's willing to talk about it now.

"What about you? All these years you've never told me about how you grew up or even where." The smile immediately falls from his face, replaced by a pained expression. I immediately regret asking, but before I can take it back, he starts to speak.

"What is there to know? My mother was junkie who would do anything and anyone for her next fix. I never knew my father. He was married when he knocked my mother up. He traveled for work and didn't live in the same town. I don't think he ever knew about me," he says, sounding like a broken little boy. I get up, walk to his side of the table, and slide in next to him. I grab his hand.

"I'm sorry, Jax. No child should ever have to be unhappy." He smiles a sad smile and continues his tale. The things his mother was capable of made me ill. Leaving him alone for days or with strangers who could've done anything they wanted to the poor kid. He was the parent. Always taking care of her and himself until she overdosed when he was sixteen.

"Did you ever try to find your father?"

"After she died, I found some papers. My mom had gone to my dad's parents and asked for money. I found out later they were loaded. He died when I was very young so she figured she'd cash in. She was so stupid, though. She only got enough money to support her habit for a couple weeks. She could have at least gotten enough to get clean and keep us living decent. She signed these papers saying she wouldn't come back for more."

"Didn't they want to know you? Be a part of your life?"

"I think so. Knowing my mom, she was the one who wouldn't allow it, but they could have fought and they didn't. They had another grandchild that was obviously more important." That's terrible. I can't imagine not wanting anything to do with your own flesh and blood. He continues, telling me how he collected all of the information he could on his grandparents and this half-sister. The way he talks about secretly following his sister around causes chills to run down my spine. He was suspicious as to whether or not they were even related, which in itself is very odd. So to make things even creepier he somehow manages a DNA test and finds out she isn't his biological sister.

"It really pissed me off to find out all this time they tossed me, their real grandson, aside for a fake granddaughter. That's how I ended up in Atlanta. I followed her there." There is something in his voice and the way he looks at me that makes the hairs on the back of my neck stand straight up. It can't be? What are the chances that there's another girl raised by grandparents that aren't biologically hers that moved to Atlanta at the same time I did? Pretty fucking slim, if you ask me.. My stomach begins to roll as sweat builds on my brow.

"What are you saying, Jax? Was Charles your father?" I ask even though I know the answer. There's something different in his eyes, like he's had a mask on for the seven years I've known him and now it's gone. He doesn't look at me with kind friendly eyes any longer. There's hate and resentment looking back at me now.

"You had the life I should've had. My grandparents, my happiness, and most of all, my money," he says, his voice full of disgust.

"What is it you want from me? Why would you pretend to be my friend for so many years?"

"I figured the only way to get what is rightfully mine was to get close to you. After I tried to reason with the Lewis' and they wouldn't get rid of you, I decided I'd just have to be patient." The thought that he actually went to them and tried to make them choose him over me makes me sick.

"What exactly is it that you think is yours?"

"You don't get it do you? You took everything from me!" he screams, his face just inches from mine. I can't help but cower. The rage that's burning in his eyes is directed right at me. In his mind, he does blame me for all of his hardships. How did I take everything from him? I didn't have any more control over any of this than he did. His parents screwed him over, not me. "They had at least set up a college fund for me, so I figured I'd be in their will too. I had it all planned out. Every last detail of how I was going to get rid of them. Then you told me your grandpa was sick and you had to go back home, so I followed you and waited. It paid off. I didn't have to get my hands dirty at all, Mother Nature took care of it for me."

I jump up from the table and run to a clump of bushes, the meal I just ate coming back with a vengeance. I can't believe he planned on killing my grandparents for money. How can he be this unstable and hide it from me for so long? Am I that stupid? It feels like I've left my entire insides in those bushes by the time I stop.

"Don't you want to hear the rest? I've been a busy guy," he says in a sing-song voice. "Thing is, there was still someone standing in my way and she had to go too. So, one night, I snuck into the house when you and dear old grandma went on one of your walks." I feel bile rising and burning in my throat again. I know where this is going and I'm not sure I can handle hearing it. He looks so proud of himself. Not an ounce of guilt showing on his face. He's a monster. "I hid in the closet of her bedroom. Before she went to bed that night, she prayed that you would move back home with her. I waited until she fell asleep, then covered her face with a pillow. Of course, everyone in this Podunk town would think she just couldn't live without her husband." Heat begins to rise in my face and my body is shaking, the rage that is running through me becoming harder to contain. Without thinking, I lunge for him.

"YOU SON OF A BITCH!" I punch, kick, and even bite anywhere I can. I've lost all control of myself. I'm yelling and crying and I have no idea if any of it makes sense. He just laughs at me, before he head-butts the side of my face and everything goes black.

Kyle

I'VE BEEN going crazy all day. Beasley left a while ago to see if he could track Amber's cell phone or credit card activity. He says he needs to know she's at least safe. We still haven't heard from her. Beasley has tried calling, over and over again. She won't answer and doesn't return any of the hundreds of messages. I know she's upset and wants some time alone, but it's not like her to just disappear. She wouldn't intentionally let Beasley worry about her. Paul stayed here to babysit me. I don't know what every one's afraid I'm gonna do.

"Are you really doing okay?" Paul asks.

"Honestly, no. I'm not." I've failed in so many ways. What if I've lost her forever? She has shed one too many tears because of me. I promised her I would never hurt her, but I did. I was being a whiney little baby. I couldn't handle the fact that there was nothing I could do to protect her or our babies. I felt like less of a man, like I wasn't doing my job as a husband or a father. I was ashamed of myself for being weak. If I were a real man, I would have just told her how I felt.

"I've lost it all. One minute, I have everything I've ever wanted, and the next, it's all ripped away from me. She'll never forgive me." If Paul weren't here, I'd be crying like the useless little bitch that I am. I walk over and take a swig of whiskey right from the bottle. Fuck it. I'm just gonna drink until I don't hurt anymore. Won't solve anything, but at least I can be numb and maybe forget for a little while. Before I can take another, the bottle is grabbed from my hand.

"You're kidding, right?" Paul snaps. "Just like that, you're giving up. *Again*. If you want to feel sorry for yourself, go right ahead. Don't expect me to throw your ass a pity party, though. Here I thought the two of you were actually meant to be together. Like fate or some shit. I must have been wrong, because if that were the case, you wouldn't be rolling over and giving up like a little bitch just because things are a little hairy." He shoves past me and almost knocks me on my ass, slamming the door behind him as he goes to sit on the front porch.

Picking up the whiskey bottle he took from me, I take another swig, then hurl the bottle against the wall, watching as it explodes into shards of glass. That's what I feel like. What if she'd be better off without me? Ever since we've been back together, she's been through one nightmare after another. Her life was normal until I came back into it. Leaving her alone may be the very best thing for her. She can have a normal drama free life again. Just thinking about walking away from her sends a stabbing pain straight to my heart.

"Sit your stupid ass down. Now! You're gonna listen and listen good, so keep your damn mouth zipped until I'm done," Beasley orders as he shoves me toward the bar stool.

Holy shit! He looks about ready to rip my head off. There's this huge vein on the side of his forehead that's throbbing swiftly along with the fast pace of his heartbeat. His face is so red, I'm a little worried he might have a damn stroke. He's pretty scary when he's mad. I decide it's probably in my best interest to do as he says. I look over and see Paul leaning against the wall, his expression a mixture of amusement and surprise.

"I know what you're thinking and I advise you to stop it right now. You leave my daughter and I will hunt you down and shoot you. Remember, I can legally carry a gun and make up an excuse to shoot your dumb ass." Paul chuckles. Beasley shoots him a look that shuts him up instantly. *Ha! Take that you smug son of a bitch.* When I look back to Beasley, he's giving me a hard stare and it makes me shrink back a bit. "You know the both of you would be miserable without each other. Ya'll tried that once for six years. Remember?" He paces as he runs his hands through his hair. "We all know you've been an ass lately, but that's over now. Reattach your balls and help me get your wife back here, then you can beg for her forgiveness. If she throws you out on your ass, you get back up and keep trying until she forgives you. Do not give up. That's not you and it sure as hell isn't my daughter." Beasley's eyes never leave mine as he sits on the stool beside me. I can't tell if he's trying to read my thoughts or ensure I'm good and scared of him.

Paul goes to the cabinet, grabs a glass and a new bottle of whiskey, and places them in front of Beasley. I give him a questioning look.

"You've had enough. I'll be doing the driving. Beasley, here, needs to calm down." He's right. Shit, they're both right. I couldn't live without her any more than she could live without me.

"I love her so much. It kills me to know I did anything that caused her pain. I would never hurt her on purpose Beasley. Never."

"I know you wouldn't, Son. It's the only reason you're not gator food right now," Beasley says so seriously. There's no doubt in my mind the lengths this man would go to in order to protect his daughter. "So would you like to know what I found out now that your nuts are nice and secure to where they belong again." His seriousness fades and he bursts out laughing. Paul and I follow. For an older man, Beasley is pretty damn awesome. I'm lucky to have him as a father-in-law and a friend. He begins to tell us what he's found. The last hit on Amber's cell phone was around Homestead last night. There's been nothing since so she must have it turned off. She probably got sick of us all calling. What was she doing in Homestead?

"I also ran her credit card activity. She only used it once in Marathon Key. I also ran Jax's, he hasn't used any of his at all and that makes me nervous."

"What's so strange about him not using a credit card?" Paul asks. I'm wondering the same thing. Out of everything, why does that make Beasley nervous?

"It's about a one-hundred and sixty mile trip to Marathon. They would have needed gas at some point. Who pays for gas anymore with cash unless they are trying to stay off the radar?" Beasley explains. He watches the two of us waiting for it to sink in. I've never seen Jax pay for anything with cash the whole time I've known him. He doesn't even tip with it at the bar.

"So, you think Jax may be trying to hide where they are?" I ask

"Yes, I do. The only purchase Amber made was at a small boutique in Marathon and I have a feeling Jax didn't know about it."

"Then it looks like we are all going on a little road trip," Holly announces from the doorway. I didn't hear them come in. Angel, Marcus, and Becky are with her. There is no way Beasley is going to let this circus tag along.

"No. The two of us will go," he says, motioning between himself and me. I can already see this isn't gonna work. Paul and Angel look pissed. Marcus, I know, wants to go but he never wears his emotions like the rest of us. I don't think anyone will challenge Beasley, though. Holly marches right up to Beasley and stands toe to toe with him. The two stare each other down.

"You may scare these panty waists, but you don't scare me, Beasley. We are all going, and that's final," Holly informs Beasley while poking her finger into his chest. I can see the corners of his mouth tip up. He raises his hands in surrender.

"Okay, but you have to promise to do as I say when we get there. I'm the cop and the father. We do this my way," he says, looking around the room at every face. He waits for everyone to acknowledge their agreement. Of course, Holly has to be stubborn and last, but she finally agrees. Beasley, Paul, and I take Beasley's truck because he has the police radio just in case we need it. The rest all pile into Angel's SUV.

I know my girl can handle herself, she's proved it over and over again, but this time is different. She's more vulnerable. She doesn't need Jax adding all this extra drama onto the full plate she already has right now. We're all missing something. I just can't figure out what it is. There has to be more to this than Jax wanting some money.

CHAPTER
Seventeen

Amber

"WHY WOULDN'T you tell me something that big, Jax? I'm your wife. Shouldn't we have discussed something so serious before you did it?" I hear Leena whine to Jax. *Wife!* They're married? No wonder they looked so cozy at the fair. I keep my eyes closed and continue to eavesdrop, hoping they don't realize I'm awake.

"You would think you would have learned how this marriage works by now. I tell you what you need to know and if I don't tell you something, it's obviously because it's none of your damn business. You have no say in anything I do," Jax snarls at her. I hear her whimper and open one of my eyes, ever so slightly. This is beginning to feel a little too familiar for me.

Jax and Leena are in the kitchen. He has his back to me, but I can see the grip he has around her neck. Here we go again. Definitely all too damn familiar. Making the mistake of looking into her eyes, I see the terror in them. He's never treated her this way before and she's absolutely frozen in fear. She sees me watching their interaction and her eyes start pleading with me to help her. Oh, no! I'm not doing this again. I'm not feeling sorry for another bitch who fell for the wrong guy and had no problems trying to ruin my life at his order. Why should I give two shits about what happens to her? She didn't care about me all the times she was trying to seduce my husband. Where was her caring side when she was screwing my husband a few hours after we buried our babies? She didn't have a single sympathetic bone in her body when she was rubbing my nose in the fact that she had my husband.

"We're just having her sign her money over to you and then we're leaving like we planned, right?" she asks. So, that's what he's wanted this whole time. Money. All of this for a few dollars that I would have gladly handed over if it meant having my grandmother with me. He must tighten his grip on her neck because pure panic washes over her face as it turns a darker shade of red. The evil laugh that comes from Jax's mouth could win Academy Awards.

"Leena, you are as dumb and naive as Amber is." She flinches when he leans in and kisses the top of her forehead. "I'm sorry, sweetheart. I take that back. You are way more naive and a lot dumber than Amber is. You want to know why?" When she shakes her head no, he continues. "I'll fill ya in anyway. You really believe I love you, that this is a real marriage. It isn't and never was. I wanted someone who would do things for me whenever I needed and the only way to do that was to make you believe I loved you. After those papers are signed, you are just as useless to me as she is," he snarls as he spins, catching me watching them. "Glad to see you're finally awake, we can get this show on the road. Sorry about the head-butt, but you really left me no choice. I didn't want to hit you, that's not my style. I've always had Beau for that," he says with a smirk as he tosses Leena on the couch next to me. What is he talking about?

"What do you mean you always had Beau for that? What does he have to do with any of this?" I question. My head is starting to spin with all of the curve balls being thrown at me.

"I suppose it won't hurt to tell you now. You won't be able to repeat it to anyone anyway. If Beau wasn't so damn stupid, we could've avoided this whole ugly scene. I did my homework, Amber." The smug bastard sits in the chair across from me. He's so damn proud of himself. "I knew about Beau's little obsession with you and his hobby. You know, the one where he liked to rape, torture, and kill women who reminded him of you." I gasp, horrified. "Maybe you didn't know that last part. Oh well. Anyway, he was completely happy with the substitutes, but I convinced him he could have the real thing. I lied a little, of course, and made him think you'd fall madly in love with him. He just had to get you away from Kyle long enough. So, I worked out a deal with him. I would help him get you and the only thing I wanted in return aside from his silence, was for you to sign everything you own to me in your will. No matter how easy I made it for Beau, he always managed to screw it up. Poor bastard just wasn't too bright, was he? And believe me, I made it a piece of cake. I all but handed you over to him. I did have fun watching all of your little minions scramble around trying to keep you safe. I just don't get it. What is so fucking special about you? Why does everyone love you so goddamn much?"

"You sound a little jealous. That's what all this is really about, isn't it?" He stands up and I follow his lead. Screw it. If I'm going down, then I'm going down swinging. His eyes are full of hatred, he's grinding his teeth, and shaking from anger. "You're jealous because *my* grandparents chose me over you. Your dad probably would've done the same if he were given the chance. Even your own mother chose drugs over you. You're jealous because I have friends who love me and stick by me. Who do you have, Jax? Leena? Not anymore after this little charade, I suppose. The only friend you've ever had was me. The person you hate the most is the only person who's ever really been your friend." *Too far, Amber*, I think to myself before his fist meets my face again. Plain blooms when he connects with my lip and the coppery taste of blood is making me queasy, but I refuse to give him the satisfaction of knowing he hurt me. I smile at him and laugh as I wipe away the blood that's dripping from my lip.

"You think you're so much better than me. Well guess what, bitch, you're not. I win. I'll be getting the money that should've been mine in the first place. I will also have the pleasure not only of watching you take your last breathe, but also knowing that your dickhead husband will spend the rest of his worthless life feeling guilty because he isn't the hero he thinks he is." Even with all that's happened, the thought of the pain Kyle will go through hurts me. I know how I would feel if the situation was reversed and I don't want that for him. Just like that, Jax causes me more pain than I thought capable. "You have a little to feel guilty for yourself. You promised Kyle you'd never jump to conclusions again about a situation, but you did. The whole thing with Leena was staged. We drugged Kyle so we could make it look like they slept together. He never laid a finger on her," he says, looking very pleased with himself.

His admission knocks the air from my lungs and as a stabbing pain enters my heart. I did it again. I'm never gonna have the chance to tell him how sorry I am. How can I get myself out of this? Thinking quickly, I remember that I packed the handgun Beasley bought for me and taught me to shoot. He made me promise to always have it close by. But how am I going to get to my bag in the bedroom? Just then, Jax's phone rings. He answers it, tells them to hang on a minute, then cups the phone.

"I know you girls aren't the sharpest knives in the drawer, but stay put. There's no way off the island, it won't do any of us any good to have you thinking you'll live through this. I'm not Beau," he snaps. Once he's in the kitchen, Leena nudges me. I want so much to just ignore the bitch. If Becky were here, she'd pop her right in the face.

"Please, Amber. I need you to see this before he gets back," she pleads. Oh, hell. I need to grow a set of balls. I look over her way and see a cell phone in her hand. It looks like it's connected on a call. How long has she had that thing going and who the hell is on the other end? As quietly as I can, I ask.

"Who is on the other end?"

"I called Kyle when I first got here and overheard the two of you talking. They were already on their way. They've heard everything. We have to stall him a little longer." She whispers.

"Just make sure Jax doesn't see that phone. If he does, you're on your own, sweetheart." I swear I hear laughter come from the phone. I wonder who all is coming with Kyle. That's a stupid question that I already know the answer to. Everybody is coming with Kyle. If they've heard everything, then he knows I know the truth. Thank God. I tilt my head down and just above a whisper say, "I love you, Kyle. I'm so sorry. Now, put that away Leena before he sees it." I have to figure out a way to get my gun from my bag. The only person I told about the gun and the lessons was Holly, so there's no way Jax has any idea I have it. Leena barely gets the cell phone out of sight before Jax returns to the living room.

"Okay, Amber, time to sign these papers. My ride out of here will be arriving in about thirty minutes."

"Fine. I'm not going to fight you, what's the use? I'm sure you'll also want the combination to my safe and the key to my safe deposit box at the bank?" He looks a little surprised. Good, if I can throw him off a little, maybe I can stall until help arrives.

"Where's the key at? And why are you being so cooperative all of a sudden?"

"The key is in my bag. I give up. I want to be with my babies and you can give me that. As far as the money goes, it's yours. You can have it all." He looks at me for what seems like forever.

"Fine, go get it. I swear, if you try anything, I won't just take off like I planned. I will find Kyle and Beasley first and make them pay," he threatens. He is one sick son of a bitch.

I slowly walk into the bedroom, feeling his eyes burning a hole in my back. Keeping my back to him, I bend over and reach into the bag. I feel around until I find my gun and a key. The key is a spare to the supply cabinet at the bar but Jax doesn't need to know that. As inconspicuously as I can, I slip the gun down the front of my shorts. Just to ensure it doesn't fall out, I make sure it's lying between my skin and panties. I turn back around and walk up to Jax.

"If you have an extra piece of paper, I'll write down the bank info and the combination," I tell him, trying to stall any way I can. He motions for me to sit at the dining room table and I do. He puts a blank piece of paper in front of me along with a pen. I write down the name of the first bank that comes to mind and a fake box number. Then I write down the old four number combination to the safe at the house. I slide the paper back to him and take the two page will he's had prepared. Praying that he's the one that doesn't make it out of this house, I sign the papers.

"This was much easier than I thought it would be." He says with a huge smile.

"Yeah, well, you could have avoided all of this if you told me who you were. I would've gladly given you the money."

"You aren't getting it, are you? It's not just about the money. It's you. I want you gone for good. Pretending to be your friend all this time has been torture. The moment I watch you take your last breathe will be like Christmas morning for me."

A simple I hate you would have done. Waiting for my chance to pull the gun on him, I try to remember everything Beasley taught me. He said the most important thing to remember is that if you are going to pull a gun on someone, you better be certain you can pull the trigger. Can I really shoot Jax? Yes, yes I can. I don't think he's having any reservations about ending my life, so I have to do whatever I can to save myself. I'll deal with the guilt later. Leena's whiney voice takes Jax's attention from me. This could be the distraction I need.

"What about me, Jax? You aren't going to hurt me, are you?"

Jax turns away from me and walks toward Leena. *It's now or never.* Taking a deep breathe, I reach for the gun, flipping off the safety as I pull it from my shorts.

"I'll make it quick, Leena, don't worry. I'll even let you chose who goes first," he says before turning back to me. Shock registers on his face when he sees the gun. He takes a small step forward and raises his hands. "What are you gonna do with that? Shoot me?" He laughs. "You don't have it in you, Amber," he snarls as he lunges forward.

Everything that happens next is in slow motion. When I see him coming at me, I only have a couple seconds to react. I don't have any other choice. I aim for his kneecap. No matter how much I want to, I still can't bring myself to kill him. He's right, I don't have it in me. I'm not him. I'm not a murderer. When I pull the trigger, I'm not expecting it to be as loud as it is and I stammer back slightly. I've only shot at the range with ear protection on. I recover and look back at him as he falls to the floor.

"You bitch!" he screams, grabbing his injured knee. There's blood everywhere. My hands are shaking. What did I just do? I still have the gun pointed at him, but I'm frozen in place. Looking at him on the floor, bleeding and in pain makes me realize something. He isn't hurting enough. He's caused every bad thing to happen in my life. He killed my grandmother. He set up everything that happened with Beau. He made me believe Kyle cheated on me. *Again.* Thinking clearer that I ever have in my life, I know what has to be done. He has to pay for it all.

Kyle

ONCE WE found the store Amber purchased her dress at, it didn't take long to find out where she is. When you have a group as intimidating as ours, people tend to give you whatever you ask for. Beasley's badge helps too. The phone call from Leena came as we were waiting for the caretaker to take us to the island. This is the longest five minute boat ride I've ever been on. I feel like I did the night we were going after her when Beau had taken her. He's made it perfectly clear she's not making it out of there alive and I'm terrified we won't get to her in time. I can't lose my girl.

The boat hasn't come to a complete stop before I'm jumping out onto the dock. The only thing I can think of is getting to Amber before Jax hurts her. As I run along the pathway to the house, I can hear Beasley right on my heels. Everyone else is not far behind him. When I get about twenty feet from the door, I hear it and my blood runs cold. The gunshot is deafening. My feet stop moving all on their own. I'm frozen in fear. Beasley doesn't stop, he blows right past me with Angel in tow. Paul comes up next to me and places his hand on my shoulder.

"Take a deep breath and let's go. We are all here with you," he encourages as he nudges me along. I have to know if she's okay. I follow Beasley through the door and immediately stop, stunned by the sight before me. It's nothing like the scenario that flashed through my mind when that shot rang out. Amber is standing in front of Jax who is sitting on the floor. Jax is holding his knee, which is bleeding profusely. I look up to Amber who's holding the gun and pointing it at Jax's chest. My sweet girl shot Jax. I don't know which emotion I feel the strongest, pride for how brave and strong she is, or fear for what she's capable of when pushed. Something in her eyes gets my attention. My Amber is standing in front of me but there's something about the cold look in her eyes that's not my Amber at all. I notice the slight shaking of her hands as she continues to point the gun at Jax and slowly move to get a little closer to her.

"Princess, we're here now. You're safe. You can give me the gun," I tell her in the most calming and soothing voice I can. For the briefest second, her eyes leave Jax and meet mine. That's when I know she can't walk away while there's the slightest chance he can ever hurt her or anyone she loves again. I get it. I feel the same way, but I know Amber. Sometimes better than she knows herself. She won't be able to shake the guilt. No matter what he's done, or how much he got what he deserved, she will allow the guilt to eat her alive. I move a little closer. "I know you've made up your mind, Princess, but if you do this, he wins." She quickly glances at me with a questioning look. "The guilt will destroy you, no matter how deserving of this he is." She looks so torn. I can't stand to see her in this kind of agony. Just like that, I know what needs to be done. I know how to make it all right again. I failed in protecting Amber and our babies before, but I can protect her now. I can make sure this monster never harms her again. She can have her sense of security along with the knowledge that he got what was coming to him.

"Kyle, he needs to pay for all of the awful things he's done," she says as the tears begin to roll down her cheeks. "He was going to kill me. He has no conscious, why should I?" She is getting more emotional now. Beasley starts to move toward her, but I put my hand up to stop him. This is our battle. I have to protect my family. I inch up behind her and whisper in her ear.

"Do you really want him dead instead of in jail?" I ask, already knowing the answer. She won't ever feel safe again if he's breathing.

"He won't ever give up until I'm dead, even jail won't stop him," she whimpers. I look back at Beasley. He nods his head in confirmation. We all know Amber's right, he won't stop until he finishes what he started. Still looking at my father-in-law, he nods again. He knows exactly what I'm thinking — it's what he wants to do to keep his daughter safe and guilt free.

"I've got your back, Son," Beasley confirms. Taking a quick look around the room at our friends, I hope they will all understand what I'm about to do. When I get to Angel, I can tell he knows.

"We all have your back. Do what you need to. There isn't one person in this room that would do anything differently," Angel encourages. I'm protecting my wife and family and I don't think I'll lose one second of sleep over it. That may make me a bad person, a murderer just like he is, but at least my intentions are good. I'm trying to save someone, not just take a life. If I have to pay for this at some later time, so be it.

"See this is your problem. You're all a bunch of spineless saps. I knew Amber didn't have it in her, but I'm a little surprised you don't have the balls to do it, Kyle." Jax chuckles.

"Princess, I'm sorry I wasn't there for you before. I'm here now. Let me make this all go away. I will carry whatever burden it brings with it so you can be free of fear. Give me the gun, Amber," I whisper in her ear as I place a soft kiss behind it. She turns slightly to look into my eyes. She's trying to see if I'm serious, so I let her know with a look that I am. I will do anything to ensure she's safe and happy. I move my hands over hers and she loosens the grip on the gun. As she slides her hands out from under mine, I can feel the tension leave her body. Beasley comes up and pulls her aside. I may be doing the wrong thing but it's for the right reasons. I wait a few more seconds to see if there are any signs of guilt or hesitation. When I don't feel either, I take a deep breath and pull the trigger. I don't even flinch as I watch the blood start to flow from his chest and his eyes close. I expect the guilt to hit, but all I feel is relief.

"Jax! No!" Leena screams and rushes to him. I turn and take Amber into my arms. The feeling of holding her makes it all worth it. She's crying hard, finally letting it all out. I let her be for a few minutes, but I really want to get the hell out of here. Before we get to the door, Leena is in our way, blocking the door. She's yelling and screaming about Jax and how much she loved him. Becky is standing off to the side of me and I glance over at her. She's looking behind me and her eyes suddenly widen. She turns and pushes me as hard as she can, sending Amber and I to the floor. As soon as we hit the floor, I hear a gunshot quickly followed by a second. I look up just as Leena drops to the floor, bleeding from the chest. I turn to look behind me and see a fresh wound to Jax's head and a gun in his hand. The son of a bitch had it all along. He was just waiting for his moment. Thankfully, Becky and Beasley saw him pull it and were able to think quickly. If she hadn't pushed us out of the way, that could be one of us instead of Leena dead on the floor. Beasley got his revenge on Jax after all and with that shot, we know he's gone this time. Helping Amber off the floor, I pick her up, cradle her in my arms, and carry her the hell out of this nightmare. It's time to finally have the life we've wanted since we were teenagers. I'm going to give that to her.

"Let's get you home, princess."

Epilogue

Amber

"KYLE, WAKE up, it's time to go." Gently, I lean down and shake his shoulder. "Baby, it's time. We need to go." Well, that gets his attention. He flies out of the bed, almost knocking me over in the process.

"Did you say it's time? Are you okay? Is there a lot of pain? Should I call the hospital?" he spits out all in the same breath. I can't help but laugh. He's so nervous, like one of those dad's you see on television running around without knowing where he's going. I'm waiting for him to drive away while I stand here watching.

"Relax. Take a deep breath." He does as I ask. When he looks into my eyes, he smiles. There's my man. "Yes, it's time, and I'm more than okay. There hasn't been a lot of pain yet and I have called Dr. Monty as well as Holly who will call everyone else." After answering all of his questions, I kiss him. Just then, another contraction hits and he's right back to being the nervous wreck he was minutes before. What is he going to do when they get really bad? "Okay, we need to get going. Paul and Holly should be here any minute to pick us up," I inform him. He still needs to get dressed. Not that I mind watching him walk around shirtless in his boxers. He stands up, takes my hand, and begins to lead me to the stairs. Poor man is so flustered he has no idea he's still naked. I slowly look down at his boxers and wait for his eyes to follow. *In three, two, one…*

"Oh shit! I need to get dressed. I'll be right down, princess," he says as he begins rushing around our bedroom. The giggle escapes me before I can stop it. I head downstairs to the kitchen and wait for Paul and Holly to get here. While I'm waiting, I start to think over the past year. I can't believe we have made it this far.

I was more than ready to shoot Jax that day. I knew he'd never stop trying to kill me as long as he was alive. It was the only way out. When Kyle took that gun from my hand and did it for me, relief washed over me. He was right, I couldn't do it without the guilt following me around forever. It's just who I am. Beasley handled the police and made sure they knew it was self-defense. Not that they really cared after hearing the long list of terrible things Jax had done.

We went straight home from there. Kyle rented a car and the two of us drove home together alone so we could talk along the way. We were able to hash everything out in those few short hours. He explained and apologized for not being there for me the way he should've when things started going badly with the triplets.

"Princess, I didn't know how to handle all of it and I was a coward. I'm so sorry I didn't support you the way I should've." He could've handled things better, but he didn't purposefully try to hurt me. It didn't take long before we were pulling over at a rest area and making out in the car like a couple of teenagers.

"Amber!" Holly yells, breaking me out of my thoughts. "Are you planning on having this baby here in the kitchen?"

"No. I'm waiting for my husband to put on some pants," I tell her. She gives Paul a look and he immediately heads up the stairs. Is my husband so flustered that he's going to need help dressing himself? The thought makes me laugh. If I wasn't in labor, I would have to go watch that.

"Let's get you out to the car," Holly says as she helps me up. As we pass the stairs, she stops and yells, "Get the lead out boys! Woman in labor down here!" We walk out to the car and Holly helps me get into the back, then slides in next to me. The guys come running out of the house like it's on fire. The only thing missing is Angel, then we'd have the Three Stooges. Paul and Kyle climb into the car and we are finally on the way our way to the hospital.

Kyle

I'M A nervous wreck. I can't believe I didn't even realize I was about to leave here half-naked. How can Amber be so calm? She's the one about to give birth and I'm the one acting like a fool. By the time Paul gets upstairs — laughing his ass off at me — I am just pulling on my boots.

"Are we a little freaked, Daddy? You do realize your wife is in labor and waiting on you to go, right?"

"Yes to both, asshole," I tease. Holly yells up to us and we both haul ass down the stairs and out to the car. I can't believe I'm going to be a dad soon. On the drive to the hospital, I can't help but think back on the day we found out Amber was pregnant again.

Three months after the incident with Jax, we decided to take the honeymoon we were never able to take. I planned the exact same trip I had before. I made all of the arrangements to Bora Bora just like before, but instead of two weeks, I booked a full month. After all we'd been through, we both deserved thirty days to ourselves with nothing on our minds but each other. Renting the same huge villa on the ocean, a private waterside balcony, a glass floor with viewing panels, and a private swimming pool, I just knew she'd love it.

The two weeks prior to leaving, she drove me crazy wanting to know where we were going. I can't remember the last time I'd seen her so excited, and that made me very happy. Finally, I was making her feel the way I should — happy and excited, not sad and miserable. Even our friends were hounded day and night for information. It was quite amusing. I finally told her our plans once the shuttle dropped us off at the airport. As expected, she was over the moon.

Our first two weeks were absolute heaven, just as I'd always imagined it would be — long walks on the beach at night, making love to her on the warm sand under the bright stars with the sounds of waves breaking around us. During the day, we would sun bathe, sight see, and snorkel in the warm, clear water. I couldn't have dreamed it any better, it was perfection. We seemed to be more in love than ever before. This trip was helping us put the past in our rearview mirror where it belonged and start fresh.

At the start of our third week, Amber came down with what we thought was either food poisoning or the flu. When three days passed without any improvement, I started to get worried.

"Princess, maybe we should call a doctor?" I suggested although I wasn't taking no for an answer. I knew I was most likely over reacting, but I wasn't taking any chances. She looked at me with loving eyes and a nervous smile.

"I don't need to see a doctor. At least not until we get home," she said with a wink. Now, I was panicking. Something was wrong and she knew it. "Don't get all worked up. I know why I've been feeling so lousy. Maybe you should sit." She patted the spot on the bed next to her. How bad is this going to be if I have to be sitting to hear it?

"You're killing me, princess. Spit it out." She looked into my eyes and took a deep breath. I could see she was a little nervous to tell me.

"I'm pretty sure that I'm pregnant," she almost whispered. I was immediately on top of the world. That's the best news I could've gotten. Then, I wondered if she was as excited as I was. Is that why she looked nervous, because she doesn't want to try again? We've only talked about it a few times since we lost the triplets. The doctor told us it was okay to try again, but be prepared for a difficult pregnancy with months of bed rest. Maybe she doesn't want to chance losing another baby and honestly, I don't blame her. I'll stand by anything she wants. Whatever makes her happy, makes me happy.

"How do you feel about this?" She thought and chose her words carefully before answering my question.

"I won't lie...I'm scared to death, but I'm really excited too. I was worried you might not be ready for this again so soon. We are just starting to get us back, I don't want to throw a wrench in that."

"Baby, I couldn't be happier," I told her as I pull her onto my lap and hold her close. "I'm scared too, but I swear right here and now, I will be right beside you every single step of the way. We'll do this together. I promise, I won't let you down this time."

"Hey, dumbass! Wake up and help your wife out of the car before she has that baby in the backseat!" Paul yells as he slaps me upside my head. Quickly, I stumble out of the car to help Amber out. I cannot believe I was so caught up in my thoughts that I didn't even realize we were here already.

Amber

KYLE HELPS me out of the car and onto the sidewalk. When I look up, I'm stunned. All of our friends are all here waiting. Angel, Marcus, Taryn, Clark, Becky, Chelsie, and Beasley. I can't control the tears that start to fall from my eyes. I love this group so much. Most of them were here with us when the triplets were born. They stood by and comforted us when we needed them the most. Now they'll get to experience this happy miracle with us too.

"Those better be happy tears baby girl," Angel says as he walks up and wipes the falling tears from my cheeks. "My offer still stands...I'm here whenever you're ready to ditch that dud for this stud." We all burst out laughing. Just the way he says it along with that cocky, sexy grin on his face is hilarious. Even Kyle is having a hard time keeping a straight face.

"Just because my wife's in labor doesn't mean I won't kick your ass," Kyle teases as he pushes him away from me. "Can we go have our baby now?" Kyle helps me into the wheel chair that Becky has rolled out for me. I don't really need it, I'm not in that much pain, but I get into it anyway.

"I've got you all checked into the maternity ward and Dr. Monty will be here shortly," Becky informs me as she begins to push me inside. Everyone falls in line behind us. By some miracle, we all fit into the tiny elevator and we're on our way to the fifth floor. As I look around the very crowded space at all of the people I love so dearly, I think back to how this day wouldn't be possible without them. They all played a part in helping us get through the last eight and a half months.

When I was a seven weeks along in my pregnancy, Dr. Monty put in a cerclage. Kyle and I were scared to death about having the procedure again, but knew it was the only way I would have a chance of carrying to term. Luckily, there were no complications this time. It also helped that I hadn't gone into labor beforehand like the last time. I was in the hospital for two days so they could monitor me, then placed on complete bed rest for the remainder of the pregnancy. I had no idea how I was going to survive the next seven months in bed. There was no way Kyle could stay with me twenty-four hours a days, he had the bar to run.

Thankfully, I had Chelsie fully running the center by then, so at least I didn't have that to worry about. I assumed we'd have to hire a nurse to come in and help when Kyle wasn't around. I had asked Becky if she knew of anyone I could hire and she was going to check on it for us. The day I got home from the hospital, our driveway was full of cars. Really knowing our friends like I do, I didn't expect anything different. What did surprise me, however, was what they had all been planning while they awaited our arrival home. Apparently, Becky told them I was thinking of hiring someone to help take care of me while on bed rest and no one was thrilled with that idea. Holly was downright pissed off that I would even consider having a stranger help out when I had all of them. It's not that it didn't cross my mind to ask, but I didn't want them to say yes because they felt obligated to do so. That wouldn't have been fair. They had a schedule made up already for the first month. Someone would be here with me whenever Kyle couldn't.

These people kept me sane through all of those months when I thought I would go crazy. Lying in bed or on the couch all the time was excruciating. The limitations I had were a nightmare, but I should've been used to it after already going through it once. However, the limitations weren't the worst part, it was the fear. The fear that no matter how well I listened to the doctor's orders, something would go wrong again. That I would do everything right, take every precaution and in the end, have to bury another child. It's something I couldn't escape, not after what we'd already gone through. Every little pain would put me on high alert. A whisper between nurses or a strange look on the face of an ultrasound tech, had me panicking. I didn't like it, but I couldn't stop it. Our friends understood and did everything in their power to keep me positive and mostly distracted. Not once did they ever fault me for my paranoia.

When Becky would come over, she'd bring a fetal doppler with her so I could listen to the baby's heartbeat. I could listen to that beautiful sound for hours. Sometimes Kyle would come home just to hear it. Holly being Holly kept me occupied by planning what she said was the hottest baby shower of all time. Then, there was Marcus and Taryn who'd bring their son, Chase, over when they visited. Not only is he the cutest and funniest kid ever, but he also showed me what I had to look forward to. What I had to hope and pray for. Angel's visits were never the same. They were as unpredictable as he is. Clark would move the couch close to the kitchen and give me cooking lessons. I really loved his visits, although everyone made sure I ate well. I'm really going to miss that. When Chelsie would visit, she would keep me well informed on what was happening at the center. She has quickly become a permanent member in our little makeshift family. She's also amazing at her job, the perfect choice to run the center. I don't worry about the place at all with her in charge.

"Earth to Amber...come in Amber," Holly says as she shakes my shoulders. "What's with all of the zoning out today?"

"Just thinking about how much I love you guys," I tell her as a nurse hands me a gown. The nurse looks at all of the people piling into the room with a 'what the hell' expression on her face. Leave it to Angel to notice the cute uncomfortable nurse and make it worse.

"To answer the question you want to ask, yes, we are all going to be here for the delivery. You see we aren't really sure which one of us is the father," Angel teases the poor nurse. The horrified look she gets on her face makes me giggle. Becky slaps Angel in the back of the head and then puts her arm around the nurse.

"Don't pay any attention to the group moron, Monica. We are all going to be here for our friend, though. This is a special day," Becky explains to the blushing nurse.

"That would explain why she has such a huge room all to herself. I'll get some chairs brought in for you all. I'll be back in just a few minutes to see how far along you are." She smiles sweetly at me, but gives Angel a nasty look before leaving the room.

ABOUT TWENTY minutes ago, the nurse asked if I wanted something for the pain. I said no. At the time, it wasn't really bad. Now the contractions are becoming quite painful and more frequent. The sudden need to push is also becoming overwhelming. When I tell this to the nurse, she starts just laughs it off until Becky steps in.

"You may want to check her out. She had her cerclage removed two days ago and she has a very weak cervix, I don't think this will be your normal delivery." Becky firmly, but nicely, puts her in her place. Luckily, the girl is smart and does what Becky suggests. She gets her gloves on and checks my cervix.

"Amber, it looks like you are right, its show time. I need to get the doctor," she says to me.

"I think I'm ready for those pain meds now," I tell her before she walks out. She turns and looks at me with a grin on her face.

"Sweetie, it's too late, we can't give you anything now," she says with a little too much pleasure in her voice. Well, I always said I wanted a natural birth, looks like I'm about to get it. Everything starts to move quickly. One nurse begins prepping the area for the baby while another preps the area at my feet for Dr. Monty. I can't believe this is finally happening. I look over to Kyle who is standing next to me, watching all of the commotion. When he notices me watching him, he smiles that handsome smile of his, then leans down and kisses me gently on the lips.

"We did it, princess. Are you ready to meet our son?" he asks with tears filling his eyes. I know how he feels, I'm overwhelmed with emotion, too. I'm scared, excited, and happier than I've ever been before, but I'm also a little sad too. I can't help thinking of the triplets. I feel a little guilty being so happy even though they aren't here. I'll have to make sure our son knows about his brother and sisters when he's old enough to understand. At least I know he will always have three of the most precious guardian angels watching over him.

"I feel like I've been waiting my whole life for this," I tell him as I pull him down for a deeper kiss. When our tongues begin to dance together, all the noise and commotion surrounding us seems to disappear. That is, until Angel decides to be a comedian.

"Umm...isn't that how we got here, you two? Can we have this baby before you start trying for the next one?" Angel jokes. He even has the nurses and Dr. Monty, who just walked in, laughing. I see Angel pull a video camera out of my bag. I'm glad someone thought of that because I forgot all about it.

"Where the hell do you think you're going?" I ask when I notice him walking south. He stops dead in his tracks and turns around with that smartass grin on his face.

"You want me to film the birth. In order to film the birth, I need to be able to see the birth."

"If you or anyone else aside from a medical professional or my husband goes past my waist, I will stop this labor and personally kick your ass. Viewing of my lady bits is off limits," I threaten.

"Okay. I got ya. I'll stay right here," Angel says with his arms raised in surrender.

Kyle

IS IT wrong to be turned on right now by Amber putting Angel in his place? She never yells at him. I think even he's a little shocked.

"Okay, folks, let's meet this little guy. What do ya say?" Dr. Monty says as he takes a seat at the foot of the bed. I think he's as excited as we are. He promised he'd help us have a healthy baby and here we are. I'm about to have everything I've ever wanted. Amber is my wife and we're happier than ever. I own the Bar and Grille that I've always wanted. And the best thing of all...I'm about to become a dad.

Dr. Monty's only told Amber to push once and now he's saying he can see the head. This is a lot quicker than I expected. Maybe this is her reward for all of the shit she's had to go through. There's no screaming, no cussing, and no telling me she hates me.

"Kyle, do you want to come watch your son come into the world?" Dr. Monty asks me. I look over to Amber to see if it's okay with her. I don't want my ass kicked for looking at her lady bits. She smiles and nods her approval as Chelsie comes over and takes my place at her side. I sit on the stool the nurse places next to Dr. Monty and put on the gloves she hands me. Glancing up at all the people staring down at me, I think this is what it must feel like to be the luckiest man alive. Dr. Monty nudges my shoulder and I see why he's trying to get my attention. A full head of black hair is starting to emerge and my heart skips a beat. It's the most amazing thing I've ever seen.

"Would you like to deliver him? It's easy from here. I'll walk you through it."

"Hell yeah, I would." He tells me where to put my hands and what to do. He lets Amber know that with the next contraction, he needs one, really big push. I'm nervous as hell, but this will be a cool story to tell my son someday.

"Here we go. Amber, you need to push as hard as you can," Dr. Monty encourages. I do as I'm told with him guiding me. He was right though, this baby is delivering himself. His whole head is out, then the shoulders, and before I know it, I'm holding my beautiful, messy son in my arms. Dr. Monty takes him as the nurse hands me a large pair of scissors. She holds the umbilical cord tight and says to cut between her hands. I never thought I'd ever do this, but with shaky hands, I do. The nurse helps take off the gloves and I immediately go to my wife.

"You are amazing, princess. He's the second most beautiful thing I've ever laid my eyes on," I tell her as I kiss her forehead. "Thank you."

"Why are you thanking me?"

"For loving me, making me the happiest man alive, and for giving me this beautiful little baby boy," I tell her just as the nurse lays our son on Amber's chest. When the tears start to fall, I don't bother with trying to stop them. I notice I'm not the only weepy male in the room. In fact, every man in the room has tears in his eyes, especially when Amber announces what we've decided to name our son.

"Everyone, I'd like you to meet Cody Lee Connor," she says while watching Beasley for his reaction. It's just like we'd hoped it would be. A huge smile breaks out across his face while tears stream down his cheeks.

Watching all of the people I love the most 'ooh' and 'aww' over my lovely wife and new son, I couldn't wipe the smile from my face if I tried. It's been one hell of a journey for the two of us, but we're still here, standing strong. If that's not true love, I don't know what is. As long as I have her by my side, holding my hand, we can get through anything that's thrown at us. Feeling the way I do right at this moment, every single ounce of pain was worth it.

THE END

Acknowledgments

There are so many people I want to say thank you to. This has been an amazing journey so far and I've met some wonderful people along the way.

First and foremost to the two most important men in my life, my husband and son, thank you for always being my biggest supporters. I couldn't have done any of this without either of you. I love you both with all my heart.

Monica James, I can't thank you enough for all of your help. Especially since you had no idea who I was in the beginning. No matter how many questions I've asked or how often, you're always willing to help me out. I appreciate that more than you'll ever know. I'm so honored to be able to call you my friend.

Chelsie Leverette, You have been my biggest supporter since day one. You were the first person to contact me to say you read First Love and loved it. I can't even explain how unbelievable that was for me. We became friends quickly and for that I am so thankful. You are always there to cheer me on when it all starts to get to me. I can't wait until September 2015 when we can finally meet in person!

Kelly Williams, You have saved me from completely losing my mind! I've been so busy and pulled in so many different directions lately that I was going crazy trying to do it all on my own. Then you came along and started to take a lot of the weight off my shoulders so that I could concentrate on getting this book finished. I am so thankful for everything you do to help me out and the friendship that's developed is just the icing on the cake.

Courtney Ledford-Houston, Thank you so much for taking the time to help me out with a scene I was having trouble with. It turned out to be one of my favorite parts in the story.

Monica Black, Thank you for the way you are able to tell me what I need to work on without being critical. You always seem to inspire me and give me the encouragement I need. I'm so lucky to have not only as my editor, but also as my friend.

To all my lovely Beta readers, you ladies are amazing. Thank you so much for taking the time to read these stories and give me feedback. You are such an important part of this process and I couldn't do it without you. **Kelly, Chelsie, Becky, Courtney, Amanda, Candi, Brandy, Chundra, Gina, and Suzanne**, I love you all!

To all you kickass ladies who are a part of my Street Team, Thank you! I appreciate everything you all do to help get my name and books out there. Most of all thank you for believing in me enough to want to support me. **Kelly, Candi, Mary, Chelsie, Angel, Courtney, Sally, Becky, and Jamie**, you girls are Rock Stars!!!

Thank you to all of the **bloggers, reviewers, and readers,** thank you all so very much. You are the ones that make this all worthwhile. You will never know how much I appreciate each and every one of you who took the time to read my stories. Every time I see a review that says someone has enjoyed my book I am overjoyed.

I know I have missed so many people, so thank you to everyone who has stood by me and given me strength and encouragement to keep following this dream!

Other Books
By Kathy-Jo Reinhart

The Oakville Series
First Love - Kyle and Amber's Story (Part 1)
Remember Me- Kyle and Amber's Story (Part 2)

Coming Soon
Protect Me- Paul and Holly's Story
Clark and Becky's Story
Angel and Chelsie's Story

Remember Me Playlist

Remind Me - Brad Paisley with Carrie Underwood
I'd Come For You - Nickelback
Gone Too Soon - Daughtry
It's All About Believin - Def Leppard
Hopeless - Breaking Benjamin
I'm Yours - Jason Mraz
Used To - Daughtry
I Won't Let Go - Rascal Flatts
Roar - Katy Perry
Bottoms Up - Brantley Gilbert
Country Girl (Shake it for me) - Luke Bryan
Tears in Heaven - Eric Clapton
Bless the Broken Road - Rascal Flatts
God Gave Me You - Blake Shelton
Never Say Never - The Fray
Broken - Linsey Haun
Wherever You Will Go - The Calling

Contact Author

Kathy-Jo would love to hear from you:

Facebook www.facebook.com/authorkathyjoreinhart
Twitter twitter.com/KathyJoReinhart
Website kathyjoreinhart.com
Goodreads www.goodreads.com/author/show/7890595.Kathy_Jo_Reinhart

This paperback interior was designed and formatted by

www.emtippettsbookdesigns.com

Artisan interiors for discerning authors and publishers.